Friends with Benefits

Also by Melody Mayer

The Nannies

Coming in September 2006

Have to Have It

Friends with Benefits

by Melody Mayer

Delacorte Press

a nannies novel

Published by Delacorte Press
an imprint of Random House Children's Books
a division of Random House, Inc.
New York

www.randomhouse.com/teens
Educators and librarians, for a variety of teaching tools, visit us at www.randomhouse.com/teachers

Library of Congress Cataloging-in-Publication Data

Mayer, Melody.
Friends with benefits : a nannies novel / Melody Mayer. —1st ed.
p. cm.
Summary: Kiley, Esme, and Lydia, seventeen-year-old nannies to the rich and famous, attempt to start a nanny placement service to earn extra money while coping with difficult children, stressed-out employers, and complicated romances.
ISBN-13: 978-0-385-73284-0 (trade) — ISBN-13: 978-0-385-90301-1 (glb.)
ISBN-10: 0-385-73284-8 (trade) — ISBN-10: 0-385-90301-4 (glb.)
[1. Nannies—Fiction. 2. Interpersonal relations—Fiction.
3. Friendship—Fiction. 4. Beverly Hills (Calif.)—Fiction.] I. Title.
PZ7.M4619Fri 2006
[Fic]—dc22 2006001881

The text of this book is set in 11.25-point Berkeley Oldstyle.
Printed in the United States of America
10 9 8 7 6 5 4 3 2 1

First Edition

In memory of my great-grandfather,
a Hollywood legend

Friends with Benefits

1

Kiley McCann

Dear Mom—

Every day I still feel like pinching myself to see if it's true: I'm really a nanny for the kids of a famous rock star! And it is real, Mom, *because* you were brave enough to let your seventeen-year-old daughter stay in Los Angeles by herself. I can't thank you enough for your faith in me.

Anyway, enough mush. Sorry we haven't had a chance to talk on the phone lately, I've just been so busy. But I wanted you to know that everything here is going great. I know that Platinum seemed kind of crazy when you met her, but that's just a rock star image she puts on for publicity. Actually, she's a nice person with good morals and values just like people back home in Wisconsin, so no worries.

You remember her kids from when you were here with me: Serenity, almost eight, is very sweet, and Sid, age nine, is so mature for his age. Bruce, who's fourteen, has been at rock and roll camp, so I haven't seen him much. I'm sure when he's home I'll get along with him just as well as I do with the littler kids.

This is great, Mom—I've made two friends here, both nannies like me. Esme works for a famous TV producer (Steven Goldhagen!!) and his wife; they have two adopted kids who only speak Spanish. I think they hired Esme because she's bilingual. Lydia (her dad is a doctor in the Amazon and that's where she lived for the past eight years!) works for her aunt, a sports commentator on ESPN. They have two kids also. It sure helps having friends here, so you don't need to worry that I'm alone or anything.

Remember that guy I told you about, Tom Chappelle, the one I met in line at the movies? Well, it turns out he's from Iowa and he grew up on a farm, so we have a lot in common. He's a model and he just did his first film role in that new movie *The Ten*. He is the one in the car on the freeway in the desert who gets smothered by locusts. We are just friends.

How is Dad doing? I hope okay and not drinking too much.

So as you can tell, you made the right decision by letting me stay here in Los Angeles. I am sooo grateful to you. You don't need to worry about anything because—

Braagh-aah! Braagh-aah! Braagh—

Kiley winced and stopped writing midsentence. The hotline phone that Platinum had installed the day Kiley moved into the guesthouse blared. All her boss had to do was lift the receiver of the red phone in the mansion's kitchen, and the matching red phone in Kiley's living room shrieked as if announcing the start of global thermonuclear war. Kiley snatched it up just to protect her eardrums from the assault.

"Hello?"

"Kiley, you bitch! If you do not have your corn-fed ass up to the main house in exactly one minute, you're fired."

Before Kiley could reply, the phone went dead.

So much for Kiley's one day off per week, which she'd planned on enjoying with her friends right after she finished writing to her mom. The phone call was just so Platinum. Everything she had just written regarding her employer and her employer's kids, other than facts like their ages, was a big fat lie. Platinum was a substance-abusing, egocentric pain in the ass. That Kiley put up with it was Kiley's own choice. She knew she could always go back to La Crosse, Wisconsin, and waitress at Pizza-Neatsa.

Pizza-Neatsa was probably where she *would* be, if she hadn't auditioned a month ago for a new reality TV show, *Platinum Nanny.* When she and her best friend, Nina, heard that *Platinum Nanny* would be doing interviews in Milwaukee, they'd primped and polished Kiley into the kind of bodacious babe they hoped would please the show's producers.

Normally, Kiley was the most natural of girls—chinos, T-shirts, and Converse All Star basketball shoes, her reddish brown hair in a ponytail. But for the interview, Nina had glammed Kiley out in a microminiskirt and stiletto boots, plus more makeup than Kiley had ever worn in her life.

Their scheme had worked. Kiley had been brought to Los Angeles to compete in the finals, the only under-eighteen-year-old in the bunch. It was insane: TV cameras had followed her everywhere. But in the end, *Platinum Nanny* was shut down by its network before any of the episodes aired; something about a bad reaction from a focus group at Warner Bros.

That was the bad news. The good news was that Kiley had managed to snare the gig anyway. She didn't even have to pile on the makeup to do it. She'd been working for Platinum for two weeks; long enough to know that there was a good chance the hotline would shriek again before she left to go to the main house—

Braagh-aah!

There it was. Kiley grabbed the receiver. "Yes, Platinum?"

"It's Sunday, Kiley," Platinum said, her tone accusing.

"True."

"Sunday is your day off. You think I don't know?"

"I thought maybe you forgot," Kiley said politely. It was entirely possible. When Platinum got drunk and/or stoned, she often didn't track what day it was, or even if it was day at all. At least her boss wasn't slurring her words. Yet.

"I didn't forget," Platinum snapped. "My anal accountant is here so I'm stuck doing this boring crap with him. Sid is in the meditation room with Persimmon."

Kiley frowned. "Persimmon?"

"Sid's new male mentor. That asshole Jeff Greenberg? I fired him yesterday. He ratted on Sid for taking a beer from the fridge."

Jeff Greenberg was a psych grad student from UCLA who Platinum had hired at the same time she'd hired Kiley. Platinum insisted that Sid have a male mentor because she was a single parent, so her son needed to "like, inhale testosterone."

"But . . . isn't it good that Jeff said something?" Kiley ventured. "I mean, Sid is only nine."

"If you keep a kid away from this shit, they'll just want it all the more," Platinum insisted. "Plus, nobody likes a tattletale. Especially me. Remember that, Kiley."

All-righty, then. Kiley sat down at the kitchen table and rested her head in the palm of one hand. "Okay, Platinum, I will."

"You'll like Percy," Platinum continued. "He's a lot more spiritual than that asshole Greenberg. Percy taught yoga at the Kripalu Center in western Massachusetts; totally balanced yin and yang, amazing third eye."

Kiley hadn't a clue what a "yin" or a "yang" or a "third eye" was.

"In case you're wondering," Platinum went on, blithely ignoring the ongoing interruption of Kiley's day off, "Serenity is at Courtney's house. She's working on this T-shirt project with Frances Bean."

Kiley did a quick mental translation. Courtney was Courtney Love, another aging druggie rock star whom Kiley had never heard of until she came to Los Angeles. Frances Bean was

Courtney Love's daughter by Kurt Cobain—another rock star, albeit now a dead one.

"So I've got it all completely covered. I know exactly where the kids are and what they're doing," Platinum concluded. "Everything's cool."

"Uh-huh," Kiley agreed. Of course, the truth was that Platinum most definitely did *not* have it completely covered. Experience had taught Kiley that when Platinum did a detailed and unsolicited infomercial on the goings-on of her two younger kids, it meant she was already semi-high and trying to pass as fully sober. Kiley thought of this as the Green Zone. Slurred words meant Platinum was in the Yellow Zone, which almost inevitably led to the Orange Zone, where Platinum went up to her room, locked the door, and didn't appear again for a good sixteen hours. There was also a Red Zone, where the rock star was rushed by ambulance to the UCLA Medical Center while the paramedics performed CPR, but thankfully this was still theoretical.

Kiley tried to be around the kids whenever Platinum ventured into the Yellow Zone; she hated the thought of them having to deal with their mother in that condition. It was ironic, really. Platinum made a big point of not bringing her lovers to the house, but thought nothing of passing out in her own vomit while her kids played with their Xboxes.

"So have a great Sunday. Go get laid or something," Platinum concluded, and then hung up.

Kiley hung up too. Apparently she was going to get to enjoy her day off with her friends after all. With Platinum, you just never knew. Working for her was crucial to Kiley's master plan. But did the gods have to make the plan quite so difficult?

When Kiley was ten years old, she'd fallen in love with the ocean on a family trip to San Diego. Her family didn't do family trips, didn't do family . . . well, pretty much anything. Her dad, Al, worked at the brewery in La Crosse and was way too fond of the product he helped make. Her mom, Jeanne, was a waitress at a diner on the road up to Eau Claire. Though Kiley loved her mother dearly, she had a lot of problems. Fears. Anxieties. Panic attacks. She wouldn't take medication for it either, having been raised a Christian Scientist. On that family trip to San Diego, Mom had been frozen by just such an attack at the Scripps Institution of Oceanography, just as she and Kiley were about to go on a tour. Kiley went on the tour by herself, blending into a throng of tourists so that the tour guide wouldn't notice her.

That was where, seven years ago, Kiley had come up with the plan. Finish high school, go to Scripps, and become a marine biologist. Side benefit of the plan: leave all things landlocked and La Crosse far, far behind. This dream had seemed entirely doable, until she actually read the Scripps catalog at the guidance office in her high school and took a good look at the tuition. There were zeros. A lot of zeros. It took Kiley but a millisecond to realize that her blue-collar parents could not afford the very white-collar out-of-state bill. Scripps wasn't anywhere close to cheap even if you were a resident of California, but at least that number was within the realm of the possible, especially with a night job and financial aid.

There was one problem. Kiley wasn't a resident of California and didn't have a chance of becoming one, absent a miracle or two. Nor did Kiley believe in miracles. Then they just started to happen to her.

The first miracle was *Platinum Nanny.* The second had been

Platinum offering her the nanny job even after the show died in vitro. If she could survive in the job, she could attend high school here in Los Angeles and apply to Scripps as a California resident.

Big if. Platinum loved the words "you're fired" more than Donald Trump. Kiley had in fact been fired twice, but immediately thereafter Platinum had retracted the edict, mostly because it wasn't easy to find someone competent to take care of Siddhartha and Serenity (also known as the Children from Hell) and tolerate Platinum at the same time.

Siddhartha—Sid for short—was a blond, angelic-looking nine-year-old brat with a belligerent attitude and a severe case of ADD, complete with bedwetting. He careened from one thing to the next and hated everyone. His only passion in life was the card game Yu-Gi-Oh!, which he played and talked about constantly.

His little sister, Serenity—no nickname, thank you very much—was more than a year younger, but bossed him around mercilessly. In fact, she bossed everyone around and got away with it. Her knowledge of the ins and outs of Hollywood was frightening. On more than one occasion, Kiley had caught her reading the trade magazine *Variety*. She was a cherubic miniature of her mother, with the same long platinum hair. Unlike her mother, Serenity had an aversion to cleanliness, and had only recently begun to take regular baths and showers.

Both kids had foul mouths well tolerated by their mother, who insisted the children were simply expressing themselves freely.

Kiley looked at the clock. Ten in the morning. Her day off had been salvaged.

There were two bedrooms in the guesthouse, both of them with twin beds covered by floral quilts. Kiley had chosen the sunnier of them and went there now to dig her swimsuit from the bottom drawer of an antique oak dresser. A plain one-piece navy Speedo; the producers at *Platinum Nanny* had provided it for one of the contest challenges.

Kiley didn't mind that the suit was more functional than sexy. In fact, she decided that she'd swim some laps at the country club. She loved to swim; it was actually the only form of exercise she did love. As she slipped the suit into her battered backpack with its EAST LA CROSSE HIGH SCHOOL CLASS OF '07 button pinned to the ratty flap, she realized that in any case she wasn't about to stuff her pear-shaped curves into some itsy-bitsy bikini at a ritzy country club where wearing a two-digit size was practically a felony.

She reached for the cell phone on her nightstand to call Lydia, but stopped long enough to check out her reflection in the mirror over the dresser. Kiley had to admit that she was happy with the lighter streaks that had been added to her hair at the Joseph Martin salon during the TV show makeover. Other than that, though, she was back to her old makeup-free self. People sometimes told her she looked like Lindsay Lohan before she went blond, anorexic, and crazy. But what Kiley saw in the mirror was just an average-looking girl, nothing special. Her middle school gym teacher back in La Crosse, Ms. Plant, had once described her as "sturdy"—about as far from "sexy" as an adjective could get.

"Screw Ms. Plant," she told her reflection. "She's not dating a supermodel. I am."

Well, that was a slight exaggeration. Maybe she wasn't

exactly dating one, but she had gone out on *a* date with one. Well, okay, not exactly a date, but close to it.

His name was Tom Chappelle. They'd met when *Platinum Nanny* had put Kiley and her mother up in a lavish suite at the Hotel Bel-Air, and then it seemed like everywhere Kiley went in Los Angeles, there he was . . . both in the flesh and on billboards and bus shelters. Tom was a model; the chief model, in fact, for a Ralph Lauren underwear campaign that left little to the imagination. He was six feet tall, with golden rippling muscles, an open face with piercing gray eyes, and a pouty lower lip. They'd run into each other at Grauman's Chinese Theatre in Hollywood at a midnight showing of *The Ten,* the summer blockbuster movie in which Tom had his first real, albeit small, role.

Afterward, they'd gone for coffee and then breakfast. It had all felt so natural—who knew that talking to a supermodel could be so easy? Maybe it was because it turned out that Tom had grown up on a farm outside Lake Mills, Iowa, just 145 miles from La Crosse. In fact, he'd actually been to La Crosse—to Kiley's school, for God's sake!—for a high school theater competition.

As for his big break into the modeling business, he'd only been discovered the previous year. An agent from New York had been scanning the midway at the Iowa State Fair, looking for fresh faces. That agent brought him to New York; he became a superstar almost overnight. When Tom recounted to Kiley how a year before he'd been getting up at four-thirty with his father and kid brother to milk the cows, his eyes shone with wonder at the impossibility of it all. The glitz and glamour of Hollywood were nearly as new to him as they were to Kiley.

That night had ended with a sunrise breakfast at the Standard on Sunset Boulevard. Afterward, Tom walked Kiley to her car, a classic 1967 platinum Mustang convertible—hers to drive as long as she worked for Platinum. Kiley had been nervous, wondering if he'd kiss her. She definitely wanted him to, even raised her face to his, hoping he'd get the hint. But he'd just given her a friendly hug and casually said he'd call her when he got back from his cross-country press junket to promote *The Ten*. That junket was supposed to last ten days, so—

Bong. Bong. Bong.

Kiley's state-of-the-art Nokia cell phone—bestowed by Platinum so that she could reach Kiley at any time—rang with its characteristic chimes of London's Big Ben clock. Kiley picked up, thinking it was Lydia. It wasn't.

"Hello?"

"Kiley, hey, it's Tom."

Tom. It was Tom. *The* Tom. She willed her heart to stop pinwheeling and tried to sound casual. "Hey. Welcome home. How are you?"

"Whipped," he said. "I talked up the movie to so many reporters in so many cities, I didn't know where I was half the time."

"Wow!" Kiley exclaimed, realizing she couldn't think of one single cute or funny thing to say. "So . . . you're back now, huh?"

"Yeah, got in last night."

Last night? He'd gotten back last night and was calling her the next morning? She'd known he had to be back in town to model in FAB, the yearly L.A. fashion extravaganza, but still, to call her so quickly? Oh my God, that was fantastic.

"I'm still so crapped out, I'm going to crash for a while," he continued. "But I thought maybe you'd like to go to a party with me tonight. I know it's not much notice—"

"Oh no!" Kiley interrupted eagerly. "I mean yes, I can go. And it's okay. About the no notice, I mean."

Shut up, she told herself. *Just stop babbling.* Now.

"Great. It's out in Malibu. So I'll pick you up around eight, okay?"

"Sure, great, fine!"

Then Kiley had a moment of panic. What if he didn't remember where she lived? "My address is—"

"Platinum's mansion," Tom put in. "I bought a Hollywood star map when I first came to town, even went on one of those bus tours of the stars' homes—don't let it get around."

They said goodbye and hung up. Kiley lay on her bed, replaying the conversation in her mind. Had that really just happened? Had gorgeous, famous model Tom Chappelle actually just called her and invited her on a *date*?

Kiley sat up quickly. Wait. Maybe it wasn't a date. Maybe it was a kick-back-with-a-bud kind of thing. Kiley remembered the friendly hug that had ended their all-night gabfest only too well. She grabbed her backpack. She'd run the whole thing by Esme and Lydia; they'd help her figure it out. Meanwhile, she sent up a quick prayer:

Dear God, please don't let him think of me as a friend, which is the kiss of death. But if he does think of me as a friend? Help me find a way to change his mind.

2

Lydia Chandler

Clad in her burnt orange Delfina nylon-spandex print bikini, Lydia stretched out on her chaise longue at the Brentwood Hills Country Club. Then she reached into her Trina Turk beaded raffia bag with bamboo handles and took out a dog-eared book. Both bikini and bag had been borrowed from her aunt Kat. Borrowed, as in: intended to return. As Lydia saw it, so long as she put said things back where she'd found them, Thou Shalt Not Steal did not apply.

The book was borrowed too. She'd found it in her aunt's closet, buried under a neat pile of T-shirts. And she did what anyone raised in the Amazon basin would do when faced with something curious. She investigated.

The book cover featured a heaving bosom–type young woman whose globe-shaped breasts were semi-clad in a lacy push-up bra, and who sat on the lap of a naked guy with rippling muscles. Lydia couldn't actually tell if the guy was *totally* naked; unfortunately, the photo ended at their waistlines. The woman faced him, her head thrown back as if she was in the throes of a very passionate moment.

The title: *Secrets of the Kama Sutra.* Talk about your must-borrow.

From the women's magazines that had been air-dropped to her and her parents, Lydia knew that the *Kama Sutra* had something to do with certain ways of having sex that supposedly led to overwhelming pleasure. Articles in *Jane* and *Cosmo* such as "Tantric Sex: Make Him Yours Forever" had taught her that much. Lydia wasn't particularly interested in making any guy hers forever, but the notion of overwhelming pleasure interested her a lot. Here she was, nearly seventeen years old, with pale blond hair choppy from the makeshift haircuts her mother had given her in Amazonia, startling green eyes, skinny but curvy figure, and an allover tan. Guys were sniffing around her all the time, letting her know how hot she was.

As she lay back on her chaise, she admitted to herself that "all the time" was a bit of an exaggeration. Said attention had only been ongoing for the past two and a half weeks, since she'd moved from the rain forest to her aunt's guesthouse in Beverly Hills to care for her aunt's two children. Back in the Amazon, local guys had found her a pathetic excuse for a female, being much too pale, and unwilling to pierce her lower lip with a stick.

Lydia hadn't always lived in South America. She'd been born the pampered princess of wealthy Texas parents. She should have lived happily ever after, moving into her teen years with a walk-in closet full of designer outfits, and boyfriends who picked her up in Porsches and Ferraris and Jensen Interceptors. That was exactly what would have happened if her damn parents hadn't developed their damn saints-on-earth complex. Her surgeon father had a heart attack at age thirty-seven, which had somehow led to a spiritual epiphany and their subsequent move to the Amazon basin. There, he worked as a medical missionary whose only mission was to improve the health of native Amarakaire tribesmen. Lydia's mother was his assistant. Princess Lydia, then age eight, was shit out of luck.

When the lifeline had come from Aunt Kat—a job offer for Lydia to be the nanny to her young cousins—Lydia had said yes faster than a giant Amazon leech could suck the life from a peacock bass.

During all those years in Ama-land, Lydia had held on to her sanity by begging and pleading for American fashion magazines from every do-gooder doctor about to come to the bush. Most obliged, packing two or three into their knapsacks. Hence, her entire knowledge of sex, pop culture, and *life* came from devouring *Cosmo* and *Glamour, Vogue* and *InStyle.*

But the truly sad thing was that Lydia, a hands-on girl, had zero hands-on experience. As in: still a virgin. Oh, the humanity! It was one of the reasons she'd pounced on *Secrets of the Kama Sutra.* She'd found her perfect first-time partner-in-crime. His name was Billy Martin; she'd met him at a nightclub in Los Feliz. Lydia had taken one look at Billy, who bore a decided resemblance to Tom Welling (she'd torn a shirtless photo of Welling out of *Star* magazine the year before and stuck it to the mud-caked wall over her straw-mat bed), and knew he'd be the one. He was also nice, funny, smart, and interesting, not to mention straight (though Lydia had misjudged that one at the outset). His parents were State Department Foreign Service officers, so he even had some sense of what it was like to be American and still feel like a foreigner.

But that first hands-on experience hadn't happened yet. It was all because of their damn schedules. Billy had just finished his freshman year at the Los Angeles Art Institute, where he was studying film and scenic design. For the summer, he had an internship with Eduardo L. Parsons, production designer of many famous films and TV shows. Parsons had been hired to design all the sets for the upcoming Los Angeles Fashion Bash (known as FAB); Billy seemed to be doing most of the grunt work. FAB opened in two days. If it had been any further away, Lydia was sure she'd be the oldest living virgin in Beverly Hills.

Where were her friends? Lydia peered around. The pool deck was crowded, but she didn't see Kiley or Esme. In fact, there were two pools at the Brentwood Hills Country Club, one of the three or four top clubs in Los Angeles. One of the pools was for families with children, one was for adults only. A breezeway connected the two of them. There were also tennis courts, lawn bowling, a gym to rival any in the city, two restaurants plus an outdoor dining pavilion, and an eighteen-hole championship golf course that had hosted both men's and women's tour events. If you had to ask how much the membership fee was, you couldn't afford it. If you didn't know several members, you'd have no chance of joining. Kat and Anya had been members ever since both were seeded tennis players. Now that Lydia was their employee, she had members' privileges too.

As she flipped open the *Kama Sutra* book, a thought struck her. Her aunt Kat was gay. She'd been living with Anya Kuriakova, the former tennis star and now famous coach, for years.

Their children, Martina and Jimmy, had been the product of artificial insemination. So what the hell was Kat doing with a book about heterosexual—

"I could show you how to do that," a male voice offered.

Lydia raised her oversized white Chanel sunglasses (thank you, Aunt Kat's closet) and peered at the drop-dead-gorgeous blond guy in sky blue surfer Jams who had just crouched by her chaise longue.

"Scott. I distinctly remember tellin' you that I'm not interested anymore," she said with a trace of her childhood Texas drawl.

"You could have changed your mind."

Lydia sighed. Scott Lyman was one of the country club lifeguards, and a former Olympic swimmer in the backstroke. She'd had a very brief flirtation with him, and considered the possibility that he might be the man to do the deed—in other words, *her*—but soon how luscious his butt looked in surfer Jams lost out to how vacuous he sounded every time he opened his mouth.

"See, Scott, the thing is, when we met I was perfectly willing to settle for eye candy—that would be you."

"Awesome," he breathed hopefully.

"But I met someone else," Lydia explained. "He's just about as perfect of a male physical specimen as you are. Plus, turns out what's between his ears is bigger than what's between his legs."

Scott gave her a knowing look. "Bummer. Some girls say that size isn't everything, but that's bull. Let me show you what a *real* man can do."

God, he was just so *dense*. She cocked her head across the

pool. "That redhead in the white bikini over there was just checking out your ass."

"Yeah?" Scott craned his head around.

"Go get lucky," Lydia encouraged him with a little wave of her fingers, and he took the hint, heading for potentially more fertile hunting grounds. Good thing. Lydia didn't want to get downright rude on the boy. If he pestered her enough . . . well, it didn't pay to get her angry, either. She'd befriended a particularly powerful shaman back in the Amazon who had herbs and potions that purportedly could make a person do or not do just about anything. While Lydia had arrived from Brazil with only a battered backpack containing a change or two of clothing, she had brought a collection of vials containing her native arsenal.

Lydia went back to studying the *Kama Sutra* chart.

Dang. That girl had to be a gymnast.

3

Esme Castaneda

As she had been every morning for the past two weeks, Esme Castaneda was struck again by the beauty and luxury that surrounded her in her guesthouse. She lay on a Duxiana bed, between the palest of pink satin sheets, under a rose and white quilt that had been handmade in Appalachia. Priceless Egyptian tapestry rugs were scattered over the burnished wooden floors. The furniture was antique, white, with hand-painted details. She'd slept with the window open; the scent of oranges from the trees outside wafted through the air. It was quiet. So quiet. It struck her anew every morning when she woke up. This was really where she lived now, fifteen miles and a few light-years from her real home in Echo Park, a Latino neighborhood—a *barrio,* really. Her parents, many people she loved, were there. But also grinding poverty. Drug addicts desperate for a fix.

Gangs that murdered each other just because they needed a group to hate.

Two weeks ago Esme had been hired on a probationary basis as nanny to the Goldhagen children. Steven Goldhagen was perhaps the most successful producer in television history. Men like Aaron Spelling, Dick Wolf, and David Kelley spoke of him with reverence. Steven and his wife, Diane, were also legendary for their charitable commitments. Each of them served on the board of their synagogue and many philanthropic organizations. For Diane, charity was practically a full-time job.

To make their complicated lives even more complicated, Diane had recently returned from a visit to Cali, Colombia, with a set of twins—two beautiful, dark-eyed girls so identical you could only tell them apart by the tiny heart-shaped beauty mark on one's cheek. They spoke no English, and neither Diane nor Steven spoke Spanish. That was why they hired Esme, daughter of their groundskeeper and their maid, and installed her in this gorgeous guesthouse on their gated Bel Air estate.

If the job worked out, Esme would attend Bel Air High School in the fall. Bel Air High, where the kids would be rich and white, with the confident air of those born to privilege. Probably the biggest thing the kids at Bel Air High had to worry about was whether Mommy and Daddy were taking them to ski in Switzerland for spring break or scuba diving in the Red Sea. There were no guns or knives, no gang wars, no outdated textbooks, no teachers forced to spend the majority of the time just trying to keep the peace.

Esme, nearly a straight-A student, had mixed feelings about the prospect. If she went to a good high school—no, a *great* high school—what might she accomplish? What scholarships might be available to her for college? The Goldhagens had opened the door to all possibilities, and invited Esme to waltz through. So why did she resent them so much?

She gazed at the still-crumpled pillow beside her, and then raised it to her face. It still smelled like him. Like Jonathan. Jonathan Goldhagen, Steve's son from a previous marriage. Jonathan was a young actor who'd already made his first feature film, a low-budget indie, well reviewed if barely seen. He was almost six feet tall, with short brown hair, startling blue eyes, and the rangy build of a tennis player. It was quite a contrast with Esme, who stood five feet four on a good day, and her raven hair, lush curves, and ochre skin. For the last week, almost every night, Jonathan had crept down the stone path from the mansion and made insane love to her in this very bed. When she awoke in the morning, he was always gone.

She put the pillow over her face, trying to block out how horrible it all was. Her mother had warned her not to get involved with the Goldhagens' son. If she knew the truth, Mama would be furious. Worse than that, Esme would bring shame on the family. Esme was already ashamed enough. That was why she hadn't even told her two new friends, Kiley and Lydia. They thought that after the night she'd hung out with Jonathan at the launch party for the premiere of the movie *The Ten* at the Santa Monica Pier, they'd gone back to being just friends, because she already had a boyfriend back in the Echo, Junior.

At first Esme had simply been too reserved to tell them. Much as she liked Lydia and Kiley, Esme wasn't a girl who chattered about her private life. Still, these two new friends were special. When Esme had really needed them to help her deal with the two *cholos* who had kicked Jonathan's ass, they'd both come through for her. But they were still Anglos. She'd never had Anglo friends before.

Besides, if she had told them, they'd want to know what she'd done about her *real* boyfriend. Junior was a few years older, a *veterano* who'd gotten out of the gang life. All the gang members respected him because he was a paramedic, and he'd come to them when they lay bleeding in the street after the latest gang war, when the L.A. cops would play deaf and dumb to *cholos* dying in the road, choking on their own blood.

Not long ago she'd told Junior the truth, that she wasn't sleeping with Jonathan. Only now that truth had turned into a lie, and she hadn't exactly filled him in on the status change. If he knew . . . She didn't even like to think about it. Junior didn't believe in beating on his lady. But that didn't mean some of his homies wouldn't do it for him. It had happened before.

The only person who knew the truth about Esme and Jonathan was Esme's best friend, Jorge Valdez. He was one of the Latin Kings, a group of guys who fought for the rights and prosperity of Latinos. He wrote rap lyrics that were actually uplifting. The *cholos* dissed him for it, called him a *chiquita linda*—a pretty girl. Jorge was man enough to take it. He was skinny, but strong, definitely straight, and very smart.

Esme's mother would faint from happiness if Esme married Jorge one day. But Esme didn't see Jorge like that. Their friendship meant too much to her. She knew what every girl knew—your boyfriend couldn't also be your best friend.

When she had told Jorge about Jonathan, his reaction had been characteristically blunt. "Do you have a death wish?"

Did she? She had no idea. Jorge's advice was to cut both guys loose. Junior, because he was going to live and die in the *barrio;*

he wasn't good enough or smart enough for Esme. Jonathan, because their differences would always make their relationship unbalanced; Jonathan would have all the power. Look at what would happen if they got caught. Diane had made it clear that Esme couldn't have male guests at the guesthouse. She'd lose her job. What would happen to Jonathan? He'd lose a few hours' sleep. Maybe. Who would suffer more? Jorge was sure that Jonathan considered Esme nothing more than a friend with benefits; probably the kind of benefits he'd never before enjoyed with an exotic Latina girl from a poor neighborhood. "Forbidden fruit," Jorge had termed it.

Every night, Jonathan came to her late and left her early, and they never talked about it. Night after night, their lust continued. What kind of girl allowed herself to be used like that? What the hell was she doing?

Yet Esme couldn't seem to stop herself. She needed Jonathan the way flowers needed rain and babies needed milk. She hungered for him. No matter how many times they had sex, the hunger only grew worse. She was disgusted with herself. It wasn't like she was his girlfriend, like they went on dinner dates, or hung out with his rich show business friends at the Derby or one of the cool clubs in Mar Vista. He claimed to have broken up with his old girlfriend, Mackenzie. Esme had met her; Mackenzie and Jonathan had been playing tennis together on the Goldhagens' private court when Esme first set foot on the property. She was everything a girl named Mackenzie should be: tall, blond, skinny, and rich. What if Jonathan was lying to Mackenzie the same way she was lying to Junior?

Esme threw back the quilt and padded through the hall to the living room, where the cuckoo clock she'd fixed herself squawked the hour—ten o'clock. Out the window she could see the tennis court with its vine-covered fence, like something out of *The Great Gatsby.* Beyond the court was the magnificent mansion of natural wood and soaring windows, surrounded by pools that reflected the beautiful flowers and shrubs her very own father nurtured and cultivated.

Oh no.

Coming down the path from that tennis court, at that very minute, was Diane Goldhagen. She wore a baby blue Juicy Couture warm-up suit, her blond hair tied back in a girlish ponytail. She didn't look happy at all.

Esme's mind raced, her heart pounding; she quickly pulled on an old gray robe—she'd been in her panties and a T-shirt—and prepared herself for the worst. She already had the scenario in her mind's eye. Jonathan had come back to the house before dawn. Diane had been waiting for him. She'd asked him where he had been. He'd told her the truth. She'd said fine, and he'd gone up to bed. Now she was on her way to Esme's to tell her that it wasn't fine at all, and Esme had maybe twenty minutes to get her brown ass off the Goldhagen property.

Esme opened the door on the first knock. "Good morning, Diane," she said, trying to cover her anxiety.

"Hi." Diane's voice was flat. "I know it's Sunday, but I've got a lot on my mind. Can we talk for a minute or two?"

"Of course."

Diane motioned for Esme to follow her, then led the way to a stone bench outside Esme's guesthouse. It was just below a date palm tree already heavy with fruit, near the paved area where a basketball hoop hung. Diane idly plucked a date from the tree and then motioned for Esme to sit down.

Esme did, with a sinking feeling in her stomach. She mentally rehearsed a plea as to why Diane should fire only her, and not let this affect her parents, who really, really needed their jobs.

"FAB starts in two days, Esme. I'm about ready to crack. We're cohosting the final charity ball on the *Queen Mary* ocean liner—it's docked in Long Beach permanently, you know—and Lateesha Nudsley, the party planner—she's a distant relative of Princess Caroline—has been driving me absolutely batty for the last week. Look, I'm using some of her ridiculous British expressions."

Esme was barely listening. Relief coursed through her arteries and out her pores. Diane's impromptu visit wasn't about her being fired after all. She knew full well that it could have been.

"Anyway," Diane went on, "the party always had a strict color scheme. Lateesha had wanted it to be black and white, but Diddy recently gave a black and white party at Mar-a-Lago down in Palm Beach and Lateesha decided black and white would be derivative, so she decided on seafoam. It's right on the invite, 'All guests must wear seafoam, aquamarine, some shade of blue,' et cetera. Can you imagine twelve hundred people in seafoam? I got a call late last night from Fred Segal himself. There are no more dresses in those colors!"

"Can you maybe have some sent in from New York?" Esme ventured.

"I did, I did," Diane reported. "But all these guests are calling in a panic, worried that they have nothing to wear. Did you see the actresses from *Desperate Housewives* on *Letterman* last night, joking about it?"

"No," Esme said.

Diane waved a hand. "Anyway, I've pretty much decided to can the color scheme; I just don't think it's going to work out and it's my own fault."

Esme nodded, careful to keep her expression neutral. Now that she knew Diane hadn't learned about her secret relationship with Jonathan, she was back to judging her boss's bizarre lifestyle. Did she actually think that seafoam dresses and actresses on *Letterman* and relatives of Princess whoever were important? How shallow could any one rich woman be?

"I'm sorry, I'm blathering on like an idiot," Diane apologized. "Ignore me; I get like this every year before FAB." She smiled and folded her hands in her lap. "Anyway, I need to tell you about tomorrow. The twins are going to be in Emily Steele's World Culture Kids fashion show. She's an amazing designer. Anyway, my girls will need some training in how to walk the runway, all that. They need to be at their agent's at one. You'll have them ready?"

"Certainly," Esme promised as she tried to digest the fact that the twins had an agent.

"Great." Diane seemed genuinely relieved. "I'm so excited about this—we've never done a children's designer before. Her influence this year is Japanese. Last year was Colombian. Isn't that ironic?"

"Ironic" wasn't necessarily the word that first came to Esme's mind. She knew Emily Steele's clothes—the twins' closets were filled with her outfits, at four hundred dollars a pop. If Diane hadn't adopted Easton and Weston (whose names had been changed the moment they arrived on American soil), they might well have grown up to be the dirt-cheap labor who would hand-embroider some future Emily Steele collection. That wasn't ironic. That was sad.

Diane left; Esme went back inside to shower, realizing just how close she'd come to disaster. As she stepped into the steaming hot water, she thought that maybe God had just sent her a wake-up call: she had to end things with Jonathan.

The only question was whether or not she'd be smart enough to answer it.

4

"Maybe he's gay," Lydia opined to Kiley, then wrapped herself in her aunt's white Irish linen swimsuit cover-up. The late-morning sun had just ducked behind a bank of puffy cumulus clouds and Lydia had skipped breakfast—very unusual for her. Low blood sugar always made her cold. As for Kiley, she'd arrived at the country club pool only minutes before and immediately started to yammer about Tom Chappelle; she was so excited that the hot young model had actually asked her out.

Lydia had quickly learned upon her return to America that her tendency to speak her mind without sugarcoating the truth could be off-putting. The way Kiley's face fell as she stepped out of her no-name jeans confirmed that, but it was too late for Lydia to take back her words about the possibilities of Tom's sexuality.

"I never thought of that," Kiley admitted. "But wait. What

about when I met him? I told you guys, he was in the next suite at the Hotel Bel-Air. I would swear there was a girl in there with him. At least she moaned like a girl."

"That proves it," Esme said sharply from the chaise on the other side of Lydia. Lydia thought she looked curvy and luscious in an aqua Shoshanna halter-top bikini that she'd told Lydia had been a gift from Diane after she'd stayed up late with the twins one night. "He's not gay."

"He could be gay and was using her as a beard," Lydia countered. "Maybe he's using both of you."

Kiley pulled her T-shirt over her head. Lydia saw she wore the same tank suit as on the day they'd met. "And a beard is . . . ?"

"Gay guys go out with a girl and a guy and pretend they're with the girl so no one will know that they're really with the guy," Lydia explained knowledgeably.

Esme closed her eyes and raised her face to the sun, which had peeked out from under the clouds. "Don't tell us," she murmured. "You read it in a magazine."

"Ha, y'all are wrong this time!" Lydia crowed. "You know X? Anya and Kat's driver? He told me he has friends who do that. He thinks it's tacky. Anyway, Kiley, maybe you're wrong. Maybe it was a guy who *sounded* like a girl."

"Kiley, don't listen to her," Esme interjected. "And toss me the sunblock. He asked you out because he likes you. Why can't you just accept that?"

"Because I don't look like . . ." Kiley cast around until her eyes landed on the actress Kate Bosworth, who was on the opposite side of the pool drying off her perfect body after a swim. It was no shock that Kate was at the club, since the membership seemed to include most of the Hollywood A-list and a good part of the B-list-striving-desperately-to-be-on-the-A-list as well. "Like *her*, that's why."

"Oh, who gives a rat's ass?" Lydia asked. She hadn't meant to hurt Kiley's feelings; she just wanted to be a loyal friend and tell it like it was. No sense not facing reality. In the Amazon basin, not facing reality could get you killed. Since she'd come back to America, she'd sometimes found it difficult to understand how exactly to act—the social rules were so different here. In Amazonia, you always watched your friend's back, so you could knock off the poison snake that had just dropped onto it from a tree. Here, you had to make sure that your words wouldn't hurt her fragile feelings. Who could figure it all out?

"You only say that because you *do* look like her," Kiley explained. "I didn't come to California to get all weirded out about my appearance."

Lydia narrowed her eyes and surveyed her friend, trying to be objective. Kiley was very cute, but she wasn't skinny and never wore makeup or sexy clothes in a town where all the other girls seemed to look like models who'd be appearing at the upcoming FAB fashion shows. But Lydia knew better. Those girls weren't naturally any hotter than Kiley. She'd seen the "Caught in Public" photo spreads in *US* magazine. Without expensive clothes, haircuts, bling, and a layer of war paint, most of the so-called stars looked—as they said in Texas—rode hard and put up wet. Lydia could fix Kiley. She was certain of it. She'd certainly memorized enough makeover articles.

"What you need is a big ol' dose of self-confidence," Lydia said emphatically. "I've got it all planned out. I do your makeup, loan you a hot outfit—"

"You don't *own* a hot outfit," Kiley interrupted. "They all belong to your aunt Kat and her wife. Husband. Whatever she calls her partner."

"Anya," Lydia declared. "She calls her Anya. Her name. They got married in Massachusetts."

"Fine, whatever. My point is, even if you did own one, I wear a size ten and you wear a size three or something."

"You wouldn't believe how roomy some of Kat's clothes are," Lydia retorted. "There's this gold Emanuel Ungaro silk tunic to die for—real low-cut—that falls from the bust in ripples and ends about here." She held two fingers to her thigh a good six inches above her knees. "Kat wears it with pants but you could wear it with a little thong. Add some strappy Jimmy Choos—what size are you? Kat's an eight."

"I'm not wearing your aunt's clothes *or* her shoes," Kiley said, making a face, "and I don't own a thong. First of all, it's just not me. Second of all, what are you going to do when she finally catches you stealing her stuff?"

Lydia raised a forefinger. "It's borrowing," she corrected. "And I'm not worried. She's doing all the big tennis tournaments this summer for ESPN, so she's traveling a ton. Like, she'll be in London for Wimbledon for almost two weeks. By the time she gets home from the studio, she's so whipped she just falls into bed."

"What about Anya?" Kiley challenged.

"Anya couldn't care less about fashion. Only makeup. Isn't that bizarre? Her clothes are in a whole different room."

"I just want to point out that you sound really defensive," Esme said.

Okay, there was some truth to what her friends were saying,

Lydia admitted to herself. But the "borrowing" wasn't going to last forever. She had big plans to—

"Lydia, a mo'?"

Lydia turned. She recognized the woman standing there, Evelyn Bowers, a publicist who had once tried to steal Lydia away from the moms—what Lydia called her aunt and Anya—with a sweet job offer. Lydia had remained loyal to the moms, realizing that without them, she'd still be eating roast monkey instead of pâté and truffles.

Not one to miss an opportunity, though, Lydia did dangle the possibility of finding a nanny for Evelyn in exchange for a serious commission. Evelyn had bit, and Lydia had sold Kiley and Esme on the idea of a nanny agency. Kiley volunteered that her best friend, Nina, might be interested. For several days now, Lydia had been trying to reach this Nina in Wisconsin to settle the deal, but the girl hadn't returned her phone calls.

From the glare in Evelyn's eyes, as she stood with her arms crossed in a size nothing white and green leaf-patterned bikini, it was obvious that the publicist was losing patience. Lydia's response was to smile up at her as if she didn't have a care in the world. The Amazonia tribesmen made an art form out of it—killing with kindness. The only thing was, often as not, they followed it up with killing for real.

"Oh, sure, Evelyn," Lydia replied easily.

Evelyn hoisted her Jamin Puech beaded silk bag with metallic leather trim farther up her bony shoulder. Lydia had seen it in a *W* layout on the most sought-after accessories. "Lydia. I'm not feeling entirely comfortable with our business arrangement."

This was not good, yet Lydia's face still betrayed nothing. "Well, then we need to have a little chat about that."

"What we need is for you to deliver me an excellent nanny as promised."

Lydia smiled. "Evelyn, this is your lucky day. After an extensive and exhaustive search, I found her. Her name is Nina Hopson."

Evelyn seemed taken aback. "Well, that *is* good news. I figured you'd flaked out on me."

"No chance of that, Evelyn," Lydia assured her.

"When do I meet her?"

"Well, there is one little thing. She lives in Wisconsin. You'll need to buy her plane ticket to Los Angeles."

This was true, *if* Nina was taking the job. Lydia had no idea if she was or wasn't.

Evelyn scowled. "Are you kidding me?"

Lydia shrugged. "I'd just hate to see you lose out on an employee of this caliber. But if you want to settle for one of those girls where you need a bank of nanny cams just to make sure they aren't abusing your children, well . . ."

Evelyn considered this, tapping one impatient foot against the white concrete of the pool deck. "At the very least I need some references for you before I—"

"Hold on a sec, Ev—hate to be rude," Lydia added, then nodded toward Kiley and Esme. "Evelyn Bowers, meet Kiley McCann and Esme Castaneda. They're two of my nannies."

Evelyn gave them an appraising look. "Are you telling me you placed these girls in their current jobs, Lydia?"

"Of course," Lydia lied smoothly. She saw Esme and Kiley exchange a glance and hoped for two things. One: that her about-to-be-first-client didn't notice. Two: that her new best friends were not about to be her new worst enemies.

Evelyn switched her bag to her other arm and shook her perfectly streaked shoulder-length brown hair off her faux-tanned face. "For whom do you girls work, if you don't mind my asking?"

Lydia jumped in before her friends could reply. "That's confidential information, Evelyn. It wouldn't be ethical to divulge it. Employer privacy and all that."

"What are you talking about? Of course it's ethical," Evelyn snapped. "That's how references get checked. So if you're not willing to provide me with—"

"I work for the Goldhagens," Esme interrupted smoothly.

"*Steven* and *Diane* Goldhagen?" Evelyn pronounced the names with slow reverence. "They hired Lydia, and Lydia here hired you?"

Lydia held her breath.

Esme nodded. "Actually, Lydia informed me that there were a number of families on her roster seeking nannies, but that the fit with the Goldhagen family seemed to be right for them and for me."

Lydia exhaled. "So true."

Evelyn fanned her face, as though the heat of being one degree of separation from the famous TV producer and his wife was more than she could take. "I heard that Diane had adopted two little girls from one of those hideous, poverty-stricken little third world countries," she recalled. "The woman is a saint."

"So, there you go, Evelyn," Lydia said, beaming. "How's that for a reference? I'm sure you don't know Steven and Diane personally, but—"

"Yes, I do," Evelyn interrupted, haughtily shaking her hair off her pinched face.

Oops. She'd been sure that Evelyn Bowers had never met the Goldhagens, otherwise she never would have said . . . Then Lydia noticed that Evelyn was tapping her foot again. It was a dead giveaway that the woman was lying her bony ass off.

Lydia dug her cell phone out of her bag and flipped it to Evelyn, who automatically caught it. "Great!" she exclaimed. "Why don't you give Diane a call right now? Diane's home, right, Esme?"

"Definitely," Esme confirmed. "She's got a ton of planning to do for FAB. All these caterers and flower arrangers for the *Queen Mary* banquet on Tuesday night."

"Well, I certainly wouldn't want to interrupt her right now." Evelyn backpedaled furiously and handed the phone back to Lydia. "It just proves once again my instincts are completely correct. You really *are* a gem! Just don't go giving my new nanny away to a higher bidder, even if it's my friend Tricia."

"You can count on me, Evelyn," Lydia assured her. "We'll talk about Tricia another time. Let her see the nanny I place with you and get insanely jealous first."

"You must have Hollywood genes, Lydia." Evelyn smiled as she stooped to perch on the edge of Esme's chaise. "So . . . Esme. You're helping your boss with this year's FAB bash?"

Esme nodded.

"I would just *kill* for an invitation."

"Just call Diane," Esme suggested. "I'm sure she'd—"

The publicist shook her head. "Oh, not now. She's far too busy."

"Let's see how things work out with the new placement," Esme said, smiling. "And then I'll see what I can do."

Evelyn grabbed Esme's hand. "Oh my God, really? That's

fantastic!" She leaped to her feet. "Call me as soon as possible, Lydia."

"I sure will. I'll call this afternoon about the plane ticket for the nanny," Lydia said sweetly. "Oh, and one more thing." Lydia rose and whispered in the older woman's ear.

"Absolutely," Evelyn agreed. She turned to Esme. "*Thank you.*"

Lydia waggled her fingers in Evelyn's direction as the publicist tottered off on her green and pink espadrilles. "I owe you. Forever," she told Esme.

Esme put on her oversized black sunglasses. "You don't owe me shit."

It took Lydia a moment to process—Esme lying for her, and then going cold. Then she got it. "It was Evelyn's stupid third world comment, wasn't it?"

"Women like her make me sick. What, she thinks her ignorant ass is the first world? Give me an effing break."

"Let me make a mental leap here," Kiley ventured. "That woman is a client for your upscale agency that doesn't exist."

"*Our* upscale agency," Lydia corrected.

Kiley turned to Esme. "You're really going to get her an invite to Diane's party?"

"Please," Esme snorted. "I'd sooner invite some *puta* from the *barrio*. In fact, maybe I'll pay for one to show up at the witch's front door and ask for her husband."

Lydia laughed. "Ex. She's divorced."

"No shocker there," Kiley said, rolling onto her stomach.

"I know it's going to be an amazing party." Lydia sighed. She'd been reading about Diane Goldhagen's annual FAB party for years, dreaming about how wonderful and glamorous it all had to be. "Can we come?"

"Lydia!" Kiley chastised her. "That's kind of out of line."

"Worth a shot." Lydia's eyes slid to Esme. "So can we? Oh, and can Kiley's friend Nina come too, now that Mrs. Bony Butt is ready to buy her a ticket?"

"Uh, excuse me," Kiley called out, "but you're putting Esme in a terrible position. Nina hasn't said yes yet. Why don't you call her again?"

Lydia was about to, when the rippling pecs of a hard-bodied lifeguard she'd never seen before caught her attention. Hmmm, he had to be new. His dirty blond hair was tied back in a ponytail; Lydia's eyes were glued to him as he ascended the lifeguard stand.

Kiley waved. "Over here, Lydia."

Lydia blinked. "Right. Waiting for Billy. I'm seeing him tonight, if he can get his boss to cut him loose for a while." She sighed as Mr. Hard Body stretched his arms over his head.

"Off-limits conversation." Esme stood and stretched. "You want anything from the snack bar? We can charge it to our bosses."

"Umm . . ." Lydia watched one of the poolside waiters edge past carrying a tray of lobster tails with the shells already cracked, and a pitcher of icy Dos Equis Mexican beer. "Lobster for you, Kiley?"

"Burger and a Coke."

"Make it two of each," Esme said as she got up. "I'm not charging lobster."

Lydia shrugged. "Suit yourself."

As Esme walked away, Lydia opened her cell and passed it to Kiley. "Can you call your friend for me? It's crucial that she says yes."

Kiley looked wary. "I don't know. I never told her what a bitch Evelyn is. Why would she want to work for her?"

"Seven hundred and fifty reasons why, actually."

Kiley's eyes widened. "I thought the pay was four-fifty."

"That was before I whispered in Evelyn's ear that the salary just went up. Plus two weeks' salary as our commission—fifteen hundred big ones, split three ways. Imagine all the lingerie you could buy and wear for Tom."

"Tom," Kiley groaned. "I managed to forget about it for a few minutes."

"You'll be fantastic," Lydia insisted. "But you'll be more fantastic in great underwear."

"Or I can save it for my college fund. Scripps costs a fortune."

"Whatever floats your outrigger," Lydia agreed as Kiley started to punch in Nina's number. "I don't know about you, but I feel richer already."

What did a nice girl from La Crosse, Wisconsin, wear to a party in Malibu when her date was a supermodel?

Kiley had no idea, it was already past seven-thirty, and Tom was picking her up. Worst of all, Kiley was still in her white cotton Kmart bra and panties. It was underwear that she knew full well belonged on a nun. What had she been thinking, that *she* could seduce Tom Chappelle? She wasn't cute enough or sexy enough or hip enough or *anything* enough. In fact, she should just call and say she wasn't feeling well, and then—

Stop, she told herself. *Don't do what Mom would do. Don't have a panic attack over a party, for God's sake.*

She marched purposefully to her closet. The only really cute item of clothing she owned was the bottle green camisole purchased for her by the TV show. She slipped it on and was reaching for her jeans when she felt the tug on her back and heard the material rip. Damn. She whipped it off and examined the damage: an inch-long gash right up the seam.

Great. This was just great. Why, why, why hadn't she taken Lydia up on borrowing something? Kiley glanced at her Timex. Fifteen minutes until Tom, if he was on time. Shit.

She scanned the closet again, though she knew exactly what she had on hand. When she'd packed to come to California, she'd brought the bare minimum, never expecting that she'd be invited to stay: three boring T-shirts, a denim bowling shirt compliments of her father's league, a University of Wisconsin–La Crosse sweatshirt, three cotton shirts, and one faux silk blouse in a bilious shade of yellow that had been a gift from her grandmother so that she'd have "something decent to wear to church." In her drawer were two pairs of khakis and two pairs of jeans. In the two weeks since Platinum had hired her, she'd acquired some white socks. That was it.

"Shit!" This time she said it aloud.

"What the hell do you have to swear about?" came a voice from behind her.

Kiley whirled around. Platinum stood in the doorway, a half-empty bottle of Taittinger's champagne in her hand. Her trademark poker-straight white blond hair fell to both sides of her high-cheekboned face. She wore an exquisite white silk scoop-necked top that fell in graceful folds to her waist, and white boot-cut jeans. Even semi-sloshed, the rock star still looked a good ten years younger than the midforties Kiley knew her to be.

"You just . . . showed up?" Kiley asked, because she couldn't think of a better way to say "Where do you get off walking into my place without knocking?" without alienating her boss.

"It's my house, baby." Platinum took a long swig from the champagne bottle, then plopped herself down on Kiley's bed. "What's happening?"

"It's still my day off," Kiley replied. "I've got a date."

"I don't have a date," Platinum pouted, narrowing her eyes as she scrutinized Kiley's bra and panties. "That's the goddamn ugliest-ass underwear I ever saw. Serenity's is hotter."

Kiley forced herself not to point out that a second grader had no business in sexy lingerie. Meanwhile, she reached for her father's bowling shirt. "Where are the kids?"

"TV." Platinum took another guzzle of champagne. "I'm so damn bored. Can I come with you?"

Okay, this was getting weird.

"Um . . . no. It's a *date*." Kiley checked her watch again. Five minutes. She needed perfume. Where was that Vera Wang perfume sample that had been in the Hotel Bel-Air bathroom? She opened a night-table drawer and started rummaging. Meanwhile, Platinum rolled onto her taut stomach, holding the champagne bottle upright against the quilt with one fist.

"Who's your date?" Platinum asked, as if they were two teen friends hanging out.

"A guy." Kiley uncovered the bottle behind her map of the Walk of Fame on Hollywood Boulevard and applied a little to each wrist.

"Where are you and 'a guy' going?" Platinum asked.

"A party. In Malibu." Kiley thought the best way to get rid of Platinum was to be curt but polite. "I think at the beach colony or something."

Platinum exploded in laughter. "A party at the Malibu Colony? No way you're going in a bowling shirt!"

Kiley flushed as she took her favorite pair of khakis out of the bottom drawer of her dresser. "Excuse me. I don't own a lot of clothes."

"Oh yeah, that's right, you're poor." Platinum sat up. "That sucks. Sure you don't want some? It's the best." She offered Kiley the champagne bottle.

"No, thanks."

Platinum shrugged and belted down some more.

Kiley immediately thought of Serenity and Sid—she knew what it was like to be home with a drunken parent. "You might want to slow down on that, you know, since the kids are here."

Platinum's eyes flashed. "I *know* you're not telling me what to do."

"No, I just meant—"

"Because you know what happens to people who tell me what to do? If they don't work for me, they can go to hell. If they do work for me, they get canned and *then* they can go to hell."

Kiley's heart thudded. It was true. She'd seen two employees come and go since she'd started as Platinum's nanny. Three, counting Jeff Greenberg.

"Sorry," she mumbled.

Platinum nodded with satisfaction, then smiled. "I forgive you. Hey, it's too damn quiet in here." She reached across the bed and flicked on the Bose Wave clock radio. Mariah Carey at ear-splitting volume. Platinum listened to about three seconds before she snapped it off. "She's such a diva. I hate that bitch, and I hate her ex more. You like her?"

"Not really."

"Good. Hey, no hard feelings about before, right?" She set the champagne unsteadily on the floor, rose to her feet, and yanked her gauzy shirt over her head. The bra underneath was a gossamer wisp of white and pale pink lace. "Here."

"What?"

Platinum held the shirt out to Kiley.

"Sorry?"

"Take the shirt. Wear it on your date."

Kiley stepped backward. "Oh no, I couldn't. I mean, thank you, that's so thoughtful of you, but—"

"It's Alberta Ferretti, for crying out loud. So take the goddamn shirt!" Platinum bellowed. "What kind of a person doesn't let another person do something nice for them?"

Oh God, this was terrible. What else could she do? Kiley took the shirt.

"Thanks. That's . . . really sweet of you."

"Horseshit. I'm never sweet, don't try to flatter me. Put it on, let's see how you look."

"Uh . . . it might be too small."

"Nah. I bought it when I was gonna get my boobs done; I was thinking big at the time. Try it."

Kiley did. It fit perfectly. Not only that, it even looked fantastic with Kiley's khakis—the contrast of expensive shirt and low-rent pants worked, somehow.

"Good," Platinum pronounced.

It did look good. Really good, Kiley had to admit, as she appraised herself in the dresser mirror. The shimmery white silk cast a light on her face, and the scoop neckline made her look curvy. Maybe even sexy. She turned to thank Platinum, but what she saw in the doorway ensured that the words never left her lips. There stood Tom Chappelle in jeans and a sky blue shirt that matched his sky blue eyes. He wasn't even looking at her. He was, however, staring at Platinum's well-filled-out Wonderbra.

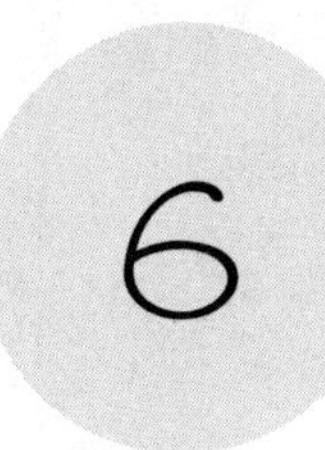

Say something, Kiley told herself. *Say* anything.

Kiley had already gotten into Tom's white Ford F-150 pick-up truck—it still had Iowa plates on it. Tom explained that buying the latest BMW or Mercedes or whatever was considered the hip L.A. car of the moment was just not him, and anyway he'd always loved his truck. He'd already pulled out of Platinum's circular driveway and was cruising west on Sunset Boulevard, en route to the Pacific Coast Highway and Malibu. Weezer wailed on the sound system, the windows were cranked open to the evening air, but still Kiley hadn't said a word.

The night she'd run into Tom at the late-night showing of his movie, she'd somehow mustered the nerve to be flirty and confident. It had all been just so perfect, so spontaneous.

This, by contrast, was planned. An actual date. That changed everything.

Tom stopped the pickup at the light at the intersection of Sunset and Barrington. His face was quizzical. "You okay?"

"I'm fine."

"You're just so quiet."

"Umm . . ." She cleared her throat. "I'm just thinking about how to handle an employer who gives me the shirt off her back—literally." She gestured to the shirt Platinum had bestowed on her for the evening.

He laughed, the corners of his eyes crinkling. "That why she was undressed?"

Okay, this was better.

"Exactly. I was gonna wear my dad's bowling shirt." Kiley fingered a wisp of gauzy silk material. "I have to admit, it's a lot nicer than anything I own. Besides, if I'd said no, I would have gotten fired."

"Kinda high-strung, huh?"

"To put it mildly."

The traffic started to move; it was pretty heavy, even for a Sunday night. Tom's eyes flicked to her again, then back to the road. "Well, it looks great. She was pretty toasted, huh? Platinum, I mean."

"Yeah." Kiley was ready to elaborate—the insanity of working for Platinum was a subject on which she could babble for hours. She knew, however, that she shouldn't. One of the conditions of her employment had been for Kiley never to discuss Platinum's private life—Kiley had to sign a legal document where she swore under penalty of penury never to be a source, even off the record, for a reporter. As for a tell-all book, forget it. Platinum had simply alluded to a close relationship with the

Los Angeles chapter of the Hell's Angels motorcycle club. Kiley needed no further convincing.

"She can't be as crazy as your tour was. How'd it go?"

"Truth is, after a while it was pretty boring. We basically had to say the same things over and over, to every TV talk show host from here to New York and back again. 'People are going to love the flick.' 'We loved working together, it was like a family.' " He shook his head.

"You mean it wasn't fun?"

Tom stopped for a light. "Yeah, I guess. My little sister Raina is completely starstruck. She wanted to come for the premiere, but my parents said she had to show her pigs for 4-H at the county fair. I just think they don't want to fill her head with nonsense."

"Some pig," Kiley joked, citing a favorite line from *Charlotte's Web*.

Tom smiled. "Good book. Templeton the rat was my hero. Just kidding!"

Damn. How could this guy look like . . . well, like this guy, and be nice and sweet and make jokes about characters in *Charlotte's Web*? If only he would be a little less perfect, she could concentrate on his flaws, and not spiral into a needy place where every atom of her body yearned for him.

She gazed out the window, not wanting to fall in love with a guy so obviously out of her league. It would feel hopeless and helpless and out of control. That was way too much like how her mom felt most of the time.

"It must be weird," Kiley mused aloud. "Six months ago you were working on your family's farm, and now . . . all this."

"Yeah, the media loves the hayseed thing. They think anyone who lives between L.A. and Manhattan is barefoot and illiterate. My dad went to Drake. My mom graduated from Iowa State. Ever see *Field of Dreams*? That's them."

Kiley nodded. "My great-aunt has a farm near Rochester, Minnesota. She grows wheat, mostly."

"Then you know what I'm talking about. Like, you told me your dad works at a brewery? I bet people make judgments about him because of that."

In my dad's case, all those judgments are true.

Kiley changed the subject again, not wanting to discuss her alcoholic father. "Tell me about the other stars. What are they like?"

"I get wiped out early on by locusts, so you can't really count me as any kind of star. Owen Wilson is great—loves to play jokes. Tara Reid is wild. She could do promos all day and still party all night."

"Are we going to her place?" Kiley asked lightly. She still didn't know their precise destination.

"I didn't tell you? It's Marym Marshall, the model. You've heard of her?"

Of course Kiley had heard of her. You had to be dead not to have heard of her. Marym was *the* hot teen supermodel, just seventeen years old. A native of Tel Aviv, she was everywhere, her image even more ubiquitous than Tom's bare torso on the Calvin Klein underwear billboards. VH1 had even thrown together a special about her life, complete with fifteen minutes of thong bikini footage from beaches the world over.

Kiley had seen the VH1 special, where Marym confirmed that her real name was Miriam Mendel and that she had been visiting cousins in South Africa before starting her mandatory stint in the Israeli defense forces. On a Cape Town beach, a vacationing *Vogue* photographer had spotted her playing Frisbee with her cousin's whippet and asked if he could take some shots.

Marym hadn't thought anything of it, until the publisher of *Vogue* called her a week later and said she could have a major career if she would just come to America. She came, bringing her father with her as her chaperone. Within three months, she appeared on consecutive covers of *Vogue,* had signed with Ford for modeling and Endeavor for everything else, and was tabbed as a thinner, taller, and more beautiful version of the young Elizabeth Taylor.

"Of course I've heard of her," Kiley confirmed. "She's amazing-looking."

"The whole stardom thing happened so fast for her—it's hard to handle, especially when you're seventeen."

Boo-hoo, poor Marym.

Kiley knew it was a little petty, but she couldn't help thinking that here she was, almost the same age as Marym. She had also uprooted her life. Not to be photographed and be put on the cover of fashion magazines, though. Instead, she had bet on herself so that she might—it wasn't a sure thing, after all—have a chance to get accepted and pay in-state tuition to a school where she could study advanced oceanography. She was willing to work. Marym was willing to get paid for the looks that she'd done nothing to earn. There was something very unfair about it.

"Anyway, this is Marym's eighteenth birthday party, and she just bought this place in Malibu—she's been living with her dad in a rental in Encino."

"So, it's a birthday party for a supermodel," Kiley declared, trying to sound chipper as Tom drove through Pacific Palisades. "Wow."

Tom reached over and tugged gently at Kiley's ponytail. "Don't worry about it, kid."

Kid? Had he just called her *kid*? What was she supposed to be, his little sister? Ugh. Maybe it was true—he had only invited her to this party to be nice, because she was new in L.A., or because he hadn't been sure when his press junket would be over and knew she'd be available on practically no notice.

"Marym and I got together for a little while, a while back," Tom added casually.

Got together? What did "got together" mean?

Then it hit Kiley. Holy shit. The screams of pleasure she'd heard that night coming from Tom's Hotel Bel-Air suite had belonged to supermodel Marym Marshall.

Kiley tried to formulate something really arch and funny, something that would show how easily she could accept his "got together" remark. Then Tom's truck rounded a curve and the most magnificent landscape spread out before them: Technicolor flowers lit by the setting sun, rocky cliffs on both sides, and a straight shot down to the azure Pacific Ocean in all its frothy majesty.

"Awesome," Kiley breathed. "It's just . . . words aren't big enough."

He glanced at her quickly, then back at the road. "I remember what you told me, about Scripps, and how much you love the ocean. Kinda makes whatever insanity you're going through with Platinum worthwhile, huh?"

"Oh yeah." Kiley drank in the panorama as Tom turned north on the Pacific Coast Highway, which paralleled her beloved ocean. She even turned down the music so that there would be no distraction. For quite a while there was a constant ocean view to their left. Once they reached the Malibu section of the highway, the view disappeared. All she could see was the ugly backs of wall-to-wall oceanfront homes.

"So how are people supposed to get to the beach?" Kiley asked.

"They aren't; that's the whole point." Tom nodded toward the homes. "It's called the Colony—chock-full of the rich and famous. They don't want to share the beach. Hence, no parking, no paths, no nothing."

"Just because you own a place on the beach doesn't mean you own the entire beach," Kiley protested. She knew she was right because she devoured everything ever written about the ocean. "There are public-access laws. You're allowed between the high-tide line and the low-tide line."

"True," Tom agreed. "But big stars aren't about to let the little people traipse across their property to get there."

"Well, that—that just sucks."

He laughed. "Fear not, O Defender of the Public Right to the Brine. There are some places where homeowners traded better beach access for the right to make their mansions bigger. There's a good path by David Geffen's estate—he's Steven Spielberg's business partner. I'll show you sometime. Ah, here we are. Marym's new place."

Tom made a sharp left turn across the PCH and pulled into a broad driveway that featured a valet stand teeming with waiting attendants. The rear of the home facing the PCH was nondescript—two stories, a few windows, nothing special.

"Where are they going to park your truck?" Kiley wondered.

"Someplace far away. I bet they'll run a shuttle van there later."

A valet gave Tom a claim ticket and drove away in his truck. Tom took Kiley's arm and led her down a narrow path on the north side of Marym's new home. As they rounded the front of it, Kiley saw that ordinary as it had been from the street, it was breathtaking from the beach; all pale wood and twenty-foot windows reflecting the slate path that led to the ocean below. At the tallest point of a center peak was a ten-foot stained-glass angel, wings spread, as if blessing the massive house upon which it flew.

They reached the front door, where a guy in a weathered leather bomber jacket and baggy jeans admired the sunset as he leaned against the doorframe. Kiley gulped. It was Leonardo DiCaprio. *The* Leonardo DiCaprio. Wait until she told Nina. She'd probably decide to work for Evelyn Bowers for nothing.

Tom put a protective arm around Kiley and whispered to her. "Hey."

"Hey, what?"

"Hey, you don't need to feel freaked about being here," he assured her.

She made a face. "I thought I was being all cool."

He leaned close. "Don't let it get around, but I'm not cool, either. I've just learned how to fake it." He squeezed her hand and gazed into her eyes with the same look he had in that Calvin poster on Sunset Boulevard; her knees nearly buckled. He was so close and so gorgeous and so . . . so out on a date with Kiley McCann from freaking La Crosse freaking Wisconsin, home of the world's largest six-pack. Kiley McCann, who hadn't even been *close* to being the cutest girl at her high school, whose one and only sexual experience with her one and only boyfriend had been such a singular disaster that she wasn't even sure whether they'd—

"You okay?" Tom asked, still holding her hand.

She took a deep breath. "I'm good."

"Excellent."

They headed inside. As they did, a couple of girls Kiley vaguely recognized from *The Apprentice* stumbled out, laughing together.

The interior was stunning: a huge open expanse of space, with soaring rough-hewn beamed ceilings and spectacular rose-colored lighting. The furnishings echoed the sea. Wooden tables holding bowls of seashells were carved into rippling waves. The chairs and couches were the color of the ocean. A mantel, perhaps twenty feet long, held more seashells, exquisite aqua glass vases that looked handblown, branches, leaves, and seedpods. Pillows on the white couches were hand-embroidered with butterflies, seagulls, and fish. A chandelier shone with amber and aquamarine glass beads, looking nothing like anything Kiley had ever seen before.

"Wow, Marym has great taste," Kiley mused.

"Nah, Harry Schnaper—he's a famous interior decorator from New York, I guess—did the whole thing for her."

Kiley's gaze swung upward. On a level perhaps twenty feet up a man in a tuxedo played a white grand piano, and sang "If I Loved You" into a mike. Kiley knew the song; she'd been in the chorus of her high school's production of *Carousel*. Behind him was a bleached-wood open bar, where a trio of bartenders mixed drinks to order. Meanwhile, waiters in tuxedo shirts and black trousers snaked through the crowd, offering flutes of champagne with mango slices floating in them, or various hot appetizers. Beautiful people milled everywhere, clad in everything from the most casual of jeans and T-shirts to expensive beaded sundresses and leather jackets. Funny how Platinum had been so wrong. Kiley really *could* have worn her dad's bowling shirt. If you were rich enough, famous enough, and good-looking enough to be invited to this party, you were by extension cool enough to wear whatever you wanted.

"See that cabinet?" Tom pointed to an antique-looking piece of furniture near the front door. It held a single giant seashell and dozens of yellow roses. "It's called a trove cabinet. It's crafted from individually carved coral-shaped wood twigs. They're silver-leafed and then attached, one by one, to the wooden frame. The doors are antique mirror glass."

"How do you know?" Kiley marveled.

"Marym told me it used to belong to Coco Chanel," he explained. "Harry found it for her at a Sotheby's auction."

Gee. Swell.

"Come on, I'll introduce you around." Tom took her arm again. Snippets of profanity-laced conversation came at her as they wended their way through the crowded living room.

"Michelle is dating another druggie . . . he trashed their room at the Century City Plaza so bad that the hotel put them on their shit list."

"Try the La Mer Essence . . . twenty-one hundred dollars for a vial but it was in the goody bag for the Grammys and I'm telling you the shit works."

"If he asks Tyra to do his shitty FAB show instead of me I'm killing him."

Tom halted at a group of four people chatting with crystal champagne flutes in hand. Kiley recognized their hostess immediately. If anything, Marym was more beautiful in person; photographs amazingly did not do justice to her violet eyes and luminous skin. Inches taller than Kiley, the model wore a red and blue silk caftan cut to her navel in front, slit up both thighs to her waist. It billowed around her willowy frame. No panty line and no bra straps—Marym obviously was wearing nothing underneath. Her jet black hair was messy in an artful way that made it look as if she'd just awakened after a night of debauchery. There was no visible makeup on her face, not even a trace of lipstick on her puffy lips.

Which, Kiley thought, *is about the only thing we could possibly have in common.*

"Tom!" Marym cried, cutting in front of an older goateed producer type in a white T-shirt, black cashmere sweater, and Live 8 concert baseball cap. "You came!" She threw herself into Tom's arms and hugged him close. Really close. For a really long time.

"Happy birthday," Tom told her, kissing her lightly on the lips. "The new place looks great."

Marym made a face. "Oh, I don't know if it suits me." Her English was perfect, with a slight, charming Israeli accent. Her friendly gaze went to Kiley. "I don't think we've met. Welcome. I'm Marym."

"Marym, this is my friend Kiley McCann. Kiley, Marym Marshall."

The model took Kiley's hand in her own slender fingers. "So nice of you to come, Kiley."

"Thanks for inviting me," Kiley replied.

Then she realized what a stupid statement that was, because of course Marym *hadn't* invited her. Tom had, but Marym either didn't notice the gaffe or was sufficiently gracious to ignore it. Instead, she backed out of Tom's embrace and peered at her jammed living room. "This is madness. I didn't know so many people would come!" She smiled at Kiley. "So, what do you do, Kiley? Are you a student?"

Kiley nodded. "In the fall, anyway. Right now I'm a nanny."

Marym's eyes went wide. "You take care of children? Oh, that must be fun. I miss my little sisters back in Israel so much." She put her hand on Tom's arm. "You know who is here, Tom? Samuel. I should find him for you."

"De Cubber?" Tom asked. "I thought he went back to France."

"He's in town to do Marc Jacobs at FAB tomorrow night. Who are you doing? Anyone besides Calvin?"

"Ralph," Tom replied. "You?"

"Vera and this crazy new designer out of Palm Springs who makes clothes with stuff she finds at the Disneyland lost and found. That is so FAB, isn't it?"

Kiley actually knew what Marym meant, since FAB was as famous for launching edgy new designers as it was for presenting the work of established favorites.

Tom and Marym chatted on about fittings and photo shoots. Kiley felt invisible. She wished she had a drink—two drinks (and she'd barely ever had a drink in her life)—just for something to do.

"Anyway, I have fittings all day tomorrow." Marym wrinkled

her perfect nose with distaste. "Oh. Want some good gossip? Sam just signed to do a big print campaign in France. That could have been you."

Tom shook his head. "No full frontal for me. My grandmother back in Iowa wouldn't be able to face her bingo friends ever again. She hasn't seen me naked since my butt fit into a diaper."

Marym laughed. "No full frontal. Only naked from the back."

"Naked?" Kiley echoed, since it seemed like the most salient word in their conversation.

"Sam de Cubber is a model," Tom explained. "And a French martial arts champion."

"You're missing a great career opportunity," Marym chided. "Americans are such prudes about nudity."

"There'll be other gigs," Tom maintained.

Marym gave a little pout. "A shame. You're not nearly as hairy as Samuel. They have to wax his back!"

Okay, so Marym had seen Tom naked—another brick of evidence for the theory that Marym had been the one in bed with Tom at the Hotel Bel-Air.

"Oh, look!" Marym waved at someone across the room. "Natalie's finally here. Thank God. Someone who speaks Hebrew besides my father."

Kiley turned to spot a young woman who she was pretty sure was Natalie Portman near the front door, looking casually perfect in worn jeans and a black ballet-style tank top.

"Excuse me; I want to say hello." Marym kissed Tom's cheek. And then, an afterthought: "Nice to meet you, Kiley." She moved off through the crowd as the piano player segued into "As Time Goes By." It was surreal; Kiley felt as if her life had acquired a sound track.

"Wow, so she's seen you—" Kiley began, trying to sound casual, but Tom cut her off before she could utter the word "naked" again. It was becoming a recurrent motif, but not necessarily in the way that she had envisioned.

"You hungry? I think there's a buffet by the bar."

Suddenly, Kiley was desperate for fresh ocean air. "You go ahead. I'll be . . . out front . . . on the beach."

"Great idea," Tom agreed.

As he edged through the crowd to the buffet, Kiley made a beeline for the front door, thoughts tumbling atop one another like a collapsing house of cards. Were Tom and Marym still an item? If so, why had he invited Kiley to this party? It couldn't possibly be to make Marym jealous. That was a ridiculous notion. Marym could have any man she wanted, and probably a good percentage of the women, too. Maybe they were friends with benefits. If so, what then? What guy would give up a friend like Marym, a friend with the kind of benefits that Kiley had heard—if not seen—her provide?

"Billy Martin, who knew you had a romantic soul?"

Billy had called Lydia's cell that afternoon to announce that his boss, Eduardo, had decreed they were actually ahead of schedule on set construction for the Yves Saint Laurent show at FAB, and that Billy could have the evening off. Did Lydia want to hang out?

Definitely.

In that case, he'd planned a surprise, which turned out to be an elegant picnic at a little-known park just south of the main drag in Pacific Palisades. The park was perched on a cliff overlooking Will Rogers Beach, and featured a view from Redondo Beach in the south all the way up to Malibu in the north. The Santa Monica Pier was only three miles away; Lydia remembered it from the premiere party for *The Ten* that she'd attended with Kiley and Esme.

Lydia had borrowed her clothes with care: a beige Marc

Jacobs cropped cotton jacket with oversized antique buttons, a pale blue Chloé sequined T-shirt, and white Hot Kiss shorts with unfinished hems. She'd recently seen the exact same Marc Jacobs jacket on Jessica Alba at the country club. Kiley had pointed Jessica out to her; otherwise, honestly, Lydia would have had no clue that she was famous.

Though Billy claimed to be a killer cook, he admitted that he'd picked up a few things at Gelson's market because time was of the essence. As the sun dropped lower in the sky, he spread out an old-fashioned red plaid blanket and unpacked a feast from a wicker picnic basket: cold roast lemon chicken, curried prawns, giant strawberries dipped in white chocolate, and a bottle of Chassagne-Montrachet '82 packed in a container that Billy claimed would keep the wine cooled to optimum temperature. He'd even brought a small boom box, from which came a male voice crooning a very sexy song.

"Who's the singer?" Lydia asked. She sprawled on the blanket, a half-eaten succulent strawberry in hand.

"Marvin Gaye. 'Sexual Healing.' "

"I like it," Lydia decided, tapping a toe to the funky beat. She bit into the strawberry again; juice ran down her chin and onto the Chloé T-shirt. Damn. Now she'd have to get it dry-cleaned before she returned it to her aunt's closet.

"You don't hear him much on the radio anymore. My dad turned me on to him. Back when Dad was in college, he was the only white guy in an R and B band."

"R and B is . . . ?"

"Rhythm and blues. Damn. You *have* led a sheltered life." Billy took a sip of the white wine from the bottle.

"It just so happens that the Amarakaire asked me to handle the drums at a fertility dance last March, so I'd say I'm not so sheltered." Lydia cocked her head toward the guitar case he'd lugged along with the picnic stuff. "Are you fixing to explain that?"

"My dad taught me."

"I thought your dad was in the Foreign Service."

"He is." Billy reached for the guitar case. "He's an eclectic guy."

So is his son, Lydia thought as Billy took an acoustic guitar from the case and started to tune it. He looked so serious, and so incredibly hot, with his chestnut hair falling boyishly onto his forehead. His pecs bulged under a blue Lucky Brand long-sleeved T-shirt with a V-neck. He had a great casual ease, so comfortable in his own skin. Unlike Scott the lifeguard, Billy wasn't trying to impress anyone, which impressed Lydia all the more.

What would it be like finally to have sex with him? Would bells go off, would the earth move? She remembered when she was a girl back in Houston, walking into the private screening room where her parents watched movies, way before anyone else had a big-screen TV. Her parents had been together on the couch. Lydia had scrambled into her daddy's lap—anything that interested adults was interesting to her. She'd never forgotten how the woman in the movie had been wearing a butt-ugly one-piece bathing suit with a built-in bra that made her breasts look like bullets. Lydia had watched wide-eyed as the couple onscreen kissed passionately in the surf. Even at age eight, Lydia had been curious about such things. Was the couple actually going to *do it*? What if the actress didn't even like the actor, or he had bad breath, or a booger was sticking out of his nose? Wouldn't that ruin everything?

But what if she *did* like him? What if she loved him, the way her mother loved her father. Then it would be the most romantic, passionate thing in the world, right? Or would seaweed get in your hair and sand in your butt and you'd feel all grungy, gross, and disgusting?

Lydia hadn't known the answer then, and she still didn't know now.

Billy strummed a funky blues beat and Lydia drummed her fingers against the blanket, keeping time. He had great hands, she noted. What would it feel like to have those hands on her?

Billy began to sing in a low, throaty voice.

> *"I got nowhere*
> *To call my home*
> *Say got nowhere*
> *To call my home.*
> *That's why I'm blue*
> *That's why I roam."*

"Who wrote that?" Lydia asked as he picked a bluesy riff on the guitar.

"Me. First thing I ever wrote. We were living in Australia then. I was—I don't know—fourteen, fifteen, maybe. My dad showed me four chords and I decided I was B. B. King. Very deep and misunderstood."

"You were singing about not having a home way back then, huh?"

Billy kept picking—the notes flew fast and furious. "Maybe I just thought it sounded cool."

"If I could sing—trust me, I can't—I would have sung about that same thing." They shared a smile of recognition. "Poor us, huh?"

"Bullshit," Billy challenged with a huge grin. "We got to live in cool places that most people never get to see. Besides . . ." He leaned toward her. "Everything you've experienced makes you the unique girl that you are."

He put down the guitar and kissed her softly. It was so sweet and sizzling at the same time that it made her toes curl. Once she'd asked her mother how she'd know when the right boy came along, especially because in Amazonia opportunities to learn about such things were exceedingly limited. Her mother had been stoking the coals under their makeshift smokehouse, drying some monkey meat.

"When I was dating your father," her mom had said, "I had a dream where I was wearing ruby red slippers like in *The Wizard of Oz*. When I saw your father, it made my shoes light up."

Lydia might not have had much experience with romance, but she thought that was the most romantic thing she'd ever heard. Looking at Billy now, she could imagine him making her *everything* light up. But then what? Would they be boyfriend and girlfriend? An official couple? If so, how would Lydia be sure that was what she wanted, instead of making up for lost time with adventures, friends with benefits, no strings, no promises, no anxieties, no expectations.

"You're lost in thought," Billy commented. His eyes were on the setting sun, just now dropping into the night.

"About . . . stuff," she said, deliberately vague. It wasn't her style, but she could see that saying exactly what was on her mind all the time could sometimes rub people the wrong way. She moved closer to Billy and they shared another sizzling kiss, and then another. This was it, finally. She felt it. The One. The Moment.

"Who's at your apartment right now?" she asked as he kissed her neck.

"My three-hundred-pound defensive lineman roommate," Billy replied.

"He has his own room, right?"

"There's a hot poker game tonight in the living room." Billy kissed her again.

Damn. Time for option two.

"Where's your parents' place again?"

"Not that far. Rancho Palos Verdes. Just past Redondo Beach." He nuzzled the pulse between her collarbones. "Of course, they're *way* far away. In Colombo, Sri Lanka."

Victory was hers.

"You, me, empty house?" Lydia prompted.

"Why, Miss Lydia. Whatever are you thinking?" he asked, doing what Lydia realized was his best Rhett Butler imitation.

"I'm thinking—"

She was interrupted by the ring of his cell phone. He dug it out of his jeans pocket and peered at the number on caller ID.

"Shit." He pressed the Send button and raised the phone to his lips. "Hey, Eduardo . . . uh-huh . . . uh-huh . . . uh-huh . . . I thought we were finished with . . . uh-huh. Well, if that's what you need . . . uh-huh."

He hung up with a scowl. It didn't take a shaman to determine it was bad news.

"My extremely talented but psychotic boss has decided that he hates the backdrop we did for Saint Laurent. He has new sketches, he wants it fixed tonight."

"But he gave you tonight off!" Lydia protested.

"In Eduardo's world, he's God," Billy grumbled. "As in: the Lord giveth and the Lord taketh away. Tonight he's on the take." He shook his head as he began to pack up the picnic stuff. "I'm really sorry to do this, Lydia. I can't wait until summer's over and this internship is history."

Silently, she helped him clean up. She felt . . . She wasn't sure what she felt. Disappointed, for sure. Shouldn't he have fought harder to be with her, considering what she was offering?

"I'll make it up to you," he promised, as if reading her mind.

Lydia's smile was arch. She was definitely taking him up on that.

"Ambulance four-four-one, I have a two-nine-eight for you, that's a two-nine-eight, copy." The dispatcher's voice crackled over the ambulance radio system at the same time that it flashed on a dashboard display.

Junior grabbed the radio microphone. "A two-nine-eight, we copy." He grabbed a pen and scribbled down the address as the dispatcher gave it, then nodded at Possum, who was behind the wheel. "Go to it, *esa*." He turned to Esme, adding, "Hold on."

Possum, Junior's paramedic partner, might have gotten his nickname for his ability to do an entire eight-hour shift without a word, but whatever aggression he felt that was unexplored verbally, he took out on the road. When the red light and the siren went on and he was driving . . . look out.

Esme knew this because she'd been in the ambulance with him and Junior before; she fastened her seat belt as Possum gunned the ambulance forward. Technically, Junior wasn't allowed to have passengers in the ambulance without clearance from his boss, but this wasn't the first time she'd come along for the ride. Sometimes there were hours filled with nothing more than skinny old guys—Junior said the ambulance term for them was "skels"—who passed out in the street from drugs or alcohol. Once, Esme had seen her boyfriend resuscitate a skel only to have him puke all over the ambulance. Then Junior and Possum had to clean up all that crap before they could take the next call.

Other times it was rush, rush, rush, from one crisis to the next. Bloody car accidents, burned survivors after an apartment fire, the aftermath of a gang war drive-by with multiple casualties lying in the street. When Esme was around for such pickups, especially if they were children, she was overcome with sadness. You couldn't stay innocent for long in the Echo. If Our Lady of Guadalupe herself was in the wrong place at the wrong time, it could be her blood forming the river to the nearest sewer or pooling on the asphalt before a crew of lethargic city workers hosed it off. If they were slow, or on another job, the dry city air made it evaporate, leaving nothing behind but a crimson stain. The police sometimes roped the spot off. It was, after all, a crime scene. They might as well rope off the entire neighborhood, Esme thought, for all the good it would do.

In the past, a night shared in the ambulance had always bonded Esme and Junior. This was where his competence and kindness to the injured and scared came into stark focus for Esme. The patients sensed his ability and looked up to him. Esme had often heard them beg for Junior to hold their hand, to stay with them. He'd do it, assuring them they'd be fine. There was just something about him that made people believe it would be all right.

After his shift ended, he and Esme would usually go back to Junior's house, have a couple of beers, and make love. But tonight, nothing felt right. Everything Junior said or did rubbed Esme wrong. The idiomatic *barrio* lingo, his habitual butchering of the English language, the low-rider magazine on the dashboard that he was reading. When had she ever seen Junior read a book? She couldn't remember.

"What's a two-nine-eight?" she asked.

"Woman in labor," Junior translated.

"Age fourteen," the dispatcher continued over the crackling radio. "Home alone, copy."

"We copy, we're on it. Damn traffic."

"You taking surface streets or the freeway?" Junior asked.

"What you think, *esa*?" Possum asked. He snapped on the flashing lights and siren and pulled into the center lane. Possum was short and Latino, built like a sumo wrestler, with tattoos covering his beefy caramel arms. Esme could see the names of three ex-girlfriends as well as his mother, and a drawing of the Virgin Mary with a glowing halo that crept under the short sleeve of his white shirt.

"Fourteen years old and in labor," Esme mused. "A baby."

"Babies have babies all the time, *niña,*" Junior said. "Ain't nothin' new there."

True. Esme had known girls in the Echo to give birth as young as age twelve. Some of them were proud of it, treating the baby like a little doll they could dress up. Usually that didn't last more than a few days or weeks. When their friends stopped oohing and aahing and they realized they could never go out, never have any fun, and that their high-tailed fine little body wasn't quite as fine anymore, that was when *Mama* or *Tía* or *Abuela* would step in and the little girl got to pretend she was a little girl again. Esme had never known anyone who actually put their baby up for adoption. And abortion? Abortion was unthinkable.

Esme shuddered. Thank God for birth control. If she got pregnant . . . She'd handled a lot in her life but that would be too much. Of all the awful things about it, the worst would be that she wouldn't know if the baby was Junior's or Jonathan's. God, how had she turned into the kind of girl who wouldn't know who the father of her baby was? Her eyes slid again to Junior, who had gone into the back of the ambulance to prepare for their call and was just now returning to his seat. He deserved better than her.

Possum turned into an alley that Esme hadn't even seen.

"On the right, up there, *esa*," Junior told Possum, hitching a thumb to the right.

A little girl stood on the small patch of dirt in front of a stucco house that had probably once been white. The heavy black bars over the windows and the front door were ornately filigreed, as if that would fool people into thinking they were there to make the house look good and not to keep the junkies out. The girl saw the ambulance and waved for it to stop. When she jumped up and down her long, inky braids jumped with her.

"*¡Mi hermana, mi hermana! ¡El bebé viene!*" she yelled, lower lip trembling.

Junior was out of the ambulance in a flash. "*No te preocupes, todo será bueno,*" he assured her. "*¿Donde está ella?¿Y cómo se llama?*"

"En su cuarto, en la casa. Se llama Esmeralda."

Possum and Junior got the gurney from the back of the ambulance and the girl led them inside. Esme waited by the ambulance. Some teen girls eyed Esme as they sashayed by with their we're-all-that struts; too much eye makeup, lips outlined in dark pencil and filled in with light lipstick, long hair hot-rollered to fall in waves over their shoulders; tricked out in short, frilly skirts that twitched this way and that at each stiletto-heeled footfall.

Looking at them, Esme felt disdain. They were such fools. Then her chest tightened. Was she really so different from those girls? What right did she have to feel superior? None. None at all.

For such a tiny girl, Esmeralda the pregnant fourteen-year-old had a big set of lungs. She screamed and cried for her mother and her savior, and cursed her boyfriend as Junior and Possum wheeled her into the rear of the ambulance. Her long, naturally dark hair had been bleached an unnatural brassy blond. Esme noticed an inch of black roots.

A hard-faced skinny woman with rollers in her hair and a cigarette seemingly glued to her lower lip came out of the bungalow next door. Junior asked if she knew where the girl's mother was. The woman explained that the mother worked nights and never got home until morning, and that was only if she didn't put in overtime. The baby's father? The woman just shrugged and sucked on her cigarette.

They got back in the ambulance—Junior let the younger sister ride in front with Possum. He and Esme stayed in the back, talking to the pregnant girl, calming her during her contractions, checking her vitals, stroking her hair, assuring her that everything would be fine.

Esme knew that Junior was a sucker for kids. She knew he'd

be an outstanding father. The knot in her stomach was shame over her own behavior.

They took the girl to County General because no way did she have insurance, and the city hospital at USC wouldn't give her a hassle. Once they wheeled Esmeralda inside, Junior let Possum handle the paperwork while he joined Esme back in the ambulance.

"How is she?" Esme asked.

"If it's a girl she's naming her Jessica," he reported. "Her boyfriend says he loves Jessica Simpson, that she's the most beautiful girl in the world."

"That's why Esmeralda bleached her hair blond, I bet," Esme said bitterly. "To look more like Jessica."

"Ain't nothing wrong with trying to please your man."

Esme lifted her heavy hair off her neck; it was a hot night. "Too bad she can't bleach her skin for him too, eh?"

Junior's dark eyes fixed on her. "Why you come out with me tonight?"

Esme shrugged. "I thought it would be fun. We never get to see each other anymore."

He reached for the bottle of water that he always kept under his seat, uncapped it, and took a long drink. "Everything's different now. You know that."

"I'm so sick of that, you say it every time you speak to me," she replied crossly.

He held the water bottle out to her; she shook her head. "So maybe you don't want me to speak to you, eh? If that's it, Esme, you just gotta say the word."

She threw her head back against the hot headrest. "Stop putting words in my mouth."

"Then stop acting like a little bitch," he shot back. "You want to be with me, you treat me with respect, *chica.*"

She didn't reply. He was right. She was treating him horribly, all because of her own guilt.

"Lo siento, tengo la culpa. It's my fault. I'm just tired," she fibbed, then leaned over and kissed him. "Mrs. Goldhagen is making me insane with all the plans for this big fancy party she's giving on the *Queen Mary.*"

"You going?" Junior asked. His tone was offhand, but Esme knew him; it was not an offhand question.

"I gotta go. I have to take the girls."

Possum lumbered out of the emergency exit and climbed back into the driver's seat. "Chow time, *esa.*" He pulled the ambulance away from the hospital and headed down Marengo toward a taco stand at the corner of Daly and Alhambra where he and Junior always ate in the middle of a shift.

Junior looked straight ahead, as if Esme wasn't even there. She couldn't figure out what was going on with him. He couldn't possibly have wanted her to invite him to the FAB party? No, that made no sense. This was Junior. He wanted nothing to do with that world—he didn't fit in there and never would. He knew who he was and wouldn't try to pretend different. She loved and respected that about him.

"I'm just the hired help," she added aloud to him, as if he had challenged her.

His glance at her was cryptic. It was almost as if he could see inside her mind, to the images of a smiling, rich gringo boy who sent shivers down her spine.

Damn Jonathan, anyway.

9

TODAY'S SCHEDULE FOR MARTINA AND JIMMY

(Lydia—do not adjust schedule without checking with me—Anya)

6:30—Wake children. Shower, dress. Apply SPF 30 sunblock to all exposed skin.

6:45—Power walk around property. Make sure children wear proper shoes.

7:00—Breakfast. Soy granola, banana for Jimmy, berries for Martina, soy milk.

7:30—Read front section of Los Angeles Times. Quiz children on current events.

8:30—Math on computer. Please supervise.

10:30–LEAP Center in Northridge. Do not be late.

12:00–Lunch at Center. No sweets, fried food, or milk products. See Martina's menu.

12:30–Socializing. Please supervise. See separate schedule.

2:30–Tennis lesson for Jimmy, aerobic dance for Martina. Make sure she does full hour, no slacking off.

Lydia pulled the neatly typed schedule off the bulletin board just outside the moms' kitchen and shook her head, then shoved it into the back pocket of her cutoffs. Of all the lipstick lesbians on the planet, why did Aunt Kat have to marry the one who channeled a five-star general in the Russian army?

Lydia stepped into the kitchen itself, a state-of-the-art facility with stainless steel everything and a mosaic tile floor. The moms' young, hippie-ish nutritionist, Alfre, was already at work, dropping fresh fruits and vegetables into the Vita-Mix Turbo blender. Lydia knew from experience that eight ounces of protein powder would soon join the mix. Alfre concocted sixty-four ounces of power drink daily; it was kept in the refrigerator for the kids and consumed instead of Dr Pepper or Coke. Anya expected the drink container to be empty by the time the children went to sleep. Usually Lydia ended up dumping most of the contents down the disposal just to keep Anya happy.

"Morning," Alfre called cheerfully. She was a slender young woman in pristine white yoga pants and a T-shirt, so constantly serene that Lydia couldn't imagine her having actual bodily functions.

Lydia sort of grunted and poured herself some coffee. It was far too early for conversation. She wouldn't even be in the kitchen except that she was too lazy to fix coffee in her guesthouse. It was enough that every morning in the rain forest it had been her responsibility to go to the river for water, and trap a turtle if they wanted protein for lunch. Lydia figured she had extra do-gooder points stored up. Her experience in the rain forest might have built character, but it also made early morning her least favorite time of day, unless of course she happened to still be up from the night before. That the previous night hadn't concluded the way she had hoped didn't faze her in the least. One of the lessons she'd learned from turtle trapping was the virtue of patience.

As she slurped the moms' preferred French roast coffee with a touch of cinnamon and plopped down at the kitchen table, she mused on the day ahead. She hadn't heard from Nina, though she'd left two additional messages. She knew she needed an alternate game plan.

The day before at the club, and then on an afternoon window-shopping expedition to the Beverly Center, she'd chatted up every girl in sight who looked remotely possible as nanny material. A cute girl from Barbados named Marie seemed promising until she shared that she was about to elope with her still-married boyfriend. A chubby girl in diaphanous purple named Chandra said she'd have to consult with her guru, her astrologist, and her numerologist before discussing a possible job. A girl Lydia met in the Beverly Center restroom—Lydia never did get her name—seemed sane and perky, two good qualities for a nanny, until she lifted her lavender silk Lanvin jersey and chiffon feathered T-shirt to demonstrate how she could make her breasts twirl in opposite directions at the same time. She proudly explained that she'd learned the skill dancing at the Spearmint Rhino in Van Nuys.

Crap. Lydia took another long sip of coffee. She had to find her savior quickly, or her get-rich-again-quick scheme was doomed.

"Can I get you something else?" Alfre asked, as she did every morning. Of course, in this case, "everything" meant disgusting crap like whipped beet and carrot juice. Compared to that, roasted grubs were appetizing.

"No thanks," Lydia replied. She checked the aquamarine quartz wall clock—6:25 a.m. She had to wake the kids in five minutes. They would moan and groan and want to sleep in. Lydia would have been happy to let them, but Anya—who clearly wore the pants in the family, especially compared to easy-going Aunt Kat—had a preternatural ability to ferret information out of the household staff. Lydia had learned this her second week on the job, when one of the maids reported that Lydia had allowed the kids to eat Cracker Jack while watching a rented horror movie. Anya had practically burst a blood vessel, she'd been so angry. Kat had taken her niece aside to explain that she didn't want discord in her home; Lydia had to follow Anya's instructions as if they were her own. If Lydia couldn't do that . . .

The implication was clear. She could go right back to the Amazon. Lydia shuddered at that prospect. Maybe down the road, when her nanny agency business took off, she could risk losing this gig. But until then, this was Anya's gulag, and the rest of them just lived in it. It meant that Lydia would have to cheat with care.

Speaking of. "Where's Anya?" Lydia asked, knowing that Kat was in New York for a production meeting about Wimbledon. Once that championship was under way in a week or so, Lydia would be alone with Anya and the kids for almost two weeks—not Lydia's notion of a good time.

"Out for a run with Oksana. You know, the Russian tennis player she's training? They're doing ten miles this morning. Did you hear? She's seeded fourteenth for Wimbledon."

That was nice. Oksana had befriended Lydia when she'd first arrived in L.A. Of course, she'd wanted to be more than friends, but Lydia found that bisexuality didn't really speak to her. Now she went to the fridge and rummaged: soy milk, protein powder, fruit, vegetables, and fresh fish. She knew the freezer wouldn't look any better. Was the occasional pint of Ben & Jerry's too much to ask for? In the cheese compartment, though, she was pleasantly surprised to discover a thick wedge of brie. She broke off half and munched on it as if it was an apple, knowing she had to finish before she woke the kids. Supposedly they were both lactose intolerant. Of course, Lydia had snuck them both milk products many times and neither had gotten the least bit sick. Breaking this news to Anya, however, would be the height of folly.

Time to wake up the kids. Lydia went to Martina's room first, since the girl was a notoriously heavy sleeper. Her room was young and girly, with tea-party toile wallpaper, thick pink carpeting, and an enormous array of stuffed animals. As Lydia watched Martina sleep from the doorway, she imagined Anya tearing down the wallpaper, burning the stuffed animals, and putting up posters of Amelie Mauresmo and Maria Sharapova.

Martina had just finished fourth grade but from the neck down was already fifteen. Of course, she made sure that people rarely saw her from the neck down, hiding her very developed breasts and rolls of baby fat under oversized sweatshirts. Her posture didn't help, either; shoulders caved in, bowed head hiding a pretty face behind lank brown hair.

Yesterday, an edict had come down from the moms . . . well, from Anya. Martina needed to drop twenty pounds, pronto. Anya handed Alfre and Lydia what she called a "healthy weight loss" regimen that included daily private aerobics, Tae Bo classes in their home gym, and a portion-controlled, low-carb, sugar-free meal plan.

Lydia wished she could tell the moms what a truly terrible idea this was for a fourth grader. One thing that had really struck home on her return to so-called civilization was how skinny the girls were in Los Angeles. What looked good in magazines looked kind of scary in real life. Her Amazonia friends ranged in size and shape from very skinny to very chubby. Girls were encouraged to eat, to be strong. One never knew when you'd have to skip a meal or two or three, when a pounding rainstorm ruined the fishing or the squirrel monkeys were too busy copulating to cooperate in the hunt.

"Wake up, sweet pea," Lydia said softly, then opened the pink and white color-block shades. Martina's room faced east; bright sunlight flooded the bedroom.

Martina groaned and turned over, burrowing into the pillow.

"I'll be back." Lydia left her to awaken Jimmy. He'd just finished sixth grade and was a good three inches shorter than his sister. Anya had recently decreed that he get a buzz cut for the summer, which made his face look rounder and his skin pastier. By his own choice, his room was strangely institutional, free of personality. Plain white walls; bare wood floor; a simple wooden desk, chair, and dresser; a single bed with one woolen summer camp–style blanket.

Lydia sighed as she looked at him. These kids had no apparent friends. They enjoyed no particular activities other than eating, and then only when Lydia snuck them something that actually tasted good. How could they possibly be her cousins? They might as well have BIG LOSER tattooed on their foreheads. Still, this could change, Lydia was sure of it. It was just a matter of finding the one thing that rang *their* chimes instead of the moms' chimes. She was sure she was just the woman to do it.

The road to find that one thing could be a really long one.

Four and a half hours later, Lydia stood in the spartan waiting room at the LEAP (Creative Leap Educational Activity and Play) Center in Northridge, out in the farthest reaches of the San Fernando Valley, and peered through the glass. Inside, Martina and Jimmy attempted to scale a climbing wall under the watchful tutelage of a young climbing instructor. The idea was for them to build confidence and strength at the same time. There were eight or ten kids at the wall, each with an expectant parent in the waiting room or standing at the glass.

Getting the kids ready to climb had been an ordeal. If not for the climbing instructor—a Cal State–Northridge phys ed major named Krissy whose clingy LEAP T-shirt revealed a pair of consistently perky nipples—Lydia doubted that Jimmy would have even put on his climbing safety harness. As for Martina, she got into her harness just fine, but each halfhearted attempt at climbing required a fifteen-minute pep talk from Krissy.

Since Krissy was in the midst of one of these pep talks, Lydia turned away from the glass window and went to the modest snack bar, where she selected a bottle of strawberry-mango juice from the fridge and brought it to the cashier.

"Wow, nice bag," the cashier commented as she put Lydia's money in the register and handed over her change. "It's a Fendi limited edition, right? How'd you score it?"

"Friends in high places," Lydia joked. She'd taken the bag from Kat's closet right before leaving for LEAP. The cashier grinned. She was fresh-faced and apple-cheeked, with glossy blond hair held back neatly by a tartan-print headband. She wore a white T-shirt with the LEAP logo and carpenter khakis. Everything about her screamed *Healthy! Normal!*

Lydia made a snap judgment. Definite nanny material.

"So, what's your name?" she asked casually as she cracked open her juice.

"Alexis. You?"

"Lydia. Nice to meet you." Lydia flashed her best Texas beauty queen smile and took a swig from the juice bottle. "You like working here, Alexis?"

"Yeah, sure. The people are nice. We even have a softball team. Kicked the butt of Burbank Twenty-four-Hour Fitness."

Lydia smiled as if she found this information captivating. But the last thing on her mind was fitness.

"Want anything to eat with your juice?" Alexis asked. "The menu is on the blackboard. We've got bean sprout and wild mushroom sandwiches, soy bars—"

"Oh, no thanks." Lydia patted her stomach. "I filled up on trail mix before I got here." This lie was rewarded with an approving nod from Alexis.

So far, so good. Lydia snuck a look over her shoulder. No one was in line—all the other mothers were gazing at their little darlings through the glass. Lydia leaned forward conspiratorially against the counter. "So, Alexis. I guess this job doesn't pay all that well."

Alexis shrugged. "It's okay. Steady. I need to work my butt off all summer—the tuition for Santa Monica College just went up again."

"What are you studying?"

"Early childhood education. I love kids."

Pay dirt.

Lydia set her open bottle on the counter. "I happen to know of a fantastic job working with kids. I'm guessing it pays a whole lot better than here."

"Huh." Alexis cocked her head at Lydia with interest and lowered her voice. "What is it?"

Lydia reached into her purse and tore off the corner of Martina and Jimmy's schedule, then scribbled her name and number on it. "Call me. This is totally for real."

Alexis held up the paper with a dubious look. "You don't even know me."

"I'm *real* in tune with the universe," Lydia said, careful to look as earnest as possible. "I have a strong vibe about you. So call me."

"Okay. Thanks." Still unconvinced, Alexis stuck the paper into her pocket.

Hmmm. Time to change tactics. "I can tell that you're not going to call me." Lydia shrugged. "Oh well. Your loss. See ya, Alexis. Have a pleasant life."

As Lydia returned to the observation window, she saw Alexis take out the scrap of paper with Lydia's phone number and study it.

Dang. It was almost as easy as finding edible hellgrammites.

Esme held tight to Weston's hand as she opened the massive double mahogany doors of the Major Modeling Agency, located on the twenty-first floor of the high-rise at the northwest corner of La Cienega and Beverly Boulevard. The agency was fortunate to be on that corner, since it came with a Beverly Hills address instead of one in West Hollywood.

First Esme shepherded Weston inside; then she held the door for Jonathan and Easton. Jonathan had insisted on bringing the twins to the agency, though he had a tennis date at the Riviera Country Club and was dressed in tennis clothes. He would drop them at the agency and then pick them up. Along the way, they had stopped in Hollywood at the main offices of Puppy Love, an upscale pet-grooming service. There they'd dropped off Diane's Pomeranian to have its nails done and hair bow changed; Diane planned to switch the current zebra stripes to hot pink with tiny pale pink polka dots, in honor of FAB's two-toned pink logo.

Fortunately, the twins had escaped the same treatment. Instead, they were wearing matching crimson silk kimonos with smiley-faced dragons hand-embroidered on the back, and thick obi sashes at their nonexistent waists. These were samples of Emily Steele designs that the girls would be wearing in their FAB fashion show late that afternoon. As for Esme, she knew she had a long day ahead with the kids; she'd dressed for comfort in jeans, a white T-shirt, and flip-flops.

It had been a strange ride from Bel Air to the agency, to say the least. Jonathan and Esme had sat together in the front seat of the Range Rover (one of the nine vehicles Diane and Steven owned, including a Lotus that Steven drove only on a special closed racecourse in Riverside). The twins had been buckled into their safety seats in the back. They had been in an ebullient mood, singing Spanish songs all the way. But Esme had found herself extremely taciturn, giving monosyllabic answers to Jonathan's questions about her plans for the day, what she had done the night before. She wasn't about to say that she'd been out with her paramedic boyfriend. Not because Jonathan would care, but rather because she was so sure he wouldn't.

Jonathan explained that he'd been at a pre-FAB party hosted by some record label. Esme stared straight ahead. Of course he hadn't invited her to this party. For all she knew, he'd been there with Mackenzie. Then he had the nerve to bring up the unfinished tattoo Esme had designed on his bicep; when could Esme finish it?

She told him she was busy in a tone that closed down the

conversation. She'd finish his damn tattoo when hell froze over. If he couldn't be public about their relationship, then he could damn well walk around with a half-done Ferris wheel tattoo on his bicep.

Esme rubbed the space between her eyes; her own hypocrisy gave her a headache. Had Jonathan come to her guesthouse the night before when she'd been with Junior, thinking they'd fall into bed per usual? If he had, he didn't say.

While Jonathan went to chat with the receptionist, Esme looked around the agency's elegant, low-key lobby. A pair of black suede couches faced a coffee table covered in what Esme had learned were called the trades—newspapers and magazines of the show business industry—*Variety, Hollywood Reporter, Publishers Weekly.* On one couch, a middle-aged brunette with a hip, short haircut and a Botoxed face sat with her toddler daughter. The girl was fidgety, alternately kicking her mother and the coffee table. Opposite them was a set of towheaded triplets a little older than Easton and Weston, dressed identically in jean overalls and red and white checkered shirts. A bored-looking brown-skinned woman with dreadlocks watched them, arms folded. The boys were completely wrapped up in their PSPs, connected to each other by a three-way game link.

She's their nanny, Esme reckoned. *All of us poor brown-skinned girls taking care of all the rich white-skinned children. Except in my case, the brown-skinned kids look like they actually could be mine.*

For lack of anything else to do, she took the FAB final banquet invitation from her pocket and stared at it.

TENTH ANNUAL LOS ANGELES FASHION BASH

June 22–23

Shows: Staples Center

Final Dinner Banquet: The Queen Mary, Long Beach Harbor

8:00 p.m., June 23

Dress: Black tie

Theme: Classic Hollywood, to Benefit

International Coalition for an AIDS-Free Planet (ICAP)

Photo Identification and Invitation Required for Admission

Banquet Hosts: Steven and Diane Goldhagen

There was no admittance fee on the invitation, but it was understood that banquet tickets were a thousand dollars each. When Esme had awakened that morning, Diane was already at the Staples Center; she'd warned Esme that she would be largely unavailable over the two days of FAB.

Esme sighed and looked at the children, wondering if they were bonding with their new adoptive mom at all. During the day, the girls rarely saw Diane. She was on the board of a dozen charities, all of which seemed to be planning major fund-raising events. The FAB final party was no exception, as ICAP was one of the most popular Hollywood causes of the moment. The year before had been for tsunami relief; in Diane's home office was a photograph of her, Tom Hanks, and Meg Ryan with the prime minister of Thailand, presenting him with a check for twelve million dollars.

It wasn't just her volunteer work, though. Diane's personal grooming regimen was itself a full-time job: workouts at the Century City Gym, facials at the spa at the Peninsula Hotel, manicures and pedicures at Spa 415, brows at Valerie's salon on Rodeo Drive, waxing at Pink Cheeks in Sherman Oaks (according to Diane, everyone knew they did the best Brazilian wax in the city), hair highlights by Raymond, ditto blowouts at the same Beverly Hills establishment, and a million other things that kept her looking perfect.

Esme snuck a look at Jonathan, who was still waiting for the receptionist. The outline of his broad shoulders tapering to a narrow V, the easy grace of his stance, the apostrophes of dimples he flashed at the receptionist when she held up a "one moment" finger to him and finished directing the phone call to the right office, filled her with a now-familiar twinge of desire.

"Hi, Jonathan!" the receptionist cried, her glossy chestnut hair held back by the headset through which she directed calls. The phone rang again. "It's insane this morning, sorry," she told him, and took another call.

So, the receptionist already knew Jonathan. Esme studied her. She was young, not much older than Esme, with round eyes that gave her a constant look of surprise. She wore a tiny citron T-shirt and lots of silver jewelry. What stood out about her, though, was the large bandage over the bridge of her nose, and a prominent bruise under her left eye.

Esme figured it out right away: *I bet her boyfriend hits her.*

"Major Modeling, can I help you?" the receptionist intoned. "Hold one moment. Major Modeling, can I help you? Hold one moment. Major Modeling, can I help you? No, he's in a meeting; I'll put you through to his voice mail."

Finally, the calls stopped. The receptionist pulled off her headset and trotted around the desk, throwing her arms around Jonathan. "Gosh, it's crazy with all the calls? How are you?"

"Terrific, Pandora. You're healing up really well."

"The doctor said in another week or so the bandage could come off?" Pandora the receptionist raised her voice at the end of the sentence, as if it was a question. "So, I can't wait to see my new nose, you know?"

"It will be fantastic," Jonathan assured her. "Barry Weintraub is *the* best."

The girl nodded. "I have to thank your stepmother again so much for . . . you know?" She touched her bandaged nose again. "Because I would have been, like, middle-aged before I could save up enough money?"

Now Esme realized: The girl hadn't been hit. She'd had a nose job. It was darkly funny, really, that Esme had jumped to the conclusion that the girl was battered before she'd considered plastic surgery. It just reminded her all over again what a totally different world this was. Plus, the clear implication was that Diane Goldhagen had either helped pay for her surgery or gotten this Barry Weintraub to reduce his fee. Just when Esme wanted to nail Diane in a box labeled Clueless and Selfish, her boss did something to prove she didn't exactly belong there.

Jonathan grinned. "Forget it. Your mom has saved Diane's butt a million times. She owed her. Esme?"

He turned to Esme, and Esme automatically stood. "This is our new nanny, Esme Castaneda. Esme, this is Pandora Carrier. Her mother worked for Diane in my dad's production office."

"*Hola!*" Pandora chirped. "Sorry, that's, like, the extent of my Spanish, you know?"

"Oh, I think I can manage in English," Esme said tartly.

"Esme's English is better than my Spanish, too," Jonathan joked, betraying nothing of a more intimate relationship between himself and Esme. Part of Esme was happy about this. Part of her was furious. He was treating her just like what she was—the hired help.

"Oh, that's great, you know?" Pandora said without a trace of insult. "Diane told me that the children are still learning English?"

Esme nodded.

"Great. Could you ask the girls if they're ready to learn how to be fashion models?"

Esme faced the kids. *"¿Vosotros estáis listas hacer modelos de la manera?"*

Both girls looked utterly blank; Esme was pretty sure they had no idea what "model" meant. She then explained in Spanish that modeling was just walking around showing people the pretty clothes they'd be wearing, but the clarification didn't seem to make an impact. Instead, Easton squeezed her crotch. *"Yo necesito la sala,"* she complained. *"Ahora! Pee-pee!"*

Pandora nodded. "Wow, that one is, like, universal?" She laughed. "Esme, why don't you take the girls to the bathroom and then I'll show you the way to Tolstoy's office?"

Esme turned to Jonathan. "Are you staying?"

"I have a meeting with a development guy over at Paramount."

"Pee-pee!" Easton repeated, crossing her legs in desperation.

Jonathan's gaze stayed fixed on Esme. "I could cancel it . . . ," he offered, "if you want me to."

Is that what he wanted? Esme wondered. No. It couldn't be. If he wanted to be with her, he'd just tell her. Obviously he had all the power. "Bye, Jonathan," Esme said firmly. "I'll call you when we're finishing up here."

Jonathan looked like there was something he wanted to say, but Easton was literally dragging Esme toward the bathroom.

Tolstoy Kocherzhinsky's actual name had been Ekaterina Kocherzhinsky when her parents had immigrated to the United States as political refugees back in the late seventies. But she'd changed it with her parents' help after having both her first and last names butchered by most of her elementary school peers. Former literature professors at Tver State University, her parents had suggested Tolstoy as a replacement, reasoning that only the rarest American would recognize that the great Russian novelist had been a man. Tolstoy had been shortened to Tol, and it had worked well for Ekaterina, who was now in her midthirties and running a powerful agency that specialized in under-fourteen clients.

Pandora ushered Esme and the girls into Tol's office, told them to wait, and then discreetly departed. The office was massive, with a 270-degree view from the Santa Monica Mountains out to the ocean and down toward Long Beach. When the agency head stepped through the glass front doors of her inner sanctum, Esme was shocked to see that Tol herself matched the outsized dimensions of the office; she was one of the first people Esme had seen in Beverly Hills with a serious weight problem. Clad in an impeccably cut black designer pantsuit, blond hair cut in a stylish shag, her makeup perfect, Tol looked like a fashion model who had been inflated with helium. In fact, Esme had a momentary flash of the oversized balloons in the Macy's Thanksgiving Day Parade.

"Ah, here are my angels!" Tol cried when she saw the girls, who merely gaped at her dimensions.

"¡Ella es muy, muy gorda!" Easton exclaimed. *"¿Por qué ella es muy gorda?"*

Esme softly chided Easton and told her to be polite. But Tol clapped with glee, which made the dozen bracelets on each of her forearms ring like chimes. "Don't you two look just precious in those kimonos. Are you girls ready to learn to walk the runway?"

"I've explained it to them," Esme said carefully. "But I'm not sure they understand. It's kind of out of their realm of experience."

Of course, so are running water and indoor plumbing.

As Tol prattled on about what a good time the twins would have at the fashion show, Esme feared a meltdown. She'd seen it happen when the twins were overwhelmed by new experiences, new people, or just too much of anything. Fortunately, the twins held it together as Tol led them down the hall to a much larger room that was a perfect small-scale simulation of the site of a fashion show, with a raised T-shaped runway and banks of folding chairs along both sides. Blue velvet curtains hung at the rear of the walkway. Along the walls were television cameras and darkened klieg lights.

"Chantal, we're here!" Tol announced.

From behind the curtains stepped a stunning, very thin black woman over six feet tall in her polka-dot stilettos; she wore a white eyelet lace dress so tight it resembled a knee-length straitjacket.

"My darlings," Chantal cooed, strutting down the runway to meet them. "These must be my little protégées!" She stepped down gingerly and hugged each girl in turn. "Delicious, simply fabulous!"

Esme noticed that Chantal had quite a distinct Adam's apple, as well as thick makeup and furlike false eyelashes. Chantal reminded her of a guy named Joaquín who'd lived down the street from her in Fresno, back before she'd come to Los Angeles. Joaquín made good money working at a female impersonators' club. He was *trolo*—homosexual—not exactly accepted in macho Latino culture. Joaquín had gotten his ass kicked on a regular basis, and one day he just disappeared. No one knew what had happened to him.

The more Esme looked at Chantal, the surer she was that Chantal was a drag queen. Esme only hoped that Los Angeles was a more tolerant environment than the Fresno *barrio* had been.

"Esme?" Weston tugged at Esme's sleeve.

"Sí?"

"*Es* boy or girl?" Easton asked.

Esme bit back her smile. The little girl was already edging toward Spanglish.

"*Yo pienso,* a boy *y* a girl," Weston answered her sister.

"Chantal?" Pandora reappeared at the door with the other kids from the lobby in tow. "Now you've got all your models?"

Chantal threw her arms open wide. "Sugarplums!" She pointed a lethally long French-manicured fingernail toward the new arrivals. "You're Houston and Austin and Dallas, right?"

God. To be named after cities in Texas. How humiliating. Well, at least none of them was named Waco.

The triplets nodded nervously as Chantal minced over to a sound system and pressed a button; strange, nasal music filled the air. "Japanese music," Chantal expounded, "to go with Emily's theme for tomorrow's show."

She eyed Esme. "You're beautiful, sweetheart. You should be in the show with the little Spanish children and hold their hands on the catwalk? I can arrange it."

"No!" Esme declared, horrified at the thought. She hated attention. It came from being the daughter of illegal immigrants. Her father was actually on the run from the law, though the law wasn't chasing him very far. Esme herself had gotten in over her head in some gang stuff back in Fresno—it had all ended tragically. No. No extra attention. "I mean, I'm sure the girls will be fine on their own. I'll explain everything to them in Spanish. And I can be backstage for them."

"Wonderful, sweetheart! I'll be backstage too. You're an angel!" Chantal threw her arms open wide as if she was about to embrace the entire planet. "All right, my stars, it's showtime!"

Serenity and Kiley were coloring. It was ironic. Platinum's daughter had every toy and electronic item any kid could ever want, but her favorite thing to do was to unearth her box of sixty-four different shades of Crayolas, sprawl on the floor, and color in a Barbie coloring book. About the coloring book, she'd sworn Kiley to secrecy.

The room itself was a thing of beauty. Like the rest of Platinum's mansion, it was all white. Serenity had a plasma television, an enormous DVD collection hidden behind a recessed wall unit, and a computer setup worthy of NASA mission control. Everything was perfectly organized and perfectly clean. Not because Serenity ever lifted a finger, but because a battalion of maids whisked through three or four times a day.

On their own, Serenity and Sid were pigs. Sid regularly deposited food, spilled milk shakes, and crusty underwear under his bed. Serenity thought nothing of emptying her closet onto the floor in search of a favored shirt or skirt. On her ninth birthday in Wisconsin, Kiley had been handed a list of chores that were a given if she was to expect a modest allowance—bring in the morning newspaper, recycle the old one, clean her room, take out the garbage, mow the lawn in the summer, and clear the snow in the winter. In contrast, she doubted that Platinum's children could spell the word "chore."

Serenity finished coloring Barbie's nails pale pink. "How was your date with doodyhead last night?"

"How'd you know I was on a date?" Kiley asked lightly.

"My mother and I talked about it. She said doodyhead was hot. She said she couldn't understand how someone like you could get such a hot guy."

So, she and Tom were fodder for mother-daughter discussions in the main mansion? Kiley fumed but did her best to hide it. "He's very . . . nice."

"My mother says he's hot," Serenity corrected. "She said she would do him. Do you know what that means? Because I do." She glanced at the crayon Kiley was using. "That color sucks. Don't use it. I don't feel like coloring anymore. I'll tell you what color to use and you do it."

Sometimes it was a challenge to like this kid.

"I told you, Serenity. You don't get to order me around."

"Well, just because you said it doesn't make it true." Serenity stood. As she did, she blithely smashed a lime green Crayola beneath her bejeweled Santa Monica HottStuff flip-flop. Kiley winced; mushed Crayola plus plush white carpet equaled cleaning disaster.

"You should take me shopping," Serenity decided, glancing

down at her flip-flop but ignoring the mushed crayon beneath it. "I want shoes. High heels. Jimmy Choo."

"Uh-huh," Kiley said pleasantly.

Why point out that Jimmy Choo didn't make shoes for children? Serenity would retort with something cutting. Kiley would chastise her. Then Serenity would do or say whatever she wanted anyway. Her mother would back her up. Platinum called it self-expression. Kiley called it spoiled brat–hood.

"Did Mr. Doodyhead try to stick his tongue in your mouth?"

"His name is Tom. And that's none of your business, Serenity."

"I know his name. He's a big model. His picture is on all the bus shelters. And he *didn't* try to kiss you!" Serenity chortled. "Knew it, knew it, knew it!"

Humiliatingly enough, that was true. Last night on the beach by Marym's home, she and Tom had walked up nearly as far as Barbra Streisand's estate. The conversation came easily, more easily as they walked away from the model's new mansion. Kiley had Tom in stitches with stories about Serenity. He'd taken her hand; she'd felt so comfortable, just like the night they'd run into each other at the movies, but he hadn't kissed her. Not then, not when he'd dropped her at home.

The dreaded F-word came to mind once again. "Friend." And most likely without benefits, because Tom showed zero interest in any. At least, not any from Kiley.

"You could be pretty, you know," Serenity told her. "I could help you do makeup and stuff."

Great. Nothing like a seven-year-old offering a mercy makeover. The women at that party last night had been so spectacular—

Tyra and Caroline and Charlize. They'd run into Mischa Barton on the beach with a Danish guy Tom knew from some modeling he'd done in Copenhagen. Each looked perfect, airbrushed, and confident.

Serenity kicked off a flip-flop, which sailed across the room and landed on Barbie's newly crayoned breasts. "Hey, did you hear me?"

"Don't do that. Are we done coloring?"

"Duh." She squinted at Kiley and studied her. "You need to lose ten pounds. You're not, like, *fat*. But only really skinny girls are pretty." She glanced at her own nonexistent tummy, two inches exposed beneath her pink belly shirt. "I'm too fat. We should diet."

"Serenity, you're not fat." Kiley began gathering up the crayons, unwilling to leave them for the maid.

"Am too. Sid said."

It was amazing, really. Serenity pulled off her know-it-all act so well that sometimes it was hard to believe she was also just an insecure, poorly parented kid who'd just finished second grade.

"Yo. I'm back." Bruce, Serenity's rarely seen fourteen-year-old brother, stuck his head in the door. Quite handsome in an offbeat, skinny rock 'n' roller way, he had spiky black hair and pale skin, and wore sunglasses, baggy jeans, and a Spits band T-shirt. "Wazzup?"

"Bruce!" Serenity squealed with joy and leaped into her brother's arms.

"Hi." Kiley rose. "Your mom didn't say you were coming home."

"Wacky weed affects the memory," Bruce opined as he lifted his sunglasses. "You torch up?"

Kiley shook her head. "Sorry?"

"Reefer, pot, ganja, four-twenty, chronic, blah blah, blah blah."

Oh. He was asking her if she smoked marijuana. "No. Neither should you."

"Who the hell are you to tell me what I should be doing?"

"You're fourteen," Kiley reminded him.

Bruce chuckled and leaned against the doorframe, one arm draped casually around his little sister's shoulders. "You're funny."

"Yeah, you're funny," Serenity echoed.

"My mom gets primo shit," Bruce confided. "She's downstairs right now with my dawg, probably sharing. The woman ain't stingy with her stash. Wanna know where she keeps it?"

Uh-oh. Yellow Zone time. Why couldn't Platinum keep herself sober around her children? Was that really too much to ask? Kiley's mind raced. Where was Sid? With Persimmon at a yoga class. At least all the children were safe and accounted for.

Kiley put the crayons and coloring book into the white Lucite toy chest. "So, you have a friend downstairs? With Platinum?"

"Yeah, babe."

Babe? Had a fourteen-year-old just called her *babe*?

"How long will you and your friend be here?"

"Hey, man, I'm gone." He extricated himself from Serenity's grasp and disappeared down the hall.

Serenity whirled on Kiley, her face dark. "It's your fault he's leaving. You treated him like a baby."

"No, Serenity—"

"Yes, you did. I hate you. You suck!"

Serenity stormed out of her bedroom, heading downstairs to

the probable den of iniquity. Kiley dashed after her, only to discover that Bruce had not exaggerated. His friend—short, stocky, spiky blond hair—and Platinum were side by side on the blindingly white Italian leather couch, with a huge white bong on the white marble table before them. Bruce's friend was doubled over laughing, because Platinum was belting out a song into a Rolling Rock bottle. Her white jeans were streaked with something red and sticky-looking; her white silk shirt was half-untucked and unbuttoned, revealing a lacy white bra. The room reeked of reefer.

The friend waved to Bruce. "Your old lady is the bomb, man." He reached for the bong and a pack of matches.

"Do me, do it to me, do it to me now!" Platinum sang into the bottle.

Serenity shrank against the stairs. Kiley realized things had progressed to the Yellow Zone and were verging on Orange. She marched over to the coffee table and grabbed the bong away from Bruce's friend. Then she crossed back to Serenity. "Come on, Serenity, let's go back to your room and figure out where we'll go shoe shopping."

Too late. Platinum reached a hand out to her daughter. "Dance with me!"

Kiley tugged at Serenity. "Come on, sweetie. Let's go. . . ."

Serenity didn't move, her eyes fixed on her mother. "Mommy?" Her voice was tiny. The doorbell rang.

"It's open!" Platinum hollered. "Come on the hell in!"

A moment later, a thirtyish guy with a scraggly goatee stepped into the living room, accompanied by a middle-aged woman in a conservative business suit. The guy carried a small audio recorder and a notebook. The woman carried a pocketbook and a portfolio. She looked absolutely appalled.

"Platinum?" she asked.

"Who the hell are you?" Platinum obviously didn't recognize her visitors.

"Karen Collins, from your record label. PR department? Thanks for leaving our names at the gate, but . . ." She turned to the guy with the goatee. "Would you excuse us for a few moments?"

"Sure," the man chuckled. "I'll wait for you . . . outside."

Kiley watched him go back to the front hallway as Bruce and his friend hustled upstairs, roaring with laughter.

"Go on up to your room," Kiley told Serenity. "I'll be there in a sec."

"But—"

"Go," Kiley commanded, and thankfully Serenity actually departed. The moment she was gone, the woman from the record label confronted Platinum, careful to keep her voice low.

"Did you forget the interview? I left you eight different messages. This is the L.A. *Times*!"

"This is the L.A. *Times*!" Platinum shrieked, mimicking the woman.

Karen flushed. "This was supposed to be the preview story for your gig at the Hollywood Bowl next week. He can hurt your career, Platinum. I'm only thinking of you."

"I'm a freaking star, get it?" Platinum gave her the finger, then turned around and pointed at her own butt. "Kiss this!"

Karen shook her head. "I give up; let someone else deal with you."

Platinum danced on the couch, ignoring the woman, lost in her own world. Kiley stepped forward and introduced herself. "I'm the nanny," she added. Her eyes slid toward the front door, knowing the reporter was waiting on the other side, and knowing what he'd seen. "Will he . . . ?"

"Write something bad about Platinum?" Karen filled in. "Who knows? Reporters have trashed stars for less, though, I can tell you that." She sagged into the nearest chair.

Kiley excused herself and went back upstairs—Bruce and his friend were behind the closed door of Bruce's room, so she went back into Serenity's room. She was playing Super Smash Brothers Mario on her PlayStation.

"Want a controller?" Serenity asked, completely composed.

"Sure." Serenity handed her controller to Kiley and got another one.

"Is there anything you want to talk about, Serenity? About what happened downstairs just now?"

"Nah."

Talk about denial. As Kiley tried to make Luigi into a lean, mean fighting machine, she remembered something from her childhood. She'd once had a friend, Michelle, who lived a couple of blocks away. Michelle's dad was a trucker and her mother was a pharmacy tech at the Revco, and neither of them spent a lot of time at home. Kiley had envied Michelle because no one ever told her she had to take a bath, or yelled for her to come home from playing foursquare after it got dark, or made her eat her vegetables. Michelle would regale Kiley with stories of going to bars with her parents, of staying up all night, of smoking cigarettes and seeing people "doing it." She'd even offered Kiley a beer as if it was the most normal thing in the world.

One day, Michelle didn't come to school. Kiley couldn't understand why, until their fourth-grade teacher explained that Michelle's parents weren't taking care of her, so Michelle would be going away to a place where other grown-ups would act responsibly.

Kiley never saw Michelle again.

At the time, Kiley had just been sorry to lose a friend, especially one who had so much freedom. Now, she understood exactly what had happened: the Wisconsin Department of Social Services had taken Michelle away because her parents had been unfit.

With her fingers still manipulating the controller, and her action figure kicking and spinning and flipping on the monitor, Kiley realized that what she'd just witnessed had been criminal. Maybe not at the level of Michelle's parents, but Michelle's parents weren't Platinum. The rock star wasn't just a bad mother, she was a dangerous mother. The kind of dangerous where, if the California Department of Social Services found out, she could lose her kids. Kiley would be out of a job, out of California, and out of her dream of attending Scripps, just like that.

That would be bad, but it wouldn't be the end of the world. However, Kiley suspected that if Serenity got taken away from her mom, it *would* be the end of that little girl's world. Kiley vowed to make sure that it didn't happen.

12

"¿Esme? ¿Soy guapa?"

Esme gave Easton a careful appraisal from head to toe. The smaller of the twins was seated on a stool in front of a portable mirror; hair and makeup people swirled around her. Weston was on the stool to her right, leafing through a fashion magazine and gawking at the pictures. Brown mascara, blush, and cherry lip gloss had already been applied to Easton's and Weston's faces. Their hair had been curled into long, inky ringlets. At the moment, their FAB stylist, a pale-skinned girl named Ivy who wore bloodred matte lipstick and black-framed geek glasses, was threading tiny red rosebuds through the curls to match the red Emily Steele embroidered silk kimono in which Easton would be photographed. As for Weston, her hair had already been adorned with tiny gold stars to match her gold kimono.

All this work was for a family photo. Then the kids would come back, take off the dresses and the makeup, and go home for a nap. Their runway show wasn't until that evening, when they'd be wearing the exact same dresses. Of course, the dresses would be dry-cleaned in the interim.

"Tú eres muy bonita," Esme told her. *"Como una estrella de cinema."*

Easton beamed, which made Esme happy, because at first the girl had been too petrified even to step inside the trailer. But a half hour into the beauty treatment, she and her sister were primping as if they'd done it their whole lives.

FAB was just getting under way. The fashion bash took place in the parking lot of the Staples Center in downtown Los Angeles, the arena where the Lakers and the Clippers played basketball, simply because it had a large-enough expanse of space to house the many tents, trailers, and other facilities needed for the event. There were four small tents (relatively speaking, of course, since they easily could seat a thousand people) for shows by less famous designers, and a large main tent that had been borrowed from the Ringling Bros. and Barnum & Bailey circus for the biggest-name designers—Ralph Lauren, Givenchy, Chanel.

The big designers, though, were not really the essence of FAB, not why hordes of the most beautiful and famous people flocked to the prestigious event as if it was a rock concert. Everyone who was anyone knew that the FAB place to be was in one of the smaller tents, Tents B and C. That was where the unknown or newly discovered designers would show their stuff. For example, last year's FAB phenomenon had been Marco Devito, formerly an abstract painter who worked in watercolors. Marco had done a show where he had applied his art to raw-silk saris. The show had received a five-minute standing ovation.

Immediately thereafter, there had been an auction of the same saris. Each sold for at least five thousand dollars, the proceeds going to the charity du jour. When the Devito line went into production, the entire stock was presold at Barneys before they ever actually made it to the store. Now there was a waiting list of six months for a Devito sari, and Marco had gone from talented but unknown painter to sought-after multimillionaire.

"Who are you interested in?" Ivy asked Esme.

"Huh?" The question caught Esme off guard. She hadn't realized that the stylist had even noticed her.

"Which young designer?"

"I . . ." Esme barely knew the names of the big designers, let alone the young ones. "I don't know."

Ivy lifted some of Easton's curls and did a little work on them with her comb. "Well, don't miss Ty's show."

"Who?"

"Ty Ahavarata. From Honolulu. He does this batik thing where he invents new colors. A friend of mine is modeling one—it's like a muumuu, but short and tight with the midriff cut out."

Suddenly, Esme remembered that Diane had been talking about this same designer at breakfast. The previous December, she and Steven had gone to the Grand Wailea Resort on Maui. Ty had been selling his traditionally cut muumuus—long and loose—at a kiosk just outside the hotel gates. It had been Diane's idea to take Ty's incredible fabric and turn it into sexy, Southern California–friendly designs.

Esme nodded. "I know who you're talking about. My boss is Diane Goldhagen. I think she discovered him. Those are her kids you're working on now."

Ivy nearly dropped her comb. "These are Diane Goldhagen's kids? *The* Diane Goldhagen? But they're . . ."

"Adopted," Esme filled in. "From Colombia."

"Your boss is . . . well, she's like a goddess to me," Ivy gushed. "I don't think there's anything she can't do. Anyway, have a great time. The kids are ready. They'll be fabulous."

A few minutes later, Esme was walking the twins out of the silver Airstream trailer. All of them had official FAB identification badges around their necks—Esme also carried a packet of passes and information about all the shows. Their next stop was Tent B, directly across the parking lot, for the family photo.

The parking lot was already crowded, though the first fashion shows didn't begin for another couple of hours. Still, hundreds of people bustled about—vendors, models, sightseers, even a few people Esme recognized from the Brentwood Hills Country Club, who acknowledged her presence with a distracted nod. They hadn't gotten more than twenty feet when Weston squealed with delight, her face lighting up.

"*Yon-o-tin!*" she shouted.

The twins adored their new big brother; he was very good with them. The problem was that their nanny adored him too. And she was about to see him at the family photo shoot, the first time she'd be with both him and his family since he'd started sleeping with her. But this time it was a case of mistaken identity—just another tall, rangy, handsome guy who looked similar from behind.

"No, it's not Jonathan," Esme told the twins. "We'll see him later."

"*¿Cuándo?*" Weston asked with anticipation as they dodged

around a rolling cart selling New York City–style hot dogs with sauerkraut.

"Más tarde," Esme reported. *"En la tienda siguiente.* At the next tent."

"¡Vámonos rápido!" Easton tugged at Esme, so anxious was she to see her brother.

They reached the backstage entrance to Tent B. Esme flashed her pass at the burly security guard, who ushered her and the twins inside.

The backstage area was a madcap scene of designers and assistants and dressers already in frantic mode. People were yelling for shoes to match certain outfits, someone was screeching that a zipper had broken, two people were arguing about which of them would be dressing which model.

For a time, Esme stood frozen with the girls, watching this chaos. She worried that the twins would have a meltdown from overstimulation, but saw that their expressions were pure wonder at it all. Then Esme spotted the Emily Steele sign, off to her right. She walked the twins there, found their dressers—two college girls, one tall and one short—and watched as they helped the girls into their kimonos.

"Have you seen Diane Goldhagen?" Esme asked the dressers. "I thought she would meet us here."

"She's in the press area, near Gate D of the Staples Center," the taller dresser reported. "That's the only place the photographers are permitted. No pictures back here. New policy."

"Okay."

Esme told the twins that they would have to take another walk, to meet their mother and brother. They didn't protest, only repeated how much they wanted to see Jonathan, and for him to see them looking like *pequeñas princesas japonesas*—little Japanese princesses.

Esme did not share their enthusiasm. She really, truly, desperately did not want to see Jonathan, not now, not like this. There were too many "what-ifs" over which she had no control. It had been difficult enough spending time with him and the twins at the modeling agency. Esme had yet to be with him in Diane's presence since they'd started . . . whatever it was that they'd started. What if Diane picked up on some look between the two of them? She'd seen Jonathan flirting with Esme; it wouldn't take a huge mental leap for her to fill in the blanks. Or what if Jonathan treated her like she was nothing more than the nanny, someone he barely knew? That would protect their secret, yes, but in some ways, it would be worse.

With great reluctance, she told the twins it was time to go. As they were about to leave, her cell phone sounded, playing the refrain to "Livin' La Vida Loca," Esme smiled; last time she'd been with Jorge, he'd programmed in the new ring. It was to fit her new life, he said. She flipped it open.

"Hello?"

"Hola," came Junior's deep, sexy voice. "What you know good, *mamacita*?"

Esme flushed, as if Junior had just caught her in bed with Jonathan as opposed to merely thinking about him. She rarely got calls from Junior. Now that she was living in Bel Air, he preferred that she call him.

"Hi," Esme said, careful to keep her voice low. "I'm working."

"That's cool," Junior assured her. "Me too. Had to fill in for some guy who ran off to Vegas with his best friend's old lady.

Loco, eh? They put me in Alhambra this morning. No one else wanted the territory. Can't blame them, there's been a lot of shit going down. But I've got the night off; Possum is with Manuel on the graveyard. Thought we could get into a little somethin'-somethin', eh?"

Sex, he meant. But unlike Jonathan, Junior would take her out, to a restaurant in Pasadena, maybe make her feel beautiful and wanted and special before he took her to his bed. And all the pretty girls who wanted her man would give her the evil eye, jealous and respectful at the same time. In Echo Park, Junior was the man. He was *her* man.

"I can't. I have to work."

"Esme." Easton tugged on her hand. *"Yo tengo mucha hambre."*

"Uno momento, Junior," Esme told him, then looked at the girl. *"Vamos a tu hermano y tu mama. Después vamos a comer. Bueno?"*

Easton nodded.

"Okay. And okay, Junior," she told her boyfriend from the Echo. "I wish I could, but I have to work."

"A'ight," Junior grunted. "That's cool. I'll catch you later, *chiquita.*"

Esme hung up, thinking how Jorge was right. It really was *la vida loca.*

The FAB press area was the size of a football field, covered by a simple blue awning supported by dozens of metal pipes. As they approached it, there was the same kind of bedlam as backstage in the tent, only on a greater scale. There had to be a dozen or more photographers, each with several assistants, working away to take the photographs that would appear in the next few weeks in newspapers and magazines around the world.

"Klieg lights on the south side brighter!"

"Change the angle of the backdrop!"

"More flowers. Not *those* flowers, you idiot, the orchids!"

Esme steered the girls through this chaos, and finally spotted Diane and Steven. Diane was chatting with a reporter—Esme guessed she was a reporter, because the tall, willowy woman was furiously taking notes. Steven, meanwhile, was wrapped up in a cell phone call, looking very unhappy about whatever was being said. No Jonathan. Esme exhaled gratefully. Maybe he couldn't make it after all.

"Easton! Weston!"

Esme realized she'd spoken too soon. There was Jonathan, two bottles of water in his hands, looking impossibly hot in a black T-shirt, Givenchy jacket, and jeans.

As soon as the girls spotted him, they screamed his name and ran to him.

"Careful, please be careful!" Ivy cried, hands fluttering. The taller dresser from the tent was on hand, still wearing her black apron with the giant pockets full of makeup and hair tools. Evidently she was there to make sure all the Goldhagens looked spiffy for the photo shoot.

As the girls were embracing Jonathan, Esme saw two workmen carrying a sofa from the less formal of the Goldhagens' two living rooms.

"A little to the left!" shouted the head of the moving crew.

In fact, one entire corner of the living room had been perfectly re-created in the press pavilion. The forest green and gold Moorish sofa that had been handmade in Fez was being carefully moved to its exact position at the Goldhagen home. This scene didn't surprise Esme; the movers had come that morning. Some design magazine had thought it would be a cute idea to move the living room to FAB and take a family portrait there. That magazine had sprung for the movers.

Esme forced herself to look everywhere except at Jonathan, but she could feel his piercing blue eyes on her even as he hugged his little sisters. She could also practically feel his hands on her, remembering how they had—

"Ready to start when you are, Mrs. Goldhagen," a flunky called out.

The reporter put her hands together in a praying gesture. "Ten more minutes, please?"

"No. Let's get this show on the road," Steven barked, snapping his phone shut and slipping it into his pants pocket. "I've got to get back to the studio. Diane?" he added impatiently.

Steven Goldhagen, late forties, thin and wiry and fond of wearing baseball caps, moved to his twenty-years-younger blond trophy wife, who pecked him on the cheek.

"Yes, yes, sweetheart, we're starting," she assured him. "Esme, keep the kids occupied until we need them, please."

Esme nodded and then went over to the girls, who were chatting away to Jonathan in Spanish. Esme knew that Jonathan's Spanish was less than serviceable, but his bright smile kept his sisters engaged.

"Girls, stay with me," Esme instructed, then translated it into Spanish, as always. She was now so close to Jonathan that she could feel the heat radiating off his body. Or maybe it was *her* heat, a result of standing so close to him.

"Hi," Jonathan said, voice low.

"Hello." Esme was careful to keep her voice neutral.

Easton tugged on Jonathan's hand. "*¡Helado!*"

"What's that?" Jonathan asked Esme.

"Ice cream."

Jonathan chuckled. "*Más* . . . how do you say . . . *tarde*!"

The girls laughed at his mix of English and Spanish. Esme explained that they couldn't go for ice cream now because they were going to have their picture taken. Easton just kept asking for ice cream. Soon balled fists and a foot stomp were added to the demand for "ice cream now." She got tears in her eyes; her lower lip trembled, signaling an impending meltdown.

Esme tried to soothe the little girl. "This is too much for them," she told Jonathan. "I don't know how they're going to survive till the fashion show."

"Why don't we duck out right after this and take them with us?" he suggested. "They'd like that, don't you think?"

Her eyes met his. "I don't know if your mother would like that." The double meaning there was, she thought, more than obvious. "Plus they're due back home for a nap."

"*Step*mother," he corrected. "I know she built in nap time for them. But ice cream first won't hurt them. Will it?"

His eyes met hers. So. He was finally asking her to do something with him in the light of day (the half-assed offer to hang around at the modeling agency didn't really count), for the first time since they had started spending almost every night, all night, together. They'd be out with the girls, true. But that made it perfect, because it could appear that the only reason they were together was for the sake of the twins.

Esme could feel her guard slipping as she smiled up at him. He really *did* want to be with her! She was about to say yes—as long as they took the girls someplace close—when someone called Jonathan's name. Someone female.

Esme turned to see Jonathan's supposedly ex-girlfriend, Mackenzie, trotting toward him. What was *she* doing here? Her hair was a sleek waterfall to her shoulders; aqua beaded chandelier earrings danced from her ears. She wore pink boot-cut pants and a pink and aqua beaded tunic that split just below her bust, revealing her skin down to the how-low-can-you-go rise of her pants. She had the kind of all-American blond beauty that intimidated the hell out of Esme.

"Hey, sweetie, I had so much fun with you yesterday." She kissed Jonathan's cheek and then turned to Esme, all fake sweetness and light. "Oh, hi. It's Esme, right? How's the nanny thing going?"

Esme narrowed her eyes and nodded her response.

"So, Esme," Mackenzie went on, snuggling close to Jonathan, "could you be a sweetheart and take the kids away for a minute? There's something I need to discuss with Jon-Jon and it's not really appropriate for them."

"Of course," Esme said icily. "That's my job. Isn't it?"

She summoned the girls in rapid Spanish, her tone so sharp that they actually stopped kicking around an empty Coke can they'd discovered.

"Thanks, Esme," Mackenzie cooed. "You're just a lifesaver. It's so hard to get Spanish-speaking help these days who aren't here illegally."

Bitch. Esme hated every blond hair on her head. But she hated Jonathan even more.

"*¡Vámonos!*" she called, and strode over to the girls, ready to lead them to the photographer's assistant.

"Esme, wait." Jonathan had walked after her. "Let me explain."

"There's nothing *to* explain."

"You don't understand about Mackenzie."

"Jon-Jon!" Mackenzie called.

"Mackenzie needs you," Esme said, shaking off his hand. "Now get out of my face."

13

Dear Mom,

Just a quick P.S. because I didn't get this letter in the mail yesterday. Remember my friend Tom from Iowa, the one I told you about? Well, there's a major fashion event here every year called FAB (we saw something about it on E!, remember, with all those clothes that no one could really wear?) and tonight Tom is modeling for Ralph Lauren! He had two front-row tickets messengered over to me. I'm very excited because the night shows are impossible to get tickets for unless you're a fashion reporter, or you're famous or something. I invited my friend Lydia to come with me because she knows all about fashion and—

"Ki-leeee!"

Not again.

Kiley heard Platinum's screech and the pounding on her front door all the way from her bedroom, where she was sprawled on the bed trying to finish the letter for her mom that she'd started the day before.

Well, it's not my day off, she thought as she put down the pen and slid the letter under her bed. *Technically, I'm working.* Serenity and Sid had departed a half hour before to go on an overnight in Santa Barbara with the kids of Platinum's CAA agent. Platinum said Kiley didn't need to go because the agent was anal and had three nannies already for her two kids: "If you're there too, you'll probably end up just killing each other."

It had been all Kiley could do not to cheer when Platinum had informed her of this. The kids weren't coming back until noon the next day, which meant that whatever happened with Tom tonight could extend to whatever happened with Tom tomorrow morning. Not that Tom had given her any indication that he *wanted* anything to happen.

The night of Marym's party had ended with a hug and a kiss on her cheek. Her freaking *cheek,* for God's sake. Kiley had been certain it was literally the big kiss-off. Yet after that, he'd invited her to his FAB show. He couldn't possibly be tacky enough to invite more than one girl, could he? Like, one babe he wanted to ravish and one little sister he wanted to kiss on the cheek? Kiley didn't have the nerve to ask.

She opened the front door for Platinum, who wore white linen pants and a plain white T-shirt; her hair was up on her head in a messy bun. Apparently she was sober, since she didn't trip on the edge of the rug.

"Hi," Kiley ventured.

Platinum pushed past her. "Your damn door was locked."

Which would explain why you couldn't barge in like you did yesterday, Kiley thought.

"So listen, we need to talk." Platinum slumped into the Danish modern couch. "I'm pissed."

Uh-oh. This could not be good. She'd told Kiley she could have the rest of the day off. Maybe she'd forgotten and she thought Kiley was just goofing off. "Is it something I didn't do for the kids? Because whatever it is, I can—"

"Blah-blah-blah," Platinum droned, making a talking puppet of her hand. "You don't need to freak, I'm not canning you. Something else."

Kiley racked her brain. "The interview yesterday with the newspaper?"

Platinum laughed. "You think that's the worst shape I've ever been in for an interview? This thing I did with *Spin* once. My friend Hunter Thompson got it for me. He died. Sid Vicious died. Kurt too. Doesn't that suck?"

"Sucks," Kiley agreed. She didn't know who any of those people were, but she was going with the flow.

"I miss Hunter so bad," Platinum murmured. "Anyway, I was totally wasted on this primo Thai stick. The reporter was such an uptight bitch that I threw a bottle of champagne at her. Five stitches. Hunter sent me a thank-you note when it ran; he soaked it in blotter acid."

Kiley blinked twice. She had only understood about half of what Platinum had just said. "Uh . . ."

"You are like walking white bread, you know that?"

"Well . . ."

"Forget it." Platinum swung her legs over the side of the

chair. "I wanna talk about your buddy. Tom Chappelle, that is. How the hell did you meet him?"

That's what this little impromptu visit was about? "Hotel Bel-Air, during *Platinum Nan*—"

"Shut up." Platinum raised her index finger and got in Kiley's face. "I don't want to hear the name of that goddamn show around here. Ever. That show is dead to you. *Understand?*"

"I understand," Kiley told her. She sat down in one of the matching chairs by the couch, just for something to do.

"So, Tom Chappelle. He's hot." Platinum ran a hand through her hair; evidently she'd forgotten that it was up in a bun. The mother-of-pearl comb holding it up fell out; her hair fell around her face. "What's up with you two? Are you screwing him?"

Kiley blushed. "Um . . . is that relevant to my job, somehow?"

"Oh, don't go all Midwest tight-ass on me." Platinum reached for the comb, which had fallen to her feet. "He invited you to his fashion show, so I figured you have to be doing him. Not that I know why, since obviously he could get, like, a babe. Do you know how hard it is to get tickets to that freaking show?"

"Extremely?" Kiley ventured.

"Try impossible. This whole FAB thing is like some closed-door society bullshit. They let you on the grounds of the Staples Center, but to get into one of the tents, forget it. Or one of the parties—especially Diane Goldhagen's thing—impossible. So hot Tom laid two FAB tickets on you. I want one."

Why, why, why had she been so stupid as to tell Platinum that Tom had given her two tickets to the main show tonight? Because she was so excited, that was why. Because she had to explain why a messenger was showing up at the gate for something that did not involve Platinum.

"Gee, I'd be happy to give you one," Kiley began slowly, "but I already asked my friend Lydia to come with me. She already said yes."

"Who the hell is Lydia?"

"Another nanny I know."

"Screw it, uninvite her." Platinum curled her hair back up again and stabbed it with the pearl comb.

"B-but I can't. I mean, that would be so rude."

"Please," Platinum scoffed. "I'm famous for being rude. Tell her your bitch of an employer forced you to do it." She stood and stretched, showing an inch of taut, tanned stomach. "I'm glad we had this chat. I'll have my driver take the Mercedes so we won't have to park downtown, unless I change my mind and want you to drive the Lotus. Be ready at seven. And for God's sake, wear something decent; the place will be swarming with photographers. I plan on giving them something to photograph. *Ciao.*" She strolled out.

Kiley slumped in her chair. Platinum had left her no choice. She'd have to call Lydia and explain.

Bitch of an employer was right.

14

"Hey, Nina, it's Lydia, Kiley's friend, callin' you again about the nanny job? Just wanted to make sure you got my message about Evelyn Bowers upping the pay to seven-fifty a week, plus the Jag. Sure beats that pizza place, huh? I'm tryin' to hold the position for you on account of your bein' Kiley's friend and all, but I have to hear from you, like, today, because I've got girls lined up wanting to grab this sucker. So I really need for you to call me back, okay? My cell is 310-555-8818. Bye now. Stay sweet!"

Lydia hung up and deposited the new Ericsson phone in the rear pocket of her fuchsia floral-print cotton-blend jeweled D&G miniskirt. Shockingly, the skirt was hers, Kat having bestowed it upon her at breakfast. Her aunt, who had been in town for all of six hours before turning around to leave for New York yet again—more meetings for Wimbledon—had explained it had been in the goody bag given to her by one of the sponsors of the upcoming broadcast. Goody bags were one of the perks of her job, evidently, as she casually offered Lydia anything in the bag; she and Anya had already taken out the stuff they wanted.

Lydia had pounced on the bag like a panther on a mongoose and secured herself a green and white apple-patterned Luella canvas jacket, a burnt orange oversized Tylie Malibu deerskin bag, Lea Extreme perfume, white Christian Roth sunglasses wrapped in fourteen-karat platinum, and Frederic Malle shower gel in Anterenea (which, according to the label, was essence of citrus, mint, and geranium).

Lydia was thrilled with the booty, but she also felt as though she deserved it. This was one of the first times Kat had treated her like her niece, like her flesh and blood. In the Amazon, blood members of the same tribe shared a special bond. They would die for each other, not just hand over perfume and clothing that they'd done nothing to earn.

She checked her watch. It was 3:15 in the afternoon. At any moment, she was expecting the girl from LEAP, Alexis, to stop over. She hoped Alexis would be on time—she had a tight schedule today. Martina and Jimmy were doing their appointed activities, which would be followed by showers, which would be followed by a special outing that Lydia had planned for them that wasn't exactly in the schedule but for which she could reasonably construct, if pressed, some educational purpose. Anya. What a pain. How uptight could one Russian lesbian be? Maybe her sex life with Kat wasn't working out, what with Kat harboring secret *Kama Sutra* how-to books and all. Sexual tension. That could be it.

Lydia went to the front door of her guesthouse and looked

outside. There was Alexis, sitting on the front stoop. Early. Excellent. This was an outstanding sign of interest and commitment.

"Hey," Alexis said when she heard the door open. "I didn't want to be late."

"Hey yourself," Lydia told her. She plopped down on the stoop next to Alexis. "For five bills a week, plus a car, plus a 90210 address, I wouldn't be late, either. Plus two real sweet kids."

"Wow, sounds great!" Alexis chirped.

Indeed. If Kiley's friend Nina wouldn't jump this puppy, that would just be her loss and Alexis's gain. Lydia would get her cut, either way.

Lydia rose. "So, come on in, we can talk about it."

She led the way inside; Alexis took in the twin black French dressers, the rust-colored curtains by the picture window, the framed circular mirrors over the dressers, and the Fortuny chandelier. "This place is gorgeous," the girl marveled.

"It's okay. I've seen Evelyn Bowers's place, and this looks like an outhouse compared to where you'll be living. Want anything? Water? Soda?"

Alexis shook her head as Lydia studied her. Strawberry blond hair was neatly plaited down her back in a single braid. She wore baggy olive green carpenter pants and a crisp little white blouse; very cute, very Southern California, very about to make Lydia so much money.

"That is awesome." Alexis took in Lydia's short, bejeweled skirt.

Lydia smoothed it over her hips. "Oh, thanks. The woman I

work for gave it to me. Yeah, she gives me expensive gifts all the time. It's just one of those nanny perks. I'm sure the same thing will happen to you. Just sit wherever."

Alexis sat on the couch, obviously impressed. So far, so good. Lydia slid into the Eames chair and crossed her legs neatly. "So, Alexis. What's your current living situation?"

"Bad. I live in a two-bedroom apartment in Westwood with three roommates. One of them never cleans up after herself—I end up having to do her dishes all the time. The other has this brain-dead skateboarder boyfriend, Ryan, who's over all the time. They use the pullout couch in the living room for sex, like, every night."

Lydia was intrigued, but since she was currently in business mode, she kept her mouth shut and simply leaned forward to circle her knees with her entwined fingers. "We're not here to talk about sex, Alexis. We're here to talk about your future."

For the next ten minutes, Lydia painted a glorious picture of what Alexis's life as a nanny to a rich Brentwood publicist would be like, and what it would be like to live on her property, notwithstanding the fact that she barely knew Evelyn Bowers and knew nothing about her dwelling save for its address.

After that, Lydia segued to the perks—membership in the Brentwood Hills Country Club, tickets to premiere parties, dinner at Koi, VIP passes to the Dungeon, etc. "Publicists are always hooked up, Alexis," Lydia promised. "You'll be on so many guest lists, you'll have to pick and choose."

"Wow," Alexis marveled. "It's just, like, amazing. It kinda sounds too good to be true."

Lydia wagged a finger at her. "There's a reason for that,

Alexis. You can imagine how many girls I have applying for every one of my openings. But I only accept certain very select girls. I mean, who wouldn't want a job like this, right?"

"Yeah, definitely," Alexis agreed. "So tell me more about . . . what's her name again?"

"Evelyn Bowers."

"Right. How are her children?"

Lydia held up two fingers and smiled. Earlier in the week, while the kids were playing in the country club pool, Evelyn had gone into some detail about her "very special" offspring.

"Well, Star is ten," Lydia began. "She's a perfect little princess. Her younger brother, Moon, age seven, is even nicer. He's like a little flower that just needs watering."

This was a big fat lie, of course. According to Evelyn, Moon had a whole list of problems that each boiled down to letters: APD—Auditory Processing Disorder; ADHD—Attention Deficit/Hyperactivity Disorder; and ABD—Antisocial Behavior Disorder. But Evelyn, being a proactive single parent, had a detailed BIP—Behavior Intervention Plan. Personally, Lydia suspected the whole thing was a crock of SHIT—Somehow Human Idiots Triumph.

Take the mother, for example. Evelyn Bowers was more intense than a barrage of poison arrows. Lydia was confident she'd ruined her son, not that she would share this information with Alexis, just as she wouldn't share it with Nina (or Kiley, for that matter, lest she fill Nina in). Some might consider this dishonest. Lydia considered it warfare. The important thing to do was to win. No one ever remembered who fought dirty and who fought clean.

"So," Lydia concluded, "what do you think?"

"It's fantastic." Alexis grinned. "What can I say except I'm just so glad that you walked into LEAP!"

"Oh, honey, I feel exactly the same way," Lydia drawled. "Now, of course, my agency gets twenty percent of your pay every week—I'm sure that's no problem."

Alexis hesitated. "Uh, I guess not. It's still a much better deal than what I have going on now."

"Great," Lydia continued. "I'll need two references, and all pertinent personal information—legal name, address, all of that. Social Security number, driver's license, et cetera. If you could get it to me by tomorrow that would be great. Then I'll arrange for you to meet Evelyn. I'm sure she'll love you."

Alexis twisted a lock of hair around her finger. "What about time off?"

"Oh, did I forget to mention that? You'll have Sundays off, and every other Saturday."

"What time do I get done at night?"

"Well, when a job is this desirable—and I'm sure you'll agree that this one is a peach—the nanny is expected to stay until the parent says they're free. Sometimes Evelyn might have a thing she has to go to in the evening, and you'd stay with the kids. You have to be flexible."

Alexis frowned. Damn.

"Well, Alexis, if that seems too much for you, I have dozens of other applicants who—"

"It's not too much," Alexis interrupted. "It's just that on Wednesday nights, well, if she needed me to stay with the kids, I'd have a conflict."

Lydia nodded smoothly. "I'm sure whatever it is you can change, right?"

"It's when my meditation group meets."

Meditation. Ugh. No one in Amazonia meditated. Close your eyes without someone watching your back, and you might never open them again.

"Well, I'm sure you can get as spiritual as you want and still make Evelyn's schedule work," Lydia said cheerfully.

"Okay . . . I guess."

Alexis stood, and so did Lydia. "I can't thank you enough, really."

"You're just so welcome, Alexis. You get that information to me tomorrow, hear, and we'll see about an interview."

Mission accomplished, Lydia thought, waving to Alexis as the girl made her way out. As they said in Amazonia: If you are going on a monkey hunt and you see a monkey, kill it. This monkey was definitely dead monkey meat.

15

"*¿Esme? Necesito agua,*" Weston whined, kicking her small legs out from under the pink and white Givenchy hand-sewn quilt on her bed. (Easton had the identical quilt on her bed. Both were gifts from Halle Berry. Esme knew this firsthand because she'd handwritten all the thank-you notes on embossed Goldhagen note cards and delivered them to Diane for her signature.)

"You already had two glasses of water," Esme reminded her. She sat on the edge of the bed, stroking her forehead and thanking the gods that at least Easton had fallen asleep quickly. Two overtired kids would have been too much to deal with.

Esme couldn't blame them. The photo shoot had been a long, tedious affair. The photographer had been a snotty perfectionist, waiting for the sun to reach a certain spot in the sky before he'd even deign to shoot. Afterward, the girls had to pee, so Esme took them to Diane's private trailer. Diane had said there were two cots in there where the kids could nap, but when Esme opened the trailer door, she saw a man on his knees frantically repinning a crimson designer gown on a very skinny, nearly naked model. "It's ruined, the dress is ruined!" he bellowed in Esme's direction, pins flying from his mouth.

Rather than try to remove him, Esme elected to simply take the girls home to nap. So far, though, Weston wouldn't close her eyes.

"Story!" Weston demanded in English. "*Conteme una historia.* Story!"

"No story. Sleeping. If you close your eyes and try to sleep, I will get you all the ice cream you can eat later." She said this in English, then in Spanish. Soon, she knew, the Spanish wouldn't be necessary.

Weston obediently closed her eyes, but Esme had no hope that it would last very long. Still, she got up and started to tiptoe out of the room. As she did, she felt her cell phone vibrate in her jeans pocket. Certain it was Jonathan—he'd called twice in the past half hour, she'd seen his number on caller ID—she gritted her teeth. She hadn't spoken to him then, and she wasn't speaking to him now.

Bastardo. No shit he was calling her. He didn't want to lose his good thing; he thought he could sweet-talk himself right back into her bed. *Que se vaya a la madre*—he could go to hell. She never wanted to see his two-timing, too-handsome face again. Esme went next door and lay down on Easton's extra bed, staring up at the ceiling. It was over with Jonathan. Over. He'd tried to speak with her after his private little chat with Mackenzie, to explain why she was there—something about an internship she was doing for VH1. Esme didn't want to hear it. Instead, she'd cussed him out in the most colorful Spanish she could muster, knowing he wouldn't understand a damn word.

He had no idea who he was messing with. He was used to these little white bitches, with their frills and fancy cars and rich daddies. Esme was a tough girl from the *barrio.* She could take pain, and she could also take care of herself.

Hot tears, unbidden, came to her eyes. God, she'd been such a fool! If the *cholas*—gang girls—back in the Echo knew how stupid she'd been, they'd kick her ass themselves. Damn stupid *puta,* they'd hiss at her. Whore.

There was a knock at the door; then it was pushed open. Weston's little face appeared.

"*Yo no puedo dormir,* Esme," Weston whispered, wide-eyed.

Esme smiled at her. "I'm not sleeping either."

Weston climbed into bed next to Esme and snuggled up; Esme felt the tension leave the girl's body. She was so trusting, so innocent. Esme prayed that this girl and her sister would not grow up to care about a boy who would use them the way she'd been used. Esme was glad they were Latinas—something she was proud to be—and she was also glad they'd be very rich Latinas. Maybe money wasn't everything, but it could buy you two important things—power and respect.

"How about if I sing you a song, *niña*?" Esme asked, stroking Weston's hair. "Maybe that would help you sleep." Her voice low, Esme began to croon a Spanish lullaby her own mother had sung to her as a baby.

Duermete, mi niña.
Duermete, mi sol.

Duermete, pedaza
De mi corazón.
Go to sleep, my baby.
Go to sleep, my sunshine.
You will always be
In this heart of mine.

She felt her pocket vibrating again. *Pendejo.* Fool. Esme kept singing.

Duermete, mi niña.
Duermete, solita . . .

"Esme?"

Her mother was standing in the doorway in her black maid's uniform. Esme studied her: legs swollen from spending so much time on her feet, ugly crepe-soled shoes that allowed her feet to expand during the day, inky hair up in a tidy bun, weary face. And still beautiful. Esme loved her so much that her heart ached.

She carefully extricated herself from Weston and went to the door. "*Sí*, Mama?" she whispered.

"Your cell phone is off?"

"Yes."

"Jorge just called me. He's been trying to reach you but you don't answer."

Esme shook her head, confused. "Why?"

"Junior. He was making a run in Alhambra. There were two boys shot. While he was working on one of them, some other *cholos* drove by and . . ."

God. Fear gripped Esme's heart. She grabbed her mother's wrist. "*¿Qué ha pasado,* Mama?"

Mrs. Castaneda looked her daughter in the eye. "Junior is at County General. It's very bad, *niña.* They don't know if he will live."

“You shouldn’t take us somewhere without telling Momma Anya, you know.”

Lydia, who sat in the front seat of the Mercedes with X, the family driver, craned around to look at Martina. The farther from Beverly Hills they’d gotten, the more anxious the girl had become. “It’s okay, sweet pea. Everyone needs to play hooky now and then. Isn’t that right, X?”

“I merely drive the automobile,” X intoned. “But if I were to venture an opinion, which, if asked by the moms, I definitely did not—playing occasional hooky is as important as a really good haircut.”

Lydia laughed. X was the funniest person she knew. He was also cute, in a skinny, spiky-bleached-hair kind of way.

She’d overheard two girls talking at the country club one day, musing on whether or not a soft-around-the-middle guy on the diving board was gay or straight. “Not hot enough to be gay," they'd decided. In Hollywood, the standard of beauty for gay men was highest of all.

"Are we there yet?" Jimmy groaned from the backseat.

"Soon," Lydia assured him.

They'd left Beverly Hills a half hour ago. A mudslide had closed Topanga Canyon Road between the Pacific Coast Highway and the top of the hill, so X had taken the 405 Freeway to the 101 to enter the canyon from the opposite direction. Now they were winding high up into the stark, barren hills. It was hard to believe it was actually a part of Los Angeles.

"You could at least tell us where we're going," Jimmy said, pouting. "What if it's just another dumb thing that we're gonna hate?"

"It's a surprise, Mr. Sunshine," Lydia replied brightly.

Of course, she had no idea if the surprise would work. These children never wanted to do *anything*. Sports were a washout. A trip to the downtown public library, a disaster. Even an afternoon at the Grove, one of the hippest outdoor shopping-slash-movie locales, had been a bust.

It was time for something more . . . out of the box, because Lydia had not found a box yet that fit her cousins.

"Straight ahead?" X asked.

"Yup," Lydia told him. "Straight through the town of Topanga."

"Hey, this place is pretty!" Martina exclaimed as she took in the quaint shops and restaurants that made up the village of Topanga.

Lydia smiled, then checked the directions she'd gotten when she'd called for a late-afternoon reservation. "There should be a street called Nectar Lane on the left where we turn."

They drove past Nectar Lane twice—the sign was obscured by foliage run amok. The blacktop quickly turned to dirt; the dirt lane ended a quarter of a mile later at a red clapboard house with a small parking lot that held several cars. A weathered sign hung from a wooden stake in the lawn:

SECTS.

"What's 'sects'?" Jimmy asked as X parked.

"Noun," X responded. "Groups of people whose religious beliefs differ from those generally accepted."

Jimmy reached over the seat and grabbed Lydia's shoulder. "It's a cult! You kidnapped us to join a cult!"

"I want to go home," Martina whimpered.

Honestly. These children were an embarrassment to the family, that was what they were. Yet Lydia forced herself to remain sweet on the outside, a lesson every Texas girl learns with her mother's milk, whether she'd been moved against her will to Amazonia or not.

"Y'all know I wouldn't do anything to hurt you." She looked back at her shoulder, where Jimmy still had a viselike grip. "You want to ease up there, bubba? X, thanks for the ride. I'll call you when we're done here."

As they got out of the car and watched X drive away, Lydia took in her cousins' closed-down faces and had a moment of doubt. Last night she'd been racking her brain for something new and different that might light some kind of spark in Martina and Jimmy. Then she remembered how a university researcher had come to Amazonia to catalog rare insects, and then had opened a bizarre restaurant-club in Los Angeles. He'd even stayed with Lydia and her parents when he'd visited their part of the river.

Lydia looked it up. There it was, in Topanga Canyon, Los Angeles's retro-hippie hangout. And now, here *they* were.

"Let's go," Lydia said cheerfully.

Martina screamed. "Eww!"

She pointed to the right, shuddering. Hundreds of wasps were flying in and out of holes in the sandy earth.

"Ground wasps," Lydia noted matter-of-factly. "Don't irritate them. It really, really hurts if they sting you."

Martina and Jimmy walked like petrified zombies to the front door, which surprisingly opened into a cozy dining room with a dance floor. At the center of the dance floor was an enormous Plexiglas cube that protected a working ant farm. A massive metal dragonfly clung to one wall; a fifty-foot caterpillar kite hung from the ceiling. Meanwhile, a glass display case on the far wall revealed thousands of crawling mealworms. There were people eating at perhaps a dozen of the tables, all of which were adorned with spiderweb centerpieces.

Jimmy's eyes suddenly lit up. "Wait, I get it. 'Sect' is short for insect!"

"See now, I just knew I had a smart cousin," Lydia told him as she ushered the kids to a small round table covered with simple white butcher's paper.

"I think I'm going to barf," Martina groaned. She wrapped her arms around her oversized black Mickey Mouse sweatshirt as if to make sure that nothing buggy would touch her flesh. Meanwhile, a waiter with a flypaper boutonniere encrusted with dead flies gave them menus and poured water that he assured them had been filtered. Jimmy opened his menu and read aloud with a mix of incredulity and undisguised interest.

"Chimichanga stuffed with pureed mealworms. Cranberry cricket polenta. French-fried bees?"

"Lydia, why did you make us come here?" Martina wailed.

"Come on, Martina," Lydia chided. "Buck up. Show a little spunk. Lots of insects are edible. I ate 'em in the Amazon all the time."

"Hat?" A boy about Jimmy's age had approached their table. He had long brown hair tied in a ponytail, and his chubby stomach pooched out the green T-shirt he wore with his khaki safari pants. He carried two baseball caps with antennae; he wore one just like them.

"Sure." Jimmy took one and put it on, bobbing his chin to make the antennae shake. "Cool!"

Lydia tried to get the other one on Martina, but the girl shrank away from her.

"We always give hats to new kids, and I've never seen you here before. I'm Paul. My dad owns this place," the kid explained.

"I know your dad," Lydia informed him. "He visited my family in Amazonia a couple of years ago."

Paul's face lit up. "No way, that's you? Cool! You guys are buggies?"

"What are buggies?" Martina whispered.

"People who love bugs, of course." He patted his round stomach. "Eat what you love, that's what Dad says."

"So do the Amas," Lydia agreed pleasantly. "They used to be cannibals."

Paul focused on Jimmy. "Hey, you wanna come up to Ant Hill after you eat?"

"What's that?" Jimmy asked.

"Kind of a club for buggy kids." Paul gestured toward the other tables—there were as many kids in the restaurant as there were adults. "Like all these guys. We finish eating, then all the kids go upstairs, talk about bugs, catalog 'em. Like which ones we like and which ones we just like to eat, like that. You in?"

Jimmy hesitated and turned to Martina. One of the few positive things Lydia could say for these kids was that they looked out for each other.

"Let's go, okay?" He kept his voice low.

"No way! It's creepy," Martina whispered.

"I know, that's what's so cool," Jimmy whispered back. "It'll be fun."

"You, not me."

Paul grinned. "Don't worry. Your sister will come around. It always takes the girls longer." He stepped away from the table. "Try the French-fried silkworms—they're the bomb."

Lydia took Paul's recommendation. Good choice. Jimmy tried the chocolate-covered Colombian ants, which were as big as praying mantises. Martina wouldn't even sip the water. When Paul came to retrieve Jimmy after the meal, he asked Martina again to join them. The girl wouldn't budge or even look at her brother and his new friend as they walked away together.

"I *hate* bugs."

"You hate *everything,* Martina."

Martina flushed. "No, I don't."

"Great. Tell me one thing that you like."

"Art," Martina said, eyes downcast. "I like to draw."

"That's something you do alone," Lydia pointed out. "I

meant something you do with other kids. How about art lessons?"

Martina shook her head. "Other kids don't like me. Plus I'm not very good, so everyone would make fun of me, plus . . ."

"What?" Lydia coaxed.

"I look weird," she mumbled into the top of her sweatshirt.

"No, honey, you just think you do. You bloomed early and it makes you feel all self-conscious. All the other girls will catch up with you soon."

Martina flushed, eyes still downcast. "I *hate* it!"

Lydia made a decision. "You know what, Martina? We're going to work on that. You and me. It'll be a secret just between the two of us."

The girl's eyes cut to Lydia. "Like how?"

"Like I don't know yet," Lydia admitted. "But whatever it is, once you start to feel more comfortable, I'm going to find some great art classes for you. You'll meet other kids who love art. You'll make some friends."

"You think Momma Anya will say that it's okay?"

Screw Momma Anya, Lydia thought. She patted Martina's hand. "You leave Momma Anya to me, sweet pea. I'll figure out some way to make things work. I always do."

"Esme, no quiero hacer esto. ¡No quiero!" Weston was sobbing, her face buried against Esme's right leg.

"Remember, this is what we practiced for," Esme told her in both English and Spanish, trying hard to sound calm and composed when she felt exactly the opposite. The girl shook her head violently and burrowed in even closer.

Esme felt as if she was going to shatter into a thousand pieces. They were backstage at Tent B, where Emily Steele's early-evening kids' fashion show was about to start. All around Esme and the girls were dressers and assistants, makeup artists and designers. Each of them was charging around, sure that their particular mission was worth their state of panic.

Tol and her trans-whatever assistant, Chantal, didn't help matters as they barraged Esme with questions. The two of them were backstage to ride herd on all the Major Modeling clients who were modeling the Emily Steele fashion line.

"What's the problem?" Tol demanded.

Esme stroked the girls' hair. "They don't want to do it."

"But every little girl in the world wants to be a model!" Tol insisted.

"Tell them this is how I began my brilliant career," Chantal suggested, shaking her long mane of hair off her face.

Just let me get through this, Esme prayed silently. She could hear Diane out onstage welcoming the standing-room-only crowd. Jonathan had to be there too, to cheer on his little sisters. Esme didn't care; he was the last person she wanted to see.

Her boss had been more than gracious after Esme explained that a friend of hers had been in a terrible accident and asked for a few hours off after the show to go to County General. Diane had told Esme to go to the hospital as soon as she could. Not that Diane was going to watch over the girls herself; not in the midst of FAB. Instead, she had asked if Mrs. Castaneda, Esme's mother, could be brought to FAB by the Goldhagens' driver and step in for Esme. After all, she could communicate with the children. That phone call had been more than an hour and a half ago, and still Esme's mother had not arrived.

Esme wanted her mother, and not just so that she could go to the hospital. Part of her wished she could bury herself in her mother's arms much the way Weston was hiding now. She had no idea what she would say to Junior when she saw him. While she'd been having sex with Jonathan, he'd been out on the streets, part of the thin line between life and death. What had Esme given him in return? Lies and more lies. Cheating and more cheating.

"And now . . . the international children of Emily Steele!" Diane's voice sang out through the sound system with its backstage feed.

The audience on the other side of the curtain applauded; there were even a few whoops and hollers.

Chantal immediately took charge, pointing to the three kids with the Texan names, dressed alike in royal blue flowing silk pants and matching vests embroidered with Chinese characters.

"Go," she said, pointing to the runway, then glared at Esme in a way that brooked no opposition. "Goldhagens on deck."

"Vamos, chicas," Esme urged the girls, alternately tugging and pushing them as firmly as she dared. *"Necesitais andar un poco. No mucho. Por la gente y sus padres.* You girls will be wonderful. Everyone will applaud because you both look so pretty. Remember, if I am not here after the show, my mother will be. Okay?"

"Bueno," Easton told her. *"Me gusta mucho su madre, Esme."*

Weston peeked through the curtain, then allowed her sister to lead her to the runway steps. A makeup artist scuttled after the girls, reapplying their lip gloss. Esme could hear the "awws" from the audience as they watched the Texas triplets model the first Emily Steele outfits.

"Esme!"

Esme turned at the sound of her name. It was her mother, hurrying over to her, still wearing her black uniform. Why hadn't she changed? Did she have to advertise that she was a maid?

"Mama." She hugged her mother, ashamed at her own thoughts.

"I had a terrible time getting through the security," Mrs. Castaneda explained in her lilting accent, "that is what took me so long."

"It's fine," Esme assured her. She could hear cheers from the other side of the curtain and knew the cheers had to be for the twins. Her mother gave her a penetrating look. "And my *niña*?"

"Not so fine," Esme said, a sob escaping her throat.

Her mother nodded. "Go to Junior," she urged. "Go."

For heart transplants in Los Angeles, you went to UCLA. For cancer care, Loma Linda Medical Center. For burns, the Grossman burn unit at Sherman Oaks Hospital. But for gunshot wounds, knife wounds, and the aftermath of automobile accidents, the destination of choice was County General. Their emergency room saw the most and knew exactly what to do.

When Esme arrived and hurried through the main entrance, the downstairs waiting area by the security desk was crowded with guys from Junior's former gang, Los Locos. There had to be at least a dozen *cholos,* including the two guys who had beaten up Jonathan a couple of weeks before, Victor and Freddie. None of them made any effort to conceal their gang status. On the contrary, they wore colors—black T-shirts and baggy jeans, with red bandannas sticking out of their back pockets. Each had the entwined *LL* tattooed onto the knuckles of his right hand—Esme herself had done many of these tattoos.

As Esme stepped toward them, they slitted their eyes at her, as if she was personally responsible for what had happened to Junior. Esme was sure that Freddie and Victor had told them all how Esme was disrespecting Junior with a rich gringo. Then Esme saw that there was another guy there, not a member of the gang. Her best friend, Jorge.

He put his finger in the book he was reading to mark his place and came to Esme to embrace her. "Esme. I'm sorry."

"He's still alive?" Esme whispered.

"Yes," Jorge assured her.

She was surprised and grateful that Jorge was here. He didn't even like Junior; he thought Esme was too good for the former gangbanger. Jorge's father was a public defender; Jorge was smart and political and planned to be mayor of Los Angeles someday. At least. He had told Esme more times than she could count that Junior wasn't going anywhere except to an early grave.

"Thank you," she mumbled into his neck.

"Having you hang alone with these homies didn't seem like an option."

She backed out of his arms, nodding imperceptibly. "How is he?"

"Better. He's out of surgery about an hour ago. The bullet hit an artery; he lost a lot of blood."

"Did he ask for me?"

Jorge gave a half laugh from the back of his throat. "No, *esa,*" he grunted. The "*esa*" part was mocking, using the phraseology of the hood for Spanish American. He lived there, and he loved the people there, *his* people, but Esme knew that Jorge was definitely not down with the gang thing. "Junior won't ask anyone for anything. Not *macho.*"

"I want to see him."

Jorge pointed behind him to the elevators. "Fourth floor. Ask at the nurses' station for his room."

"You want to come?"

Her friend shook his head. "I'm not here for him, Esme. I'm here for you."

Junior wasn't the biggest guy in the hood, just the most respected. Esme was used to thinking of him as taking up a lot of space with his presence. But when Esme reached his room, she was struck by how small he appeared under the sterile sheets, in a room he shared with an elderly, sleeping patient. One of his legs was elevated and wrapped in surgical gauze; a tube ran from that leg to a bag that hung from a pole. That bag slowly filled with a pinkish liquid. An IV snaked from another bag into his arm. There was a heartbeat monitor attached to his finger.

"Esme," he muttered when he saw her.

She went to him and took his hand, careful not to disturb anything. "What you go and do, *Papi,* eh?" she asked, falling into the idiom of her neighborhood without even thinking about it.

"Nothing good." He smiled faintly.

She kissed his hand. "What happened?"

"SOS, *chica.* Blood in blood out. They checking this baby G with the CWs. I get the call; he's not more than thirteen, all wet behind the ears and shit; an' I catch a bullet in my leg. No biggie, eh?"

Esme did an instant mental translation: same old shit. The Bloods, one of the most dangerous gangs in L.A., were initiating a new young member. He'd only be admitted if he killed someone, so he picked someone from their rival gang, the Crips. Junior had gotten the call on his radio; he'd raced his ambulance to the scene, only to get caught in another Bloods strike while he was loading the victim into his ambulance. The message was clear: If we kill someone, leave him to die.

"It never ends, does it, Junior." A statement, not a question.

"For you it does." He managed a weak smile. "You got out. You stay the hell out."

Guilt flooded her again. "I told you before, the Echo is still my home. This is just a job to me. A job."

"An' I told you to forget that shit, Esme. You keep that in your head, how you gonna do in the fall when you go back to school, eh?"

If she kept the nanny job, she'd be able to go to Bel Air High. If she made the grades there—and she knew she would—maybe she'd get a scholarship to college. After that . . . she had no idea. No idea at all.

Junior reached out to touch her hair. "You come from where you come from, *esa*. But now you need to look to where you're going."

Love for him, for all that was familiar and hers, flooded through her.

"You could do it too, Junior," she insisted. "You're so smart. You could . . . you could go to college, be a doctor, do anything."

He shook his head. "That ain't me, *chica*. That's you." His eyes started to droop. "They give me some shit for the pain, it's knocking me out."

"I'll try to come back later. If you need me just have someone call my cell. I'll come."

He shook his head again. "You got work. Don't mess that up."

"Junior—"

"Go."

She waited until he nodded off before she tiptoed out of the room.

Every once in a while, Platinum just took an instant liking to someone.

This had happened with a girl who'd appeared in a music video that Platinum had shot a couple of months ago. Her name was Lori Sheel, and she was a conceptual artist. In the video, Lori had demonstrated her conceptual art, which consisted of rolling around naked in a kiddie pool filled with Marshmallow Fluff and inviting people to lick it off. Lori, Platinum decreed, would be babysitting Sid and Serenity while Platinum and Kiley went to the main FAB fashion shows that evening.

Kiley didn't know the neighborhood and was glad she'd thought to Mapquest the address. A skinny, pale young woman dressed entirely in layers of filmy purple waited at the side gate to a boxy two-story apartment building off Fairfax in Hancock Park. Her wheat-colored hair was tipped lavender. Oversized purple sunglasses protected her eyes from the sun. When she got into the Lotus and reached for the seat belt, a purple-hued tattoo of a Greek goddess peeked out from the cuff of her shirt. She explained to Kiley that her body was her canvas. Literally. Currently, she was in her purple phase.

Lori assured Kiley that she'd taken care of Platinum's kids before, so Kiley merely dropped her at the front door and returned to the guesthouse. It took only a moment for her to spot two white boxes on the living room coffee table. The larger one had the word "Versace" engraved in raised gold script. The smaller box said "Harry Winston." Under it was a note scrawled on a platinum calling card.

K—

Wear this tonight.
You're driving the Lotus.

—P

Kiley stared at the boxes for a moment. She'd thought about what she'd wear that evening, but it hadn't taken long. By default, it would be the bottle green camisole, which she'd carefully mended. If you looked closely, you could see the tiny stitches, but still it was the best she could do.

Evidently, her boss had something else in mind.

She opened the larger box and unfolded the perfumed lavender tissue paper. Inside was a black sequined silk dress—strapless, very short, with a flounced hem of sequins. A ruffle over one thigh was cut so high Kiley guessed a girl would need a bikini wax to wear it safely. She peered at the label. Yep, Versace. She was holding a real Versace in her hands. She noticed something else black nestled in the fragrant tissue, and pulled it out: a matching black silk thong. She had been right about southern exposure. Also nestled in the tissue paper was the sales slip. Kiley stared at it, mouth agape: $2,900 without tax.

Gulp.

With trembling hands, she opened the smaller box: hammered gold wrist cuffs and a matching hammered gold choker. There was another sales slip: $3,600.

My mom's last car cost less than all this.

How could she possibly wear this stuff? For one thing, the dress would never fit. For another thing, she'd feel like an idiot. And for another thing—

The red house phone squealed. Kiley snatched it up before her ears were damaged.

"Yes, Platinum?"

"Like what I left for you?"

"It's . . . amazing."

"Cool. Just for God's sake don't get it dirty, because you're gonna return it to the store tomorrow. *Ciao.*"

"Wait, Platinum! I don't think the dress will fit."

"It'll fit."

"And also I don't have any—"

Platinum had already hung up.

"Shoes," Kiley finished into the silence.

She undressed, took a shower and did a serious shave of all possible hair-exposing parts other than her head, then stared down at the dress. After she pulled it over her head and shimmied into it, she risked a peek in the mirror. Holy shit. It really *did* fit. It was cut in an amazing way so that a woman who was a size four could wear it, but so could she. It looked really . . . good. At least it would have, if the white straps of her utilitarian bra hadn't been hanging out the top.

What to do about the bra straps? She tried tucking them inside the dress, but they bulged, and white showed through the gossamer silk. There was only one solution. Off came the dress, off came the bra, and back on came the dress.

"Damn," she told her reflection, unable to decide if she looked cute or ridiculous.

There was a knock on the door. Kiley went to open it.

"What size?" Serenity demanded, a pair of high-heeled shoes dangling from her left hand. Lori was with her, holding a pair of metallic gold kitten heels.

"Uh . . . eight."

"The Michael Kors," Serenity decreed, pointing to the shoes Lori was holding. "Too bad you don't wear a nine. You could have worn my mom's Zanottis."

Not knowing what else to do, Kiley took the gold shoes. "Thank her for me."

Serenity put her hands on her nonexistent hips and scrutinized Kiley's face. "You need makeup, you know, or else you'll look all washed out and poopy."

"Thank your mother for me."

"No problem," Serenity told her. "Me and Lori are going to have so much fun tonight!"

As Serenity beamed, Kiley thanked them again and shut the door.

Great, she thought as she padded back into the living room. Competition from a conceptual artist. It was clear who Serenity thought should win. *Tomorrow when I bring back the clothes and the jewelry, maybe I should turn in the guesthouse keys, too.*

Kiley sat on the couch, pushed out of her flip-flops, and slipped on the new shoes. They fit. Now all she needed was the—gulp!—matching thong. Gingerly, she stepped into it and pulled it up. It felt weird, but so far, so good. Yeah, this could work. Maybe this would make Tom see her in a whole different light. *Girlfriend* light. Take-her-to-bed-and-make-her-scream light.

Not that she was altogether certain that she even *had* such a light, since it had never been turned on. Why couldn't a girl dream, though?

Makeup was next. She didn't have much, but she arranged what she had on the kitchen table, along with a small vanity mirror that she'd found in the bathroom. She flipped on the local evening news while she sat down to do her face. The news was the usual. A bank robbery in Pacoima. A police pursuit that had tied up traffic on the west side all afternoon. A gang-related shooting in Alhambra that had left two dead and a paramedic injured. The model Marym Marshall . . .

Huh?

Hearing the familiar name got Kiley to grab the remote, spin around to the television, and turn up the volume. There was the rear of Marym's new home in Malibu, shot from the Pacific Coast Highway. By the side gate were a half dozen people carrying picket signs.

". . . and the protesters claim that with the transfer of the property to supermodel Marym Marshall also comes an easement that would give them access to the beautiful and exclusive beachfront. While many celebrities live up here in Malibu and favor environmental causes, few are willing to give the public the right to traverse their backyards to reach the public beach property between the high-tide and low-tide marks. The protesters hope that with the new owner will come a more public-spirited attitude."

The camera went to a Latina reporter in Marym's driveway. "While the supermodel didn't answer the door to do an interview with us," the reporter said, "the protesters claim they will be back out in force tomorrow at sunrise. They intend to, as one of them told me, 'make some noise' to affirm their right to enjoy the ocean as the law permits. Juanita Perez, KLA News."

Kiley clicked off the TV. She remembered the amazing beach behind Marym's house—how walking on it had made her feel. If there was one thing in life about which she felt proprietary, it was the ocean. *Her* ocean. What Marym was doing was deeply wrong, that much Kiley knew. In fact, *she* should join that protest!

She mused, mascara wand in hand. Marym had certainly been nice to her at the party. Plus, she was a good friend of Tom's. What would he think if Kiley joined the protest? It couldn't possibly increase her "girlfriend material" quotient with him.

But no, she couldn't think like that, *wouldn't* think like that! She had nothing but disdain for girls who changed everything about themselves for a guy. It was bad enough that she felt so insecure about Tom. He'd just have to take her or leave her, the *real* her, who believed that the ocean belonged to everyone.

Kiley absentmindedly pulled the thong out of her butt—why did girls wear these things? She would stand up for what she believed in and go to that sunrise protest tomorrow morning, and she'd *definitely* wear something else.

A VIP parking pass came with the tickets to Tom's Ralph Lauren show at FAB. The lot was right behind the tent, so Kiley thought she and Platinum would have an easy time getting from Platinum's white Lotus to the credentials checkpoint.

No such luck. The Staples Center blacktop was an insane scene. Barriers held back hundreds of fans, who were dressed in everything from black tie and evening gowns (as if to mimic the stars they were there to gawk at) to cutoff T-shirts and Daisy Dukes. They screamed for their favorite celebrities—Christina Aguilera, Penelope Cruz, Mischa Barton, Eva Mendes, and both Williams sisters, who obligingly stopped and posed for photos.

There were plenty of media in attendance too. The parking lot was rimmed by television remote-broadcasting trucks parked tail to nose, all of them with microwave relay antennae on top to send FAB pictures to their home stations across the country. Radio stations, too, had flocked to the fashion show, with vans broadcasting into the crowd via rooftop loudspeakers. Kiley found it disconcerting, as they edged their way toward the main tents, to step from rock 'n' roll to soul to hip-hop and back to rock 'n' roll. The dozen Hollywood opening–style searchlights that crisscrossed the sky added to the otherworldliness of the event.

Strangest of all for Kiley was to be there with Platinum. Kiley had thought her own outfit was over the top until she saw what Platinum was wearing, or rather, barely wearing: the tiniest white feather bikini specially made for her by Scott Wilson of London. Over that, a diaphanous feather-trimmed gown. The sky-high white Balenciaga heels with attached diamond ankle bracelet made Platinum over six feet tall. Photographers pushed each other out of the way to snap her picture; fans pressed forward screaming Platinum's name. To Kiley's dismay, the rock star looped her arm through hers; there was no escaping. "Hey, Platinum!" someone in the crowd shouted. "That your new girlfriend?"

Platinum smiled enigmatically while Kiley blushed and prayed that none of the live-remote trucks was broadcasting back to La Crosse, Wisconsin.

As they finally cleared the entranceway and approached the credentials table for the Calvin Klein show, Kiley spotted Lydia and Esme waiting for her on the other side. She waved, grateful to see them—Kiley realized Esme must have given Lydia a ride. Meanwhile, Platinum went to chat with Colin Farrell and his latest girlfriend.

"Dang, girl," Lydia drawled appreciatively, looking over Kiley's dress. "Who'd you do to get *that*?"

"It's a loaner from Platinum and I *definitely* didn't do

her," Kiley explained, glancing down at herself. "Does it look ridiculous?"

"Honey, *I'd* do Platinum to get those threads," Lydia proclaimed. She gestured toward her own citrus floral crepe de chine sundress. "Tracy Reese. Yes, borrowed. Did you hear from Nina?"

Kiley shook her head. "She hasn't called you?"

"No. I left another message. I gotta tell you, she's running out of time here."

"Maybe she's not interested," Esme suggested. "Not everyone wants to be a part of all this." She gestured to the crowd of beautiful people filing into the main tent.

Kiley noticed how tired and tense Esme looked. "Are you okay?"

"Fine," Esme said stiffly, looking away.

"That's the same load of crap she handed me," Lydia reported. She nudged an elbow into Esme's side. "Give it up, girlfriend. We're on your side, whatever it is."

Before Esme could reply, Platinum had joined them. "Hi, I'm Platinum; you guys are Kiley's friends?"

Lydia grinned. "I've seen you in so many magazines. You're hotter in person. I'm Lydia Chandler. This is Esme Castaneda. That outfit is amazing—"

"Can we just cut to the freaking chase here?" Platinum interrupted. "Which one of you works for Goldhagen?"

"Me," Esme replied.

"Cool," said the rock star, shaking her waterfall of platinum hair off her face. "So listen—what was your name again?"

"Esme."

"Right, Esme. Somehow my publicist screwed up and forgot

to get me on the list for Diane's party on the *Queen Mary* tomorrow night. My *ex*-publicist, actually. I'm sure you can fix that for me. Right?"

"Honestly? I really don't think I—" Esme began.

"—can even go myself," Lydia interrupted, finishing Esme's sentence. "That's what Esme was about to say."

Kiley saw Esme shoot Lydia a lethal warning look, but Lydia ignored it and drawled on. "The same goes for me and Kiley. Of course, we're all invited. But we don't have a thing to wear. Now, if you were to give the three of us a small budget of, say, ten thousand dollars for clothes, shoes, and what all, I think Esme might be able to help you. Maybe."

For a moment Platinum was shocked into silence. Meanwhile, Kiley was ready to wring Lydia's neck—Platinum was supposed to *bribe* Esme to get the ticket she coveted?

Platinum's eyebrows furrowed, her eyes narrowed.

I am so fired.

Then Platinum threw her head back and laughed hysterically. "Oh my God, you rock, I *love* the balls on you!" she shrieked, grabbing Lydia into a hug. Then she opened the small white embroidered raw silk purse she carried and took out a credit card. "American Express Platinum," she said with a smirk, flipping it to Lydia. "Your budget is six thou. For all of you. Go over it and I'll send a guy named Cheech to break your legs."

Kiley couldn't believe this was really happening. "We're supposed to go clothes shopping on your credit card?"

"Did I stutter?" Platinum snapped back. "Hell, yeah. For a ticket to the *Queen Mary* FAB party? I'll give you a couple of hours off tomorrow—that's just the kind of bitch I am. What the hell, I'll even throw in the dress you've got on—you already got photographed in it so it would be a bitch to return, and I never wear black anyway." She turned to Esme. "So, we cool?"

Esme barely nodded.

"Have the ticket messengered to me; I don't trust those freaking doormen with their freaking lists, you know what I'm saying?" Platinum spun on her heel and saw Courtney Love about to go into the tent. Courtney beckoned to Platinum, and the two superstars entered together.

Lydia flashed the American Express card at her friends. "Am I good or am I good?"

"Do I look *happy*?" Esme glared at Lydia.

Lydia's face fell. "Uh-oh, you're pissed."

"You had no right to do that," Esme seethed.

"But you said Diane told you to put whoever you wanted on the guest list." Lydia grimaced. "Wait, you *can* get her in, right?"

"I'll just give her name to Diane's personal assistant, and see that the ticket gets messengered to her," Esme replied.

Lydia pumped a fist in the air. "*Yes!*"

Esme set her jaw. "It should have been my decision, not yours."

"Esme, I just got us a shopping spree from a woman who probably lights her joints with thousand-dollar bills," Lydia pointed out. "She'll never miss it."

"That isn't the point," Esme began, and then stopped, staring hard at Lydia. "You know what, never mind. I have to go to Diane's trailer and pick up the kids."

Esme turned, but Lydia put a hand on her arm to stop her. "Esme, wait." She turned back. "Something bad happened," Lydia stated. "I see it in your eyes. The shamans call it reading the soul."

Kiley saw Esme flinch as if Lydia had hit her—or maybe just hit the truth.

"What is it?" Kiley asked.

Esme hesitated, as if she was going to tell them something; then she just shook Lydia off. "I have to go."

"At least come shopping with us tomorrow," Lydia called after her as she walked away. "I'll call you!"

Kiley winced. "She's really ticked. You were kind of out of line, huh?"

"Oh, she'll get over it," Lydia insisted, waving away Kiley's concern. "That's not what's really on her mind, anyway."

Kiley saw the last of the line snaking into the tent. "Let me know when you figure it out, Madame Witch Doctor. I have to go sit with Platinum and pray that she doesn't throw her nearly naked body at Tom's feet."

"Cool. I'm off to meet Billy. Tonight I finally get laid, isn't that great?"

Kiley laughed.

"Tomorrow we'll celebrate the loss of my virginity and spend six thousand dollars—a perfect day."

Lydia saw Billy waiting for her by a side entrance to the main tent. She smiled. He was one delicious hunk of boy. If Tom Welling was a ten, Billy Martin was an eleven. He had on dusty jeans, there were paint speckles on his black T-shirt, and his chin was spotted with two days' growth of sexy stubble.

"Well, well, well, if it isn't Billy Martin," Lydia said.

"Lydia Chandler. Didn't I meet you in a hut in Amazonia? You were wearing a loincloth? Very hot," he teased.

She went along with the joke. "But so last year." She gave

him a soft kiss. "How can you be so straight and still be so funny?"

"Someone told you I'm straight?" He gave her a look of mock surprise.

Lydia furrowed her brows and wagged a finger at him. "This is a test. I repeat. This is only a test." Then she kissed him, and felt it all the way down to the toenails she'd painted with Scarlet Lady Red nail polish.

He held her close. "I could do that for a few more hours."

"What a great idea."

Billy chuckled. "You are one of a kind."

"You're the lucky boy who gets me. Please tell me your roommate the football player isn't home."

"He's not."

"Excellent." She took his hand. "Let's go."

He held back. "We're gonna have to table that."

"Tables, chairs, beds, let's do it all," Lydia agreed.

Billy groaned. "My boss is screwing with my love life. I gotta work."

"No!" Lydia cried.

"Yes. Eduardo went over to the *Queen Mary* to check out the set for the main ballroom and had a hissy fit. He wants it redone. Tonight."

Lydia stopped, disappointment welling up in her throat. "This is the second time—"

"I know." Billy sighed. "Welcome to the life of an underpaid intern."

"But he said you could have tonight off. That's so unfair!"

"Tell me about it," Billy agreed. "Eduardo Parsons thinks an internship means slave labor. I know it's gonna look great on my résumé, but I'm not sure it was worth it. Thank God it's all over tomorrow."

"Oh, baby," Lydia cooed sympathetically, and kissed him again. "Want me to zap him with one of my witchy-woo potions?"

"Listen, I'm going to make this up to you tomorrow night, I promise. I'll be putting the finishing touches on the damn set all day, so I'll already be there. We'll meet at the boat, okay?"

Lydia sighed. "You'd better, Billy Martin. According to this article I read in *Cosmopolitan*, a woman doesn't peak sexually until she's forty-five, but a man peaks at around age twenty. I don't think we want to let the best days of your life slip away."

The portly limo driver opened the door to Diane's trailer at FAB. "I'm looking for Mrs. Estella Castaneda."

Esme saw her mother give a little wave. "I'm Estella," she murmured.

"I'm to drive you home," the driver said. He wiped a bit of perspiration from his forehead with a white bandanna. "Diane Goldhagen's orders."

"Could you wait outside a moment?" Esme asked him. "Five minutes, no more."

"Certainly," the driver said.

As he closed the trailer door, Mrs. Castaneda shook her head. "I could have gotten a bus. It's just as easy."

"No, you cannot get a bus," Esme insisted. "You did me a favor and your boss has gotten you a ride home. Accept it."

Certainly her mother had earned her keep. When Esme had come back to the trailer, Easton had been in its bathroom. She'd gotten stuck inside. When Esme had finally opened the door, she'd found that the little girl hadn't gotten to the toilet in time.

Esme couldn't bear to scold her. She was doing the best she could, and it had been a very long day. Esme just helped get Easton cleaned up, put her wet clothes in a plastic garbage bag, then wrapped her in a cashmere sweater of Diane's that she found in a closet. It gave Esme perverse pleasure to think of Diane's dry cleaning bill.

Mrs. Castaneda took her daughter's hands. "Esme, there's something you should know. While you were at the hospital, Jonathan came looking for you."

Esme flushed and looked away. She'd assured her mother that nothing was going on between her and Jonathan. At the time, except for an intense flirtation, it had been true. Her mother had instructed her not to let nothing turn into something.

"Esme, mi querida. Por favor, sus ojos en mis ojos. Look at me." Mrs. Castaneda gently turned Esme's face toward hers.

She'd never been a very good liar with her mother. She was sure that her mom could see the truth in her eyes. Or at least the part of the truth where nothing had, in fact, turned into everything.

"Esme. You take time off work to go and see Junior, and then your boss's son comes after you. What are you thinking?"

"I can't talk about it now," Esme insisted.

"Yes, you can." Her mother's face hardened. "I will not allow you to throw away this chance over a boy."

"It's not up to you!" Esme defended herself. Her head was throbbing. "Just leave me alone about it. Please, Mama. Please."

Her mother didn't say another word to her—which, in some

ways, was even worse. She got her things, kissed the girls goodbye (they were transfixed by *Shrek 2* on Diane's portable DVD player), and left the trailer.

Forty-five minutes later, she had the twins back at the Goldhagen estate. They fell asleep like a pair of kittens, arms and legs thrown around each other. Esme carefully untangled them and carried one, then the other, into the house and upstairs to their respective rooms. Rather than making them change into nightgowns, she just covered them with their quilts and put them to bed. Each was so tired that she didn't even open her eyes.

As Esme was working, her mind was on Junior, as it had been all evening. She was dialing the hospital on her cell before she was even out of Weston's room.

"Yeah?" He answered the phone.

"It's me," she told him, sitting down at the top of the stairs to talk. "How are you?"

"Looking good, *Mama*."

"No complications?" Esme had been warned that this was the doctors' concern.

"De nada," he assured her. "If I don't run a fever, I get sprung in a day or so."

"I'll come home to take care of you," Esme declared.

"You will not, *chica,*" Junior retorted. "You will stay right where you are."

"But, Junior," Esme remonstrated. "Who's going to—"

Esme heard the front door close downstairs.

"I've got to go," she told Junior quickly. "I'll call you later." She hung up.

From downstairs: "Esme, you here?"

Steven. Not Jonathan. Thank God.

"Hey, Esme," he greeted her easily when she came downstairs. He must have come straight from work, since he was carrying a stack of scripts under his arm. "Got the princesses to sleep?"

She nodded and leaned her elbow against the banister. "They were so tired."

He shook his head. "Between you and me, making those girls jump through hoops today was insane."

Esme was silent. She agreed but wasn't about to side with Mr. Goldhagen against his wife.

"Anyway, you were great today, Esme. I'll stay with the girls—you can go."

"I don't mind—"

"Boss's orders," he said with mock severity. "Can't have you working around the clock. Listen, I know you've got to watch the girls at the party tomorrow night, so take some time off during the day."

"If you're sure . . ."

He was. She thanked him and said good night.

Five minutes later, Esme inhaled deeply as she walked the gravel path toward her guesthouse. Orange blossoms. Roses. The scent of money, of all the freedom money could buy.

The scent of Jonathan.

She whirled around to confront him.

Only he wasn't there. Just the memory, in this very spot, of the night they'd first kissed. Her mind was playing tricks on her.

When she reached the guesthouse, she saw that the basketball—the one Jonathan always used—had rolled under a rhododendron. She retrieved it and impulsively turned on the floodlights that lit the driveway and its basketball hoop. She dribbled, shot, and made the basket. Dribbled again, away from the basket, and hit a three-pointer. And another.

Esme Castaneda had a great many skills. She could take a car engine apart and put it back together. Bake bread from scratch without a recipe. Design tattoos. She even knew how to take a bullet out of a wound and stanch the flow of blood. She could speak two languages fluently and get straight As and be a nanny for the children of the most powerful man in Hollywood.

What she couldn't do was fool her heart into thinking that she wasn't out there shooting hoops, hoping that Jonathan would come back.

21

Kiley edged along the crowded front row and slid into the empty seat next to Platinum just as Elton John's "Crocodile Rock" began to blare from the sound system. She took in the T-shaped runway, now bathed in giant pools of animal-patterned spotlights. Upstage from the runway, six twenty-foot-high surrealistic trees, each painted a different animal print, dripped crystals where the leaves should be. The fashion show had a wild-animal theme—that much was obvious.

The music grew louder; a spotlight circled from stage to audience and back again. The lights dimmed, and Kiley felt a little thrill of anticipation. Here she was, in a tent jammed with a thousand celebrities, sitting next to one of the biggest rock stars in the world, courtesy of one of the hottest male models in the world.

The runway parted; a hidden surface rose. On it, Elton John himself, clad in a zebra-patterned faux-fur cape and matching faux-fur-trimmed glasses, was playing a leopard-striped grand piano and singing the music they'd been hearing through the sound system. The crowd roared its approval.

Platinum leaned closer to Kiley. "Can you believe he used to try to pretend he was straight? He grabbed my ass at Mick Jagger's birthday party, like, twenty years ago."

Kiley was too stunned to reply as Elton finished his number; the crowd stood and cheered. "He's so toast," Platinum said through her smile.

Elton blew a kiss, the platform disappeared again, and models began to strut out onto the stage, this time to recorded Remy Zero. Fooled once by Elton John, people craned their necks to see if the band was actually in the tent. This time, though, the music was coming from a CD.

First out was Heidi Klum, in a python-print minidress with a heavy brocade coat thrown over it; a live snake coiled around her shoulders.

It was a FAB conceit to use hip actresses as well as models in the runway shows. Next out was Scarlett Johansson in a cow-print A-line silk dress cut down to her crotch, with hair extensions so long they were wrapped around the dress like embroidery.

Katie Holmes was next in a camouflage-print evening suit with a bare midriff, set off by a sequined camouflage eye mask.

"Who could actually wear these clothes?" Kiley asked Platinum.

"No one," Platinum replied. "It's supposed to be over the top. All those couture bitches get stuff made exactly how they want it anyhow."

The last model was Marym. She wore a snow leopard–print

ball gown whose twenty-foot train was carried by six little boys in white dinner jackets. This one was a real crowd-pleaser. Kiley heard many murmurs of approval; then a wave of applause swept through the tent.

Platinum leaned in again. "She's had more work done than Elton John."

"Marym?" Kiley was taken aback. "How do you know?"

"Please," Platinum snorted.

"But . . . she's only eighteen."

"She was this skinny little slut with a huge honker who finally screwed the right guy she met on some beach, I forget where," Platinum explained. "He bought her the new nose, the cheekbones, and the tits."

"I don't believe it," Kiley declared. For some reason she felt like she should defend Marym, which was ludicrous, considering that she was planning to picket Marym's beach home at sunrise. Plus, there was the niggling worry that Tom was more into Marym than he was into her. Literally.

The music changed to Bruce Springsteen's "Born in the USA," and the lighting changed to pools of red, white, and blue. The trees began to shed their skins—Kiley had no idea how this worked—revealing statues of George Washington, Thomas Jefferson, and Abraham Lincoln. The female models came out again, one by one. This time they wore casual American-themed outfits: Heidi in a worn leather bomber jacket over a red-striped bikini, Scarlett in a blue and white nautical-patterned circle skirt with a safari jacket, Katie in red wide-legged, high-waisted silk pants with diamond-studded suspenders over bare skin (another big crowd-pleaser), and Marym in a glittering red, white, and blue bikini, which, according to the program that Kiley had found on her seat, was made of thousands of diamonds, rubies, and sapphires, and insured for ten million dollars.

Marym looked fantastic. As far as Kiley could tell, all her body parts looked real.

The girls gave way to the guys. Unlike the girls, Kiley recognized none of them but Tom, who was the third one out. He had on an unbuttoned red and blue paisley shirt, revealing a tan, ripped six-pack; his oversized pants slithered tantalizingly low. They'd spiked up his hair and hidden his gorgeous eyes behind black sunglasses. He slouched and posed; Kiley could actually *feel* the women in the audience wanting him.

I'm with him, Kiley thought. *Me, Kiley McCann.*

According to the program, Tom was followed by some European model named Marcus—hadn't Tom mentioned him at Marym's party? He wore a long distressed black leather greatcoat over naked skin, and bleached-out jeans ripped at the knees.

The guys did their clothing change, but stayed with the same theme. Tom posed right where Kiley was sitting. This time he stopped, lifted his sunglasses, and flashed a half smile right at her. She blushed furiously. What that look did to her insides was right out of one of the torrid romance novels her mother read. Maybe that light switch of hers really was in perfect working order.

Tom replaced his glasses and strutted to the other side of the runway. Then Platinum nudged Kiley. "Did you see him check me out just now? I should send him the bra I was wearing when we met with my phone number on it."

Crap. Had Tom been looking at Platinum, and not at her? In the real-world scheme of things, it made a hell of a lot more sense. So what if Platinum was more than twenty years older than Tom? On Planet Platinum, such things were meaningless.

Insecurity flooded Kiley. Maybe this wasn't a date. Maybe Tom had invited her as a friend, a pal, a—damn him—kid sister. The idea that she could compete with Platinum was beyond ridiculous. If that was so, what should she do when the fashion show ended? Tom hadn't said. Was he planning to take her out? Kiley knew there were VIP parties that night. She didn't want to put him in an awkward position, nor did she want to look like a nerdy cheesehead, even if she felt like one.

Okay, so she'd find him and thank him for the tickets, and then act like she was leaving, and if he wanted to stop her, he'd stop her. That could work. She turned to tell Platinum, but her seat was empty. Huh. Well, it wasn't Kiley's problem. For once, Platinum could take care of herself.

The show ended when Ralph Lauren came out onstage with Marym on his arm. All the other models came too, applauding the designer.

The lights went up and people began to move out of their seats. It took nearly ten minutes for Kiley to snake her way out of the tent. A guard directed her to the backstage entrance. But since she didn't have a backstage access pass, she could go no further. She felt like an idiot. If Tom wanted her to come backstage, he would have arranged for the pass, right? Which meant she should just leave before she humiliated herself—

"Kiley!" Tom bounded over to her, buttoning his worn denim shirt. "I saw you out there. I'm so glad you came!"

"Of course I came. You were great."

"It's not exactly brain surgery."

"But it probably pays better," Kiley pointed out.

Tom laughed. "How screwed up is that? Hey, I'm sorry I didn't get you a backstage pass; it just slipped my mind. But it's a zoo in there, anyway. So, you ready?"

Kiley hesitated. "For what?"

Tom bounced backward on the heels of his Nikes. "Tell me I didn't forget to tell you about the thing."

"The *thing*?"

"Heidi and Seal are giving a thing on the beach; supercasual. I'm not into the big FAB stuff. I mean, if you want to go to J.Lo's bash at the Beverly Hills Hotel we could—"

"No, no, the beach sounds great, perfect," Kiley said quickly. Yes! He *did* want to be with her!

"I just have to find Platinum and see if she can drive herself home or if—"

"Where the hell were you?" Platinum demanded, pushing rudely through people when she spotted Kiley. "What, I'm supposed to go hunting for my freaking nanny? What's that about, huh? You want to explain that to me?"

Uh-oh. Yellow alert; Kiley could tell already from Platinum's manic voice. She must have snorted something or other in the ladies' room just now. Damn. Kiley couldn't very well have Platinum drive herself home if she was high on something.

"Sorry," Kiley replied; taking the blame seemed like the lesser of evils. "I'll drive you home now, okay?" She turned to Tom. "Maybe you could follow us in your car?"

Platinum flung herself at Tom, who had no choice but to catch her. "You are so freaking hot, man! I just wanted to roll those pants right down your legs, that's how hot you are. Man, I could eat you with a spoon."

"Thanks. I think." Tom gently extricated himself from Platinum's embrace.

Oh God, how embarrassing. Kiley felt her cheeks flame.

"Sorry," she mumbled to Tom.

Platinum turned and rubbed her butt against Tom. "This place is nuts! Isn't it insane?" She whirled around again. "Hey, let's go somewhere! I want to dance. You want to dance, right? Let's freaking dance, baby!" She lifted her hair onto her head and shimmied up and down like a stripper. "Whoo-hoo!"

Kiley saw Marym slide past the backstage guard, then stop when she saw Platinum rubbing against Tom. She looked amused. "I didn't know you two were acquainted."

"Screw off, coke ho," Platinum spat at Marym. She flipped her middle finger at the model just as a photographer snapped her shot. She whirled toward him. "Hey, shoot this, asshole!" She reached under her flimsy gown and lifted her bra top, flashing her breasts at the photographer, who obliged by taking another picture.

Oh. God.

"We should go, Platinum," Kiley said quietly.

"Hey!" Platinum's face lit up; she didn't bother to pull her bra top down again. "Let's get the kids and have a party! Shit, yeah, that's what we should do!"

Not Yellow. Orange.

"Tom, I'm sorry, but—"

"No, it's okay. I know you work for her, so . . ."

"It's not just that. It's her kids. I have to make sure they're okay."

"You want me to follow you back in case you need any help?" Tom offered.

God, no. She didn't want to involve him in this nightmare. Besides, he was just being nice.

"I got it covered," she assured him.

Marym moved closer to Tom. "We understand, Kiley. We'll miss you at the party."

Yeah, I bet, Kiley thought.

They looked so perfect together. It wouldn't even matter that Kiley was going to picket Marym the next morning, because, let's face it, she couldn't compete with Marym anyway. There was really no point in trying.

Marym hooked an arm through Tom's, as if to prove Kiley's point. Then Platinum moved off into the crowd, and Kiley had to go after her.

Kiley recognized the stretch of the Pacific Coast Highway as she neared Marym's Malibu mansion. It was still so early in the morning that the sun had not risen above the hills; a bank of fog was poised offshore, threatening to drape the coastline in a blanket of gray. But the road was clear, with just a few cars traveling in either direction. Obviously, the time to get from point A to point B in and around Los Angeles was when the rest of the city was sleeping.

As she drove along, she had a lot of time to think about what had happened the night before. She'd found a coked-up Platinum flirting with the FAB parking valets. Once they'd gotten home, Platinum had ordered Kiley to crank one of her CDs to ear-splitting volume, then danced all over the living room with Serenity and Lori. Sid and Bruce came home from someplace and wandered through the living room without stopping; Platinum didn't acknowledge their presence. When Kiley went to see what they were up to, Bruce had slammed the door in her face. There was nothing she could do about it. It wasn't like she could discuss it with their mother.

Serenity finally whined that she was tired; Kiley took her off to bed, leaving Platinum and Lori to retire to Platinum's suite to do God only knew what. Kiley didn't want to leave Serenity alone, so she fell asleep in Serenity's desk chair, her head on the white desk. She'd woken up with a start and checked the luminous hands of the clock on Serenity's dresser—4:30 a.m. The little girl was sleeping peacefully. Kiley figured she had just enough time to shower, change, and hit the road for the demonstration in Malibu.

Damn Platinum anyway. She had to be the most selfish person Kiley had ever met. She might love her children, but she didn't really think about anyone except herself.

Before reaching the final stretch of the PCH by Marym's house, Kiley stopped to take in the view. The stretch of beach was deserted save for a pair of early-morning surfers on their long boards, enjoying the peace and the four-foot swells. Kiley left her shoes on the floorboard and walked barefoot down to the water's edge to gaze at the ocean and the surfers in their black wet suits. One of them acknowledged her presence with a friendly wave; Kiley waved back. Then he caught a perfect wave and rode it toward shore. Just as he kicked out of the wave, two silvery porpoises broke the water to his left, shimmering in the early-morning light, seemingly timing their jumps for the exact moment when the surfer's ride ended. It was so perfect that Kiley laughed in pure delight; this was just the kind of moment she had dreamed about when she'd decided to come to California.

No one, certainly not Marym Marshall, had the right to keep

access to this ocean to herself. Kiley got a funny feeling in her stomach. She couldn't think about Marym without thinking about Tom. Maybe she should have mentioned that she planned to go to this protest . . . but no. That would have felt like asking his permission, or something. She was doing the right thing; she was sure of it.

The demonstration leaders had placed helpful signs along the Pacific Coast Highway—FREE THE BEACH! MARYM MANSION: 1 MILE. As she approached the mansion itself, she saw a few police cars with their lights flashing. Across the road, a long line of parked cars and TV broadcasting trucks snaked back along the east side of the highway. Since there was no place else to park, Kiley pulled her white BMW 550i (actually, Platinum's BMW—Kiley never drove the Lotus unless specifically instructed to do so) behind the last car in the row, and then crossed the highway at a makeshift crossing point run by a California highway patrolman. "Just stay off her private property," the young cop advised Kiley as she started to cross. "And you won't have any trouble."

There were already fifty or sixty people in front of the mansion, walking a ragged picket line. As Kiley joined them, one of the event leaders, a young woman with bright pink hair and multiple facial piercings, carried a bullhorn and led a call-and-response chant.

"What do we want?" she bellowed, in a voice that belied her diminutive stature.

"Free beach!" shouted the demonstrators.

"When do we want it?"

"Now!"

The chanting continued. For a moment, Kiley stood off to

one side, not knowing exactly what to do. It wasn't like she'd ever been part of a protest before. Then a bearded, bearish-looking man in his forties walked over to her, grinning.

"Don't just stand there." He pointed to a pile of ready-made picket signs. "Pick up a sign and join us!"

Kiley did. A moment later, she found an opening in the line of picketers, and was shouting "Free beach! Free beach!" along with the rest of the demonstrators. Part of her felt ridiculous. But part of her felt great. She'd been on the beach on the other side of Marym's house. It was glorious, much nicer than any of the others between Malibu and Santa Monica. The sand was crystalline, the ocean pure and unpolluted. The California legislature had given everyone the right to enjoy that beach. It didn't seem fair for rich people to own houses that blocked the way in for ordinary people like herself. If she hadn't been invited to Marym's party with Tom, she'd never have had the privilege.

She thought of her mother, back in La Crosse. Her mom would love to see that beach sometime—if a panic attack didn't make the trip impossible. Life was so damn unfair. Her mom was such a good person, but she was stuck in La Crosse at a dead-end waitress job, crippled by panic attacks, and married to a guy who was married to a bottle.

Well, that wasn't going to be Kiley's life. She wasn't going to be the kind of person to sit around and be crippled by . . . by *anything*. She hoisted her sign a little higher, glad that she was willing to stand up for the right thing.

"Free beach! Free beach!" Kiley found herself among the loudest of the chanters, feeding off the energy of the crowd. One of the television cameras came in tight on her face, and a blond reporter in a short skirt asked for an interview, but Kiley shook her head emphatically. That was going too far—she didn't want to make a spectacle of herself. Most of all, she didn't want Tom to see her on TV before she had a chance to talk to him.

The girl with the pink hair had no such reservations. She pushed over to the cameraman; a moment later, she was being interviewed by the blond reporter. Suddenly, some of the demonstrators cheered, shouting to one another.

"What's happening?" Kiley asked the guy with the beard.

He smiled. "A light just went on in the upstairs window. That means the bitch is home. She saw us out here, I bet." He cupped his raised hands together. "Free beach! Free beach!" he yelled up at the window.

Kiley's instinct was to hide; what would Marym think if she saw her? *I can't let that matter,* she thought resolutely. *Marym may have beauty and money and even Tom, but I have the ocean.*

Kiley winced. Her mental tape was sounding just a little too Joan of Arc.

Now that the demonstrators knew Marym was home, some of them edged up onto her driveway, which prompted a quick response from the police. They got between the home and the people with the picket signs.

"Why are you protecting her?" the girl with the pink hair screamed at the police. "You should be helping us! Tell her to open the way to the beach!"

Several other demonstrators started to chime in. "Free beach! Free beach! Free beach!"

Kiley could feel the mood change from ebullient and fun to something more ominous. Across the road, more people were parking to join the demonstration, moving closer to the property line.

"We really shouldn't go any closer," Kiley told the pink-haired girl.

The girl stared back at Kiley as if she'd just grown horns. "Whose side are you on?"

"Stay off the property!" a cop warned again.

"What are you gonna do, arrest us?" the bearded guy taunted, getting in the cop's face.

This was not good. Arrested was something Kiley definitely did not want to be. She'd made her point. It was time to leave.

Then she realized something. She'd probably see Marym that very night, at the FAB closing party aboard the *Queen Mary.* She was looking forward to the party, but she wasn't looking forward to seeing Marym.

"This will be so great," Lydia assured Alexis as they stood together on the doorstep of Evelyn Bowers's home—a beautiful Mediterranean-style villa in Brentwood. Evelyn had warned Lydia that she lived on Rockingham, the same street where O. J. Simpson had his home back in the nineties, but she said that these days there were very few tourists; the murders were, in Hollywood terms, ancient history.

The two-story home was white stucco, with expansive windows and blue trim, set far back from the street behind a row of ten-foot hedges. Hedges similarly blocked the view of the neighbors, so the place felt more private than it actually was.

Lydia pressed the buzzer; Evelyn answered so quickly that Lydia suspected the woman had been waiting just inside the front door.

"Welcome, welcome!" she said when she saw that it was Lydia and Alexis. She beamed first at Lydia, and then at her new nanny. "You must be Alexis. It's a pleasure, an absolute pleasure."

She ushered Lydia and Alexis inside. Lydia was pleased with how Alexis had chosen to dress for this meeting with her potential new employer—she was wearing conservative black trousers and a white shirt. Lydia had suggested that Alexis bring a small suitcase with her—to show that she was ready to start work immediately, should Evelyn decide to hire her. Alexis had complied.

Lydia had tried to give Kiley's friend Nina one last shot by calling her in La Crosse while she was drinking her morning coffee in her aunt's kitchen. Just like all the other times, there had been no answer. When Lydia had gotten Nina's voice mail, she didn't leave a message. Instead, she called Alexis and said the job was hers, if she could get through a personal interview that morning with Evelyn Bowers. Then she called Evelyn and set the meeting. It had been as easy as trapping a stunned thorntail iguana after it had tumbled from the jungle canopy in a storm.

"The children are gone," Evelyn explained after she ushered Lydia and Alexis inside. "I thought we'd have more privacy that way. Let me take you on a tour, then we can talk. Sound good?"

"Sounds great," Lydia agreed. She'd told Alexis to let her do all the talking at this stage. Back in Amazonia, a visiting doctor had brought a copy of *Forbes* magazine with him to read. Lydia was desperate for anything new, so she'd begged for him to leave it when he departed for America. It was from a *Forbes* article that she learned that the person in a power position should always do the talking in any meeting.

The house was exquisite. The living area led to an open courtyard that boasted soaring palm trees; there were five bedrooms, six and a half bathrooms, an ultramodern forest green kitchen that opened directly to a sunken family room with the biggest plasma TV Lydia had ever seen, and a sunroom with a massage table and glass ceiling. The backyard featured a lap pool and a paddle tennis court.

"It's awesome," Alexis said, clearly unable to keep herself from commenting.

Evelyn smiled. "Well, I'm so glad you like it, Alexis. Right this way." She led them past the pool and through a sliding glass door that led to what appeared to be a home office.

"Oh, so you work here," Alexis said.

"Publicizing . . . what do you publicize, exactly?" Lydia asked, feeling she should add something.

Evelyn waved airily. "Various . . . groups. Freedom forums. I believe very strongly in personal freedom."

"Oh, me too," Alexis agreed, clearly eager to please.

Lydia peered at a large framed poster on the wall. It was all black, with red letters that read: YOUR LIFE. YOUR CHOICE. IT'S THE AMERICAN WAY. Lydia scrutinized lettering at the bottom of the poster so small as to be barely legible: The American Tobacco Association.

Cigarettes? Evelyn Bowers publicized *cigarettes*?

Alexis checked out the fine print on the poster too, then turned a questioning face to Evelyn.

"Hey, I used to do publicity for Greenpeace," Evelyn said defensively. "But when my husband left me for that ditzy bitch in Burbank—see what that does for your bank account."

"Whatever floats your canoe, Evelyn," Lydia said easily. "Right, Alexis?"

"Uh, smoking really messes up people's health," Alexis began, "but all you're doing is telling people that they have the right to *choose* to mess up their health, right?"

Evelyn beamed. "We're going to get along famously, I can tell already." She turned to Lydia. "I'd like to talk privately with Alexis for a while, if I might."

Lydia nodded. "I'll go sit by the pool. Let me know when you're done." She retraced her steps to the pool, slipped off her aunt's Enzo Angiolini leather wedge sandals with rhinestones, and stretched out on a chaise. Fifteen minutes later, a beaming Evelyn strolled outside, arm in arm with Alexis.

"She's just charming," Evelyn gushed, patting Alexis's hand. "She's going to be perfect for my children. When can she start?"

Lydia gave Alexis a pointed look.

"I actually have a small suitcase in my car," Alexis responded. "I can start immediately, if necessary."

"Aren't you a gem!" Evelyn cried. "This is going to be the best job you ever had."

Alexis smiled.

"So you both live happily ever after, and I'm just tickled over it," Lydia intoned. Since Alexis had driven over, she figured she could call X for a ride home. "I'll just leave you with Alexis for her orientation. All we have left to do is for me to collect—"

Evelyn smoothly took a small envelope out of her pocket, stepped over to Lydia, and handed it to her. "I think you'll find everything you need in there. I made the check out to Lydia Chandler."

"Fine," Lydia said smoothly, pocketing the envelope. Of course, she didn't exactly have a bank account in which she could deposit the check, or even an easy way to cash it. She didn't even know how to open a bank account, and she still had to contact her second cousin who was a lawyer in Dallas about drawing up some business documents, release forms, and the like.

Well, Aunt Kat might help her with all this. She'd have to be impressed that Lydia had started her own successful business. Plus, Lydia was certain that once she waved that big ol' check in front of Kiley and Esme, they'd be in too.

"But it's nine-thirty." Martina bit her lip anxiously and rechecked her Hello Kitty watch. "I'm supposed to be home for my aerobics lesson."

"I won't tell if you won't." The taxicab pulled into a strip mall at the intersection of San Vicente Boulevard and La Cienega. Lydia paid the fare and gave the driver a two-dollar tip.

"Why are we here? Where are we? What are we doing?" Martina demanded as they exited the cab.

"You aren't exactly a happy camper these days, right, sweet pea?"

Martina shrugged behind her veil of hair.

"You *hate* aerobics, don't you?"

Martina nodded, eyes downcast. "That woman who comes to our house to teach me, she's so mean. She patted my stomach and said, 'We need to get rid of this.' "

Lydia was incensed on her sensitive cousin's behalf. How

dare Betsy Boomer, of Bodies by Betsy fame, say such a thing? Did she have no idea how damaging a remark like that could be? Lydia would have reported it to Anya, but Anya and the trainer were friends. Besides, Anya would not only share the trainer's opinion, she'd applaud it.

"I hate her too," Lydia said, smiling. "Okay. You remember I told you I was going to find something more fun for you to do, right?"

Martina nodded cautiously.

"Do you trust me?"

Martina nodded again.

"Okay, then, come with me." Lydia wrapped a protective arm around Martina's shoulders and led her down a few doors to one of the strip mall's storefronts, thinking how lucky she was that Jimmy had a tennis lesson on the home court and Anya was working out this morning with her protégée, Oksana, at the Beverly Hills Hotel tennis center. Three whole hours with Martina to do what she wanted. That should be a good start.

The storefront windows were obscured by billowy jewel-toned curtains. The door was painted black save for a small sign: FATIMA'S.

The night before, Lydia had been giving herself a facial with MTV on in the background. A show called *Made* caught her eye. The idea of the show was that kids could get the coaches, teachers, whatever they needed to reinvent themselves. In the first segment, a girl who was dreadful at sports wanted to become a cheerleader. While being a cheerleader struck Lydia as a particularly insipid waste of time, she was impressed by the girl's transformation. In the second segment, a klutzy girl wanted to be good enough to audition for her school's dance team. *Made* brought in a dance coach named Fatima who had her own belly dance studio in West Hollywood. When Lydia saw Fatima, very round and nurturing, she'd turned the sound up and watched, transfixed. Bugs worked for Jimmy. Why not belly dance for Martina?

She'd found the information on Fatima's studio, which was near the Beverly Center, and called, explaining the particular challenges her fourth-grade niece was facing. Fatima had been very encouraging. And now . . . here they were. Lydia hadn't said a word about it beforehand, not wanting to give Martina time to think it over and then scuttle away to her room.

Martina stopped dead in her tracks. "Fatima?"

Lydia nodded. "You'll see."

"No! I can read. It's *Fat*-something."

Poor baby. She had the self-esteem of a maggot.

"It's a woman's name, sweetie," Lydia assured her. "I swear."

"It's not a fat camp?"

"Promise."

Martina reluctantly allowed Lydia to lead her inside. The room was plain, with a wooden plank floor, a ballet barre, and a wall of mirrors. Middle Eastern music played through the sound system and the air smelled of pungent incense. Fatima herself, clad in purple harem pants and an ornately jeweled purple bra, was dancing in the center. She looked to be in her midforties, and far from beautiful in the Hollywood sense. Her dark hair fell in waves nearly to her waist. She wore black eyeliner drawn upward at the outer edge, and matte red lipstick. Her nose was noble, her expression serene. She had bells on her fingers that rang as her hands dipped and swirled around her body. A ring of women and teen girls seated on floor cushions—maybe a dozen—clapped as Fatima danced.

All the color drained from Martina's face. She turned to bolt.

"You don't have to do anything, I swear," Lydia whispered. "I want you to look at the girls in this class. Just look. That's all."

Martina allowed Lydia to pivot her back toward the group. Lydia saw it register with Martina that she was not the fattest person in the room. Some of the girls were thinner, but a few were much larger. One woman had to weigh at least three hundred pounds.

When the music ended, the group applauded Fatima heartily. She took a graceful bow, then hurried over to Martina and Lydia. "You are Lydia?"

Lydia nodded. "And this is Martina."

Fatima took Martina's hand. "Welcome."

Martina's cheeks went crimson as the studio owner placed a forefinger gently under her chin to lift it. "Such a beauty you are."

Martina shook her head.

"Oh yes, I never lie," Fatima insisted. With one arm around Martina's shoulders, she turned to the group. "Everyone, this is Martina. She is ten years old."

They all called out variations on welcome.

"You have beautiful skin," said a blond-haired girl with braces.

"Your face is so sweet," said a woman with cornrows in her hair.

"You will grow into your beauty like a flower," the very overweight woman decreed.

"I can already see that you'll be graceful," offered an Indian girl with a red dot between her eyebrows.

Martina looked bewildered.

"We greet our guests by saying positive things about them," Fatima explained.

"That's nice," Martina whispered, almost smiling.

Good God. This actually might work.

"Please, come join us," Fatima said, urging Martina forward. "You don't have to dance. No one has to do anything here unless they wish to. There are no judgments. When you choose to join in, you just pick a skirt that is beautiful to you." She pointed to a costume rack that held dozens of brightly colored, flimsy skirts that tied at the waist. Lydia noticed how all the women and girls wore similar skirts over their jeans.

Martina allowed Fatima to usher her over to the group, where a pretty, extremely curvaceous black girl urged Martina to sit next to her. "My name is Tonya," the girl told Martina, loud enough for Lydia to hear. "That's my mom." She pointed to the three-hundred-pound white woman.

"I have two moms," Martina replied solemnly.

Fatima got the group's attention and explained a basic belly dance move, swiveling the hips as if playing with one of the round hoops that the Amas loved to swirl on themselves. When the group got up to try the move, Martina shyly asked Lydia if she could help her pick a skirt from the rack of belly dance costumes. They agreed on a pale pink one, which Lydia tied around Martina's waist. Five minutes later, Martina was pivoting her hips and laughing hysterically with her new friend, Tonya.

The forty-five minutes of the class sped by. When Fatima announced the end of the class, Martina groaned along with everyone else. Lydia sidled over to Martina to help her out of her skirt. "Fun?"

Martina nodded happily. "Everyone here is really nice, don't you think?"

Tonya scurried over. "Martina, do you think you can come to my birthday party next week? It's at my house in Westwood."

Martina's face lit up. She turned to Lydia. "Can I?"

"Of course, sweet pea," Lydia assured her.

After Lydia scribbled down the information, she and Martina departed, with Martina yammering nonstop about her new friend Tonya and what she would get Tonya for her birthday. Lydia's original plan had been to call a cab immediately and return to Kat and Anya's house, but the girl was in such a good mood that Lydia suggested they stop at Jerry's Deli, across from the Beverly Center, for a snack. She didn't have to ask twice.

It was a ten-minute walk to the famous deli, and Lydia realized that between the walk and the class, this was probably more exercise than her niece had done in a year. The hostess seated them on the patio parallel to Beverly Boulevard. Lydia called for a cab to pick them up in thirty minutes, then people-watched as they waited for a waitress to take their orders. Meanwhile, Martina buried herself in the enormous Jerry's menu.

"Do they have soy shakes without sugar?" Martina asked.

Lydia made a face. "That's not a snack. A snack is something that actually tastes good." She pointed to the long line of luscious baked goods and ice cream confections on the menu. "Pick something from there."

The waitress appeared—an older woman with a big smile and a gruff manner. Lydia ordered an extrathick chocolate milk shake. Martina said she wanted to order one too, with extra whipped cream and nuts. But her lactose intolerance . . .

"I've given you lots of stuff with milk in it, sweetie," Lydia confided. "You never got sick once."

"And the calories . . ."

The waitress made a face. "*Scoff* at calories. Ha-ha-ha!"

Martina laughed as the waitress went back inside the restaurant. "I'm so glad you came to live with us, Lydia," she said softly.

"Me too," Lydia agreed. She felt great. Helping her little cousin to feel better about herself was *fun,* she decided. Maybe she had some of her parents' do-gooder genes after all.

"This is the best day of my life!" Martina announced, just as a silver Porsche skidded to a stop at the curbside, right by where she and Lydia were sitting. A familiar athletic female form, dressed in gym shorts, a T-shirt, and a Russia Davis Cup team jacket, came pounding out of the driver's side. Anya.

"Is going to be *worst* day of your life!" Anya thundered. "What is going on?"

Lydia saw Martina's face turn green, which was her signal to turn on the charm. "Anya!" she said brightly. "Imagine running into you here."

"Do not—do not make to ignore question," Anya sputtered, her Russian accent as thick as Lydia had ever heard it. "What is going on?"

"We're just . . . having a healthy snack," Lydia chirped.

Anya pointed at her daughter. "You are supposed to be at aerobics lesson."

"We . . . decided to go for a power walk instead," Lydia improvised. "Since it's such a beautiful day."

"To West Hollywood from Beverly Hills? Where is Jimmy?"

"Tennis lesson," Lydia said meekly.

"You left child alone?" Anya shrieked.

"He's hardly alone," Lydia pointed out. "I mean, Alfre is there, and the maids, and, um . . . the tennis coach. And he's home. Where he lives. Not in some public park."

"I'm sorry, Momma Anya," Martina whimpered.

Anya pointed at her daughter. "You are in very big hot water."

There were tears in Martina's eyes. Lydia felt terrible. "Please don't blame her," Lydia pleaded. "This is my fault, not hers. I won't deviate from your schedule anymore. I promise."

"Your promises are not worth toilet paper!" Anya thundered. "You are big liar."

Lydia tapped a finger against her lips. "Now, see, I think that's a little harsh—"

"Is not harsh enough. Maybe you think I am stupid!" Anya reached into her bag and plucked out a yellow legal pad. "You are not only big liar, you are big thief. I keep running list since you come."

She thrust the pad at Lydia, who had no choice but to take it.

ITEMS MISSING SINCE LYDIA COME

1. *Jimmy Choo stiletto sandals, baby blue python*
2. *Frost French Jeans, distressed denim*
3. *Marc Jacobs pumps, black*
4. *Vintage Gucci minishift, psychedelic print*

5. *Hourisan Manolo Blahnik sandals, silver gray*
6. *Delfina bikini, burnt orange*
7. *Trina Turk beaded raffia bag, bamboo handles*
8. *Langercroft Irish linen bathing suit cover-up, white*
9. *Emanuel Ungaro silk tunic, gold*
10. *Marc Jacobs cropped cotton jacket, beige*
11. *Hot Kiss shorts with unfinished hems, white*

Lydia's first reaction was relief. Anya had missed at least half the clothing items she'd borrowed, including the pale blue Chloé sequined T-shirt with the strawberry juice stain from her picnic with Billy. She'd meant to send it to the dry cleaner's, but now remembered that it was still wadded up in the bottom of her closet.

Her second reaction was surprise. Nothing about *Secrets of the Kama Sutra,* which meant two things—that the book definitely belonged to Kat, and that Anya didn't know anything about it. All this left the question, of course, of why Kat would have a book secreted away that revealed the ins and outs of glorious—and strictly heterosexual—sex.

Her third reaction was indignation. Who kept a secret running list like this? She'd replaced most of the items right back where she'd found them, in her aunt's closet. Maybe not in the exact spot, but she *was* family, after all.

"It's called borrowing." Lydia defended herself, head held

high as she handed the pad of paper back to Anya. "I returned everything."

Anya looked smug. "You are liar."

"Well, *almost* everything," Lydia amended. "What am I supposed to do, run around Beverly Hills in a loincloth?"

"Your aunt returns from New York day after tomorrow; she will stay home for few days, we will deal with you then."

Deal with? As in: send back to Amazonia? No. Her aunt Kat wouldn't do that to her on her partner's say-so. Would she?

Just then, the waitress returned. "Two extrathick chocolate shakes with extra whipped cream and nuts," she announced, setting them down and taking off again.

Lydia thought Anya was going to burst a blood vessel when she saw the thick, luscious milk shakes.

"They're both for me," Lydia explained blithely. "One for now, one for later. Martina's only drinking water. I swear it."

Anya's only response was a glare that could reignite the Cold War. "Come," she finally told her daughter. "We go home. Lydia, you squeeze in car or not. I not care."

For once, Lydia had no quick answer. She left the milk shakes on the table, tossed down a few dollars, and meekly followed Martina to the Porsche.

24

"Thanks for the ride, X," Kiley said. The chauffeur had driven Kiley, Esme, and Lydia to Rodeo Drive in the Beemer. He'd just returned from driving Anya and the kids to a Nike company picnic in Studio City; Anya had an endorsement deal with them. It had seemed to Lydia that Anya's hostility toward her oozed from her pores all the way home from Jerry's.

Lydia considered calling Aunt Kat; she had the cell number. But first she had to figure out a way to play the situation that would work to her own advantage, and she didn't quite have that down yet. Most of all Lydia wished she could pick up the phone and talk to her mother. Weirdly enough, she actually *liked* her mother and respected her opinion. But there was no phone service in the little village where her parents lived, only a ham radio that ran off a generator.

Lydia's eyes slid to Kiley and Esme, who both looked like little kids about to unwrap Christmas presents. Kiley had called

Esme that morning to see if she'd come on the shopping outing, and surprisingly, considering her mood lately, Esme had said yes. Well, Lydia was not about to rain on Esme and Kiley's parade. She squared her shoulders. She would figure it all out and everything would turn out fine, no doubt.

X stopped the Beemer at the corner of Rodeo Drive and Wilshire Boulevard and the girls got out. Lydia came around to the driver's window. "You rock." She leaned in to kiss his cheek.

"How could you not love me?" X asked rhetorically. "I introduced you to Billy Martin."

"Exactly," Lydia agreed. "Now I'm about to find the hottest clothes on Rodeo Drive for him to remove, compliments of Platinum's Platinum card. What're you going to do?"

X shrugged. "Drive over to Westwood and stare at college boys, then go pick up your aunt and the kids in Studio City. *Ciao.*"

The Beemer moved off into traffic, and Lydia gestured with a flourish toward the long row of boutiques as she took Platinum's credit card out of her pocket, all her worries instantly on hold. "Behold, the most expensive stores in the world. Behold, Kiley's boss's American Express card in my hand." She looked reverently toward the blue skies over Beverly Hills. "Lord, you can take me now."

Kiley swiveled, taking in the splendor. She seemed overwhelmed. "We could get a lot more for our six thousand dollars if we shopped somewhere a little cheaper."

Lydia wagged a finger at her before she edged out of the way of a group of Japanese tourists led by a guide. "Kiley, you have the mentality of a girl destined to be middle-class her whole life. That instinct is to be squashed, understand?"

"I agree," Esme chimed in. "Today I'm throwing caution to the wind. I've been thinking much too much about . . . everything. I just want to have fun. With someone else's money."

"Now, there's the spirit!" Lydia cheered. "Besides, like I already told you in the car, that girl Alexis is Evelyn Bowers's new nanny. Which means if I don't get thrown out of the house, once I get my aunt to cash Evelyn's check, we'll be in the chips, ladies."

"Thrown out of the house?" Kiley echoed.

"Nothing, forget it," Lydia insisted. "Just a little run-in this morning with the merry matron from Moscow; nothing I can't handle." She flashed a brilliant smile. "Now, shall we?"

They started north on Rodeo Drive, past a brick staircase laden with Japanese tourists, bubbling fountains, a latte cart, and what Kiley suspected was an out-of-work actor dressed in garish red nineteenth-century livery garb, who acted as the Rodeo Drive goodwill ambassador. Tourists clamored to have their photo taken with him, preferably in front of Tiffany's.

The boutiques were to their right. Shining glass storefronts displayed the most minimal and expensive clothing: One suit in the Armani window. Two dresses in the Gucci window. A single camisole in the Dior window. Lydia bypassed them all but came to a quick stop at the entrance to Chanel. Ground zero, site of her humiliation at the hands of the snotty saleswoman. When Lydia had shopped there with X and tried to charge her purchases to the credit card the moms had given her, the card was declined. That was when Lydia learned she had a one-hundred-dollar limit. The smug face of the French saleswoman had lived on in Lydia's mind. It was time for some payback.

She quickly explained her previous Chanel shopping experience to Esme and Kiley. Revenge was going to be sweet.

They entered the shop. And there she was, the same black-clad skinny young saleswoman. Her glossy chestnut hair was blunt cut to her chin; her cosmetic-free skin shone with patrician perfection. She flicked her eyes over them; clearly, she didn't remember Lydia. Excellent.

The saleswoman pressed her fingers together and gave them an almost imperceptible nod. "May I help you, *mesdemoiselles*?" she asked in her posh French accent.

"Hey! How y'all doin'?" Lydia asked in a booming, exaggerated Texas drawl.

The saleswoman winced. "Zere is no need to shout, *mademoiselle*."

Lydia smacked the saleswoman in the bicep. "Well, butter my buns and call me a biscuit, you're acting like you don't remember me! I was here just a ways back with my friend? Tried on a whole passel of stuff! And then my danged credit card didn't work. You had your nose all stuck up like the cat done dragged in a skunk."

Lydia turned to wink at Esme and Kiley, who had to stifle their laughter.

The saleswoman sucked in her cheeks and tried to regroup. "I may recall zis."

"Sweet!" Lydia exclaimed. Then her brow furrowed. "Now, let me just ask you a little ol' question, sweet pea. When we try on clothes, do y'all have to put 'em all back afterwards? Because that must be plum hard work."

"It is my job, *mademoiselle*."

Lydia grinned and punched her arm again. "Yeehaw! Because

we're fixin' to try on pretty much everything in the store." She opened her arms expansively to Kiley and Esme. "Ladies, go to town."

The saleswoman was smart enough to stay out of their way as they each gathered more clothes than they could comfortably carry and brought them into the huge dressing room, which was lined with 270-degree sets of mirrors. Once they were inside and the door safely closed behind them, Esme and Kiley were hysterical over Lydia's performance.

"You could be an actress, seriously," Kiley said.

Esme pulled her T-shirt over her head. "That was some show."

Lydia bowed with a flourish. "We can't afford a lot of this stuff, but we're trying it all on anyway."

Esme laughed. "I like the way you think. I'd say our budget here should be, say, a thousand dollars apiece. That'll leave another thousand apiece for shoes, jewelry . . ." Her voice trailed off, and a cloud of shame crossed her face. She stopped midsentence. "I can't believe I just said that. I shouldn't buy a thing. I should take my share of this money and give it to my mother."

"No, you should not," Lydia decreed, thrusting a pleated python camisole at Esme. "I'm as generous as the next girl—"

"No you're not," Kiley put in. "You were born rich."

"True," Lydia acknowledged. "But I also know what it's like to use an outhouse on a daily basis. Ha! Topped ya there, didn't I?"

"No arguing today," Esme said. "I mean it."

"Fine," Lydia agreed. "And once I get the moms to cash the check from Evelyn Bowers, you can both give your share to *your* moms, if that's what you want to do. Proving"—she shot Kiley a significant look—"that I know how to be generous . . . with someone else's money."

Lydia pulled on a lilac silk camisole with embroidered straps as Kiley stepped out of her jeans. Lydia took in the sight of Kiley's white cotton underwear and pointed at her. "When bad underwear happens to good people."

"Leave her alone," Esme chided as she wriggled into a white linen pencil skirt.

Lydia nodded thoughtfully. "You have a point. I used to worry about fire ants crawling into my noonie cuz I didn't wear underwear at all. Who am I to talk?"

Esme laughed. "Your *noonie*?" She pointed at Lydia's lacy pink thong. "And where did you get that little number? Borrow it from your aunt?"

"Nope. She gets free stuff sent to the house all the time. You know, companies hopin' she'll wear their clothes. You know Trash lingerie on La Cienega? This was in a box from there that never got opened. The note that came with it was dated two years ago. I thought it was a shame to let it go to waste."

Kiley took the red, white, and green floral-print silk halter dress with a fitted skirt from its padded hanger and slipped it over her head. The dress was pretty, but the underwear definitely didn't work.

"You need lingerie," Lydia decreed.

Kiley reached to the side to zip her dress. "I don't really want to spend my share of this windfall on underwear. Waste of money."

"Says the girl hoping and planning to undress for the hottest model on the planet," Lydia said. She scrutinized Kiley and shook her head. "I changed my mind. That doesn't work; you look lumpy. And I don't mean your underwear."

"Really?" Kiley checked out her reflection in the three-way mirror. "You're right. Not that it matters. My lumpy ass and I are not going to be getting naked with Tom anytime soon. Maybe ever."

She filled them in on last night's horror with Platinum, and how close Tom and Marym had been—literally and figuratively—when she'd gone off in search of her drugged-out employer.

"The Tom-Marym thing is all the more reason we need to get you into some sexy undies," Lydia declared. "There's an Ama saying: fight fire with fire, not with bananas."

Kiley laughed and started to hang up the sundress.

"Let Miss France in the World-Class Bitch Pageant do it," Lydia advised. She reached for a pale green eyelet-lace dress with spaghetti straps and a full skirt and tossed it to Kiley. "Try this one. If Tom doesn't want to take those straps down with his teeth, I'd be wondering about his sexual preferences if I were you."

"Do we really have to talk about boys?" Esme asked. "Don't you ever just get tired of them?"

"No," Lydia replied. She checked out Esme's rear view in the skintight pencil skirt. "If I had an ass like yours, I'd serve dinner off it."

Esme shot Lydia a jaundiced look and unzipped the skirt.

Lydia shook her head. "There *is* something going on with you. A guy thing?"

"Drop it," Esme said. "Everything is okay."

Lydia put her hands on her hips. "Everything *isn't* okay. Come on, we're supposed to be friends, you have to—"

"Fine!" Esme spat. "But only to shut you up. Junior got shot. Are you satisfied?"

Kiley was shocked. "When? How?"

"Why didn't you tell us?" Lydia added. "Is he in the hospital?"

Esme pulled off the skirt and waved away the details. "Yes he's in the hospital, it was an accident, he's okay. No big deal. And I don't really want to talk about it. Can we finish shopping now?" She reached for a black cocktail dress with a fitted corset top.

"I can get X to take us to the hospital, if you want," Lydia offered.

Esme fingered the material of the dress and shook her head. "He should hate me."

Kiley touched Esme's arm. "Why would you say something like that?"

Esme raised her face, her eyes flinty. "Because I'm a lying bitch, that's why."

Lydia hung a silk shirt on a hook. "You can't go talkin' about our friend Esme that way."

"It's true." Esme stepped into the black dress. "Never mind. I don't want to talk about it."

"But—" Lydia began.

"But nothing. I'm sorry I even brought it up."

For a long moment the dressing room was quiet. Lydia didn't understand Esme. It was clear that she didn't trust them; not enough to share what was going on with her, anyway. Was it because she came from a poor neighborhood, or because she was Latina? Or both? For Lydia, who easily embraced everyone, it was hard to fathom Esme's attitude. She hoped Esme would explain when she trusted them more, and she hoped that would be soon.

Twenty minutes later they'd decided on their purchases: the black corset-topped cocktail dress for Esme, a white strapless tulle for Lydia, and the pale green eyelet-lace sundress for Kiley, who said she liked the fact that her outfit wasn't as dressy, because she could wear it for other occasions.

They made their purchases—Lydia was smug when Platinum's credit card went through—and happily left heaps of clothing in the dressing room for the snotty clerk to rehang.

Next stop, per Lydia's decree: a taxi to the corner of Melrose and Crescent Heights Boulevard, to a huge, vine-covered store called Fred Segal.

"It's actually a whole bunch of different boutiques all mixed together," Lydia explained as they stepped through the front door. "You've got your Fred Segal Couture, your Fred Segal Feeling, Fred Segal Fun, Fred Segal Sparkle, and so on. Nicole Kidman bought her daughter her first pair of high heels here, and when Mary-Kate and Ashley are in town, it's their favorite place to shop."

"Which magazine did you get that from?" Esme teased.

"Not a magazine. TV. *Entertainment Tonight*," Lydia said. "They did a whole show from here last week. So, Kiley needs lingerie, we all need shoes, jewelry, what else?"

"A spare million," Kiley said, fingering a price tag on a simple sheer embroidered shirt. "This costs eight hundred and forty-seven dollars!"

Lydia looked at it too. "Well, yeah. But it's Oscar de la Renta. Come on, shoes are this way."

It took them an hour to try on dozens of shoes. Kiley found out that more expensive did not necessarily mean more comfortable. Esme bought red Constança Basto sling-backs with a three-inch heel; Kiley found some silk and beaded Michael Kors sandals that barely had a heel at all—there was only so far she was willing to go to put fashion over comfort.

Lydia, of course, went all out. She explained that Stuart Weitzman had designed a shoe he called the Cinderella slipper for Alison Krauss to wear to the Academy Awards, when she was nominated for writing the theme song for *Cold Mountain*. The slippers were four-and-a-half-inch stiletto sandals studded with 565 platinum-set Kwait diamonds. That shoe went for two million dollars. Lydia settled for the Weitzman "in the style of" version, which was festooned with rhinestones and cost high three figures instead of low six.

After that, they hit the jewelry counter. By the time they finished purchasing their "cheap chic" earrings and necklaces, as Lydia called them (meaning, she explained, they could not yet afford real gems), they taxied back to Awilda Salon in Beverly Hills for blowouts and manicures. Kiley's dress had been considerably less expensive than the other girls'; both her lingerie and Esme's shoes had been on sale. That was why they still had enough money left for hair and nails, after which they would be completely busted. They didn't have enough money to leave a decent tip; Kiley hated that part. But Lydia assured her that as soon as their nanny business took off, they'd come back and tip double.

Kiley's stylist there, Amiko, was so diminutive that even in heels she could barely reach the top of Kiley's head. But she turned out to be as talented as she was tiny; Kiley shook her head back and forth like a shampoo ad, admiring the way the light bounced from the casual waves Amiko had created. Just as Amiko was hitting Kiley's hair with the glossing spray, Kiley's cell phone rang.

Her first thought was: *Platinum.* Her second thought was: *Orange Zone.*

"Hello?"

"Kiley, it's Nina!"

"Nina!" she shrieked, more loudly than she'd intended, because she was so surprised and happy to finally hear from her best friend. At the next station, Esme's hair was being flat-ironed by Dominic. Esme turned with an inquisitive look when she heard Nina's name. Lydia's hair had gotten done first; she was at the nearby manicure station drying her nails.

"Now she calls?" Lydia queried.

"What happened to you?" Kiley asked into the phone. "Lydia called, I called—"

"I know, I know, I'm so sorry," Nina babbled. "My parents took me to my aunt and uncle's farm in Lake Mills, Iowa, out in the middle of flipping nowhere, up the road from the Laugens' place. You remember we went on a hayride there one year?"

"Yeah, we were, like, ten," Kiley recalled. "Your aunt made us help her can peaches for hours."

"Same place," Nina said. "My uncle had surgery, my aunt

needed help, so I was, like, stuck there for days—sheer torture. Anyway, they don't have cell service, so I was flipping stranded, and a storm knocked out their power and— Look, never mind, it sucked, but I'm back in La Crosse."

"Glad to hear it," Kiley said. "Listen, about the nanny job—"

"I'm so taking it!" Nina interrupted. "My parents are driving me insane. Plus if I have to spend one more night working at Pizza-Neatsa I'm going to spew mozzarella. I told my mother I wouldn't have sex until I'm out of college if she lets me come to L.A. for the summer to hang with you. So, anyway, I called you first but now I'll call your friend Lydia. I'm so psyched!"

Kiley glanced over at Lydia, who was listening intently to Kiley's half of the conversation. She didn't even need to get into the fact that the gig would not be just for the summer, and that Nina wouldn't exactly be "hanging" with Kiley. "Uh, there might be a problem, Nina."

"No, there can't be a problem. Whatever it is, I'll fix it!"

"Well, Lydia didn't hear from you. So she offered the job to someone else, and this other girl took it. In fact, she already started work. Hold on, Lydia's right here. She can explain."

Lydia gestured for the phone and Kiley tossed it her. Careful not to smudge her freshly painted nails, Lydia confirmed that there was no longer a job opening. However, Lydia had another client who might be interested in a nanny. Was Nina interested? By the way Lydia was nodding, Kiley could tell that the answer was yes.

"So there's hope, right?" Nina asked when Kiley took the cell back from Lydia.

"Sounds like it," Kiley agreed. "Don't go to Iowa again."

"Don't rub it in," Nina groaned. "How's that hot model guy you bagged?"

"Still hot, and I didn't bag him."

"Yet. When you do, call me and give me details. I have no life."

Kiley laughed. "It probably won't happen at all, but if it ever does, you'll be the first to know." They said their goodbyes and hung up.

"This could work out," Esme said, rising from her salon chair. "Nina could work for Evelyn's friend."

"Exactly," Lydia said. "Ladies, we are going to be rolling in clover. This is only the beginning of our empire!"

Maybe it really *would* work out, Kiley thought. She hadn't been very enthusiastic about the nanny placement service because she felt utterly unqualified to be part of one. But on the other hand, things were going so well, so fast—maybe she'd actually be able to save up money toward her Scripps tuition.

As Lydia settled their bill, Kiley checked out her reflection in the mirror behind the cashier's desk. She loved her hair. She loved her new dress. She was going to an impossibly hip party that night and she was going to look damn hot.

Maybe she could be comp for Marym Marshall after all.

There was an air-conditioning vent on the floor of Lydia's guesthouse. After she put on her dress for the party, she stood directly on top of it. The chiffon skirt of the strapless white dress whooshed around her legs, like Marilyn Monroe's in a famous photo the moms had hung in their dressing room. They also had framed photos of Greta Garbo, Vivien Leigh, and Angelina Jolie (the one of Angelina was signed—at least they shared good taste in women).

Lydia stepped into the incredible Stuart Weitzman rhinestone and Lucite heels—they made her legs look a mile long. She'd already used Kat's Stila and MAC cosmetics—bronzer, eyeliner, mascara, and gold-peach lip gloss. Her choppy white-blond hair had been coiffed into a sexy, edgy style, half up and half down, exposing her new Luis Marais gold hoop earrings.

"I'd definitely do me," she opined, giddy with excitement

and anticipation. Tonight, finally, she'd know what all the hooting and hollering was about. The boy who would introduce her to pleasure was a boy she really, truly liked. That hadn't been part of her criteria for this experience, true, but it was a lovely bonus.

Not only that, but now that the nanny placement service was taking off, she'd have money to buy the hottest designer everything. Today she'd purchased her first Chanel. Tomorrow would be . . . let's see . . . what did she covet the most? A Leigh Bantivoglio camisole set—she'd read that Julia Roberts owned three. Or maybe she'd rather have a Goa embellished lace miniskirt like the one Jada Pinkett Smith had worn to the Emmys.

She was spritzing herself with her aunt's Jo Malone perfume when the phone rang. She dove across the bed to answer.

"Hello?"

"Lydia, Evelyn Bowers."

"Hey, Evelyn." Lydia sat on the edge of the bed, admiring the way her new heels elongated her calves. "How's life?"

"This is not a social call, you twit."

Uh-oh. Lydia kept her voice cheerful. "Gee, I was just on my way out, Evelyn, maybe we could have a nice little chitchat tomorrow?"

"Do you have any idea what Alexis did today?" Evelyn demanded. "She held a goddamn séance with my son!"

Double uh-oh. "That sounds fun," Lydia said in her perkiest voice.

"Fun?" Evelyn echoed. "She asked Moon who he wanted to speak with who was no longer with him. He said his father, so

she summoned him up from the great beyond and let Moon talk to him. The only 'beyond' that Moon's father is in is Santa Barbara!"

"Right," Lydia agreed meekly. "He's not dead."

"Moon didn't understand that Alexis—who calls herself a spiritualist, by the way—meant 'dead.' Now he's hysterical because he thinks his father died and no one told him. I had to bring him to his therapist to calm him down."

Crap, crap, crap. "I'm sure we can rectify this, Evelyn—"

"No, Lydia, we can't." Evelyn advanced on her. "Alexis has traumatized my child. She keeps a skull in her room, for God's sake!"

"A fake skull, I'm sure—"

"Do you think I care?"

Lydia fought her rising panic. "I'll call Alexis right away, Evelyn. She'll need to keep her hobbies private and not bring them to—"

"Hobbies?" Evelyn echoed. "You *must* be joking." For a moment, the phone in Lydia's hand was silent. When Evelyn spoke again, it was in low, measured tones. "Let me make myself perfectly clear, Lydia. Alexis has been fired. And I already stopped payment on the check I gave you."

"B-but you can't do that," Lydia sputtered. "We have a contract."

"Don't screw with me, little girl," Evelyn said. "You are toast, over, finished, and much deader than my son-of-a-bitch ex-husband. Don't ever try to place one of your so-called nannies with another mother within a hundred-mile radius, or you'll never eat lunch in this town again." She slammed the phone down in Lydia's ear.

Lydia hung up. Damn. Just when things were looking up. She really didn't see why Evelyn was so upset. Maybe talking to the dead and whatnot was unusual in Beverly Hills, though from what she'd read over the years, she'd say that California was pretty out there when it came to spiritualism. Lydia knew that some other cultures would find a woman who decided to carve open her chest to insert a couple of silicon beach balls the epitome of true insanity.

It all depended on your point of view.

The line of limos at the Long Beach marina waiting to drop their passengers at the *Queen Mary* snaked back practically to the freeway. Esme sat in traffic for a while, but finally she'd become impatient enough to climb out of the Mercedes and walk the twins the final quarter mile to the red-carpeted gangway between the filled parking lot and the venerable old ocean liner.

It was already an hour into the FAB closing party. Diane wanted to make sure the girls got in a long nap before the festivities. Esme thought it was ridiculous to bring them at all, since this was hardly an event for children.

"Big," Easton said in English, gazing up at the massive luxury liner, which had last crossed the Atlantic in the sixties before being turned into a floating hotel and restaurant. They reached the credentials table, where six handsome young men in white tails were welcoming the famous and the infamous aboard.

"Muy grande." Weston whistled.

Esme chuckled; they spoke the truth. The *Queen Mary* was more than eighty thousand square feet in size, with fourteen different art deco salons decorated with warm wood paneling, original oil paintings from the twenties, larger-than-life murals, and brass and nickel-silver fixtures with etched lead-glass accents. Many spectacular parties had taken place aboard the luxury liner. But none would be more spectacular than Diane Goldhagen's closing-night party for FAB.

The entire ship had been decorated for the event by famous set designer Eduardo Parsons. Diane and Eduardo had worked together to mesh the fashion world with the art deco decor of the luxury liner. In the ten-thousand-square-foot central ballroom, Lenny Oran's Orchestra would play music from the twenties on a central revolving stage. The room would be lined with mannequins clad in museum-quality art deco dress—columns of silk, satin, and brocade, dripping with precious gems; short, fringed hemlines; and multiple strands of long pearls. Eduardo had created a larger-than-life mural backdrop for the mannequins—famous faces, books, films, and music of the era: Louise Brooks, Scott and Zelda Fitzgerald, Dorothy Parker, Buster Keaton, Charlie Chaplin, and the flapper cartoons by John Held Jr. from the cover of *Life* magazine. In fact, Lydia's boyfriend, Billy, had helped put up the backdrop.

There were the celebrity participants who had volunteered to be part of the show to help raise money for the AIDS charity. Some of them would be seated in swings hung from the ceiling, clad in costumes from the Paris Folies-Bergère of the twenties—rolled-down stockings, red-rouged cheeks, bobbed-hair wigs, and fake beauty marks. Others, in twenties black tails, would be guest waiters, snaking through the crowd during the cocktail hour with teacups of booze; during Prohibition, when alcohol was illegal, people drank their liquor in teacups in case the place was busted by the cops.

Guests were encouraged to tip liberally. All the celebrity waiters' money would be deposited in a twenty-foot Lucite martini glass so that everyone could watch the sum grow.

All this Esme knew merely from being in proximity to Diane as she planned the event with Lateesha. It was one thing to hear about it, another to experience it. The twins' eyes were wide open as they climbed aboard with Esme, and Esme wasn't much less overwhelmed herself.

"No te preocupes, Weston," Esme assured the older of the twins as she felt her hand tighten in a death grip. *"Tu mamá y papá están aquí. Vamos a ver."*

Even the security guards smiled as the twins stepped onto the deck—they looked incredibly cute. Their flapper dresses had been specially designed for them by Donna Karan, as a favor to her friend Diane. Easton's dress was pink and Weston's was baby blue; each featured straight tubes of silk that ended in two inches of ribbon fringe. The girls liked to twirl and feel the ribbons swishing against their legs. Luckily for them, the fashion of the twenties wasn't at all uncomfortable or binding. Esme suspected that if straitjackets had been stylish in that era, that was what the twins would have been wearing.

"Welcome aboard, welcome aboard," more gorgeous young men called, handing the women wrist corsages of rare flowers as they boarded. Esme followed the throngs into the main body of the ship, then asked a uniformed officer—they were everywhere she turned—where she might find Diane Goldhagen's stateroom. That was where Diane wanted the twins brought.

"Oh, I think I can show you the way," a voice offered from behind Esme. A voice she knew all too well, in the dark of night, whispering things to her that made her lose every inhibition she'd ever had.

Her back stiffened with resolve. It wasn't as if she hadn't known that Jonathan would be there.

"*Yon-o-tin!*" the girls cried, running to him.

"Wow, look at you guys," Jonathan crowed as he knelt to embrace them, looking comfortable in an impeccable Armani tux. "You're gorgeous." His eyes met Esme's. "Actually, you're all gorgeous."

Esme was glad she'd spent the money on the incredible low-cut Chanel cocktail dress, and equally glad of her new red pumps. Her hair had been styled into sexy waves down her back; her makeup was perfect. She held her head high.

Let him want me, she thought, *let him know what he's lost.*

"That's not necessary," she said, making her voice as cold as possible. "I can find your mother's stateroom myself. Girls, come." She held out her hands to them. They both shook their heads and held fast to their big brother.

"You know how stubborn my little sisters are," Jonathan cajoled. "I think we're all in this together. This way, miladies." He cocked his head toward the far end of the passageway.

"You take them, then," Esme declared, not about to let him call the shots. "I'll be there in fifteen minutes." Before Jonathan could say anything else, she turned in the opposite direction and followed the signs to the main ballroom. Her heart was pounding; she felt short of breath. She was glad to be away from him and planned to spend the night as far from him as possible.

There was a grand staircase leading to the ballroom, like something out of *Titanic.* Nothing Esme had heard from Diane prepared her for what she saw when she entered the ballroom. There were easily a thousand people on hand—the biggest stars in the world were talking and laughing and sipping drinks from bone china cups. A full orchestra in white formal wear was playing something slow and romantic; a singer dressed in a long white-sequined skintight gown crooned into the microphone. It was a paparazzo's dream: Hayden Christensen was dancing with Kristin Kreuk, Sofia Coppola was chuckling at something Bruce Willis had just said, Salma Hayek—Esme's mother's favorite actress—was in earnest conversation with Denzel Washington. In addition to the famous faces there were hundreds of others that looked as if they *should* be famous.

It was difficult for Esme to take it all in. Long Beach was a tough town. How could it be that people lived like this, partied like this, while only a few miles away gangs were killing each other, homeless people were begging for spare change, and girls were being beaten by their boyfriends or their fathers? How could it be that Junior got shot trying to be a good guy and Jonathan got everything, would always get everything, even if he was a bad guy?

There was no justice. Her honest, intelligent parents worked six days a week to serve people like this. Goodness and hard work weren't rewarded. The world was never going to change. This party had cost hundreds of thousands of dollars. Oh, sure, the rich people could tell themselves they were doing it all for charity, but that was crap. They could have just given the money to charity anyway. No. They wanted an excuse to have a party this splendid, to be seen and photographed at it, so that the rest of the world would see it and envy them. It was a world of haves and have-nots.

Was this what she wanted, to go to Bel Air High School and then some expensive university, so that she could become one of them?

"Esme!"

Lydia's voice rang out over the music; she waved from across the ballroom. Then Esme saw her stand on her tiptoes and whisper something into the ear of the guy she was with—tall, broad-shouldered, and, from what Esme could see, very cute. Lydia took his hand and led him through the crowd and up the staircase to Esme.

"This is the best night of my entire life!" Lydia cried, throwing her arms around Esme.

Esme grinned; Lydia's energy and excitement were always infectious. Plus, her friend looked even more spectacular in the strapless white Chanel dress than she had that afternoon in the shop. As Lydia introduced Billy, who wore a deliberately oversized black silk sport coat, a black T-shirt, and jeans, Esme was struck by the kindness in his eyes.

Jonathan didn't have kind eyes. Jonathan—that bastard!—was not kind.

"Nice to meet you, Esme," Billy said, flashing twin dimples. "I've heard a lot about you."

I've heard that Lydia plans to lose her virginity to you tonight,

Esme thought. *One of the differences between Lydia and me is that Lydia would say it aloud and I wouldn't.*

"This is the most incredible party!" Lydia exclaimed. "Y'all, it's like I've died and gone to heaven. How'd you get cut loose from your girls?"

"Jonathan took them to see their mother."

"Jonathan Goldhagen," Lydia explained for Billy. "Remember you told me you saw that movie he was in?"

"*Tiger Eyes,*" Billy filled in. "Bad flick. He was good, though."

"He has a thing for Esme but Esme already has a boyfriend," Lydia told Billy. "Now, if it was me, I'd split my time between the two of them. Life is too short to limit your options. But Esme is a much better person than I am."

Billy laughed.

"Is Kiley here yet?" Esme asked, because she really, really wanted to change the subject.

"Haven't seen her. Or our financial benefactor, Platinum." Lydia took hold of Billy's hands and wrapped them around her slender waist from behind. "Oh, I have news. Evelyn fired Alexis because Alexis talks to the dead. Plus, she threatened to close down our nanny empire."

Empire? Esme thought. Lydia was prone to hyperbole.

"You don't sound very upset about it."

"Oh, I'll figure something out," Lydia said breezily. "Besides, for right now I'm just too dang happy to let Evelyn Tobacco Queen Bowers spoil things." She craned around to Billy. "I wonder what we need to do to get one of those staterooms all to ourselves."

"Donate at least five thou to ICAP," Billy replied. "I read the little card on the tables. It's kinda out of our budget range."

"Well, considering that you busted your really cute ass decorating this place, I'd say they owe you," Lydia quipped.

"Me and Eduardo's staff of fifty," Billy said. "Not gonna happen."

Lydia looked past Esme. "Oh my God, there's Cameron Diaz. I *love* her!" The orchestra segued into an upbeat tune. "Let's go dance, y'all!"

"Can't," Esme told her. "I have to go check on the girls."

"Right, you're on duty," Lydia recalled. "Well, that sucks. Can we sit with you at dinner, at least?"

"I'm sure I'll be with the Goldhagens so I can watch over the girls during dinner. That is, if they last that long." Esme hugged her friend. "Have fun. I'll try to find you later."

Esme left her friends as they descended to the dance floor. She headed back toward Diane's stateroom and the twins. She wished she could just keep walking right off the ship. She'd go . . . where? To Junior, who would get out of the hospital the next morning? To Jorge, to cry on his shoulder? To her parents, who would be home relaxing, playing dominos maybe, after a hard day slaving for the Goldhagens?

But she couldn't do any of those things. She had work to do. She vowed that if she ran into Jonathan, she would look right through him.

Billy held out Lydia's ruby velvet chair for her, and then took the adjacent seat. Dinner was being served in twenty different locations around the enormous ship.

The FAB banquet guests had found their dinner seating listed with the dozen concierges outside the ballroom reception. Those who were electronically inclined could pick up the new BlackBerry that was a party favor for each guest and find their table by pressing a preprogrammed sequence of buttons.

There was a definite pecking order, even among the richest and most famous of the Hollywood elite. The largest donors and the biggest celebrities, plus some of the top models, were seated in the immense and famous Sir Winston's Salon. Middling stars and those whose donations only came to five figures were mostly in the Regent Room or the Royal Salon. Billy and Lydia were seated a level down from those rooms in the Queen's

Salon, a small but elegant room with ivory-colored tablecloths, gold flatware, and gold serving plates at each place setting. A single red rose adorned each woman's plate; an expensive Cuban cigar adorned the men's plates. The salon held tables for two or four, along with velvet banquettes along the wall for larger parties.

"Trade ya," Lydia said, plucking up Billy's cigar. "I've always wanted to try one of these puppies."

"Take both," Billy offered, lifting her rose. He gently stuck the stem behind her right ear. "That suits you more than it would suit me."

"Have you always been this nice?"

"Oh, I've had more than my share of screwups, just ask X. He knows 'em all."

It was so great that Billy and X were best friends. Both of them were so hot. It got Lydia to wondering. "Have you ever had sex with a guy?"

"Have you?" Billy countered.

"Now, see, that's not a fair question because I told you that you were going to be my first."

"No, Lydia Chandler. I have not had sex with a guy. You think just because X is gay we have to be screwing each other?"

Lydia thought about that one for a moment. "If I was a guy and X was my best friend, I'd definitely have sex with him once. Just to find out what it's like."

He laughed. "You probably would."

Lydia loved that this didn't seem to bother him. "How old were you when you first did it?"

"Sixteen," Billy replied, sipping from the crystal water goblet at his place setting. "And that is all you're getting out of me."

"Waited until you were sixteen. Huh." Lydia was intrigued. "I thought all boys were horn dogs."

Billy chuckled. "Come on, Lydia, you did not."

"Do you just have a low sex drive?"

They'd sat side by side instead of across the table from each other, so Billy could slide an arm around her shoulders and lean close to whisper in her ear. "My sex drive has been in overdrive ever since I first laid eyes on you."

Lydia shivered deliciously. "That gave me chill bumps. Dang. I'm so glad I didn't have sex with Scott the lifeguard."

Billy laughed. "Me too."

Lydia heard her stomach growling. "I'd be willing to skip dinner and move on to dessert—that'd be you—but I forgot to eat all day because I was so excited." She plucked the menu from the center of the table and read it aloud, squinting at the words that had been done in calligraphy with black ink. " 'Foie gras with caramelized apple, sautéed in Calvados. Mesclun salad with sliced scallions, red and yellow pepper, and goat cheese, garnished with hand-cut avocado and crab chunks. Chateaubriand. Braised rabbit with purple potato compote and mixed berry Chambord sauce. The Queen's soufflé with Grand Marnier and Kahlua.' " She gave Billy a quizzical look.

"Not a clue," he admitted. "But hey, I'm game."

A waiter in a white dinner jacket used tongs to place hot scones, fragrant with rosemary, on both of their white china side plates. Billy broke off a piece of his and buttered it. "How about you, Lydia, open to trying new things?"

Lydia lowered the menu. "When my parents lost their minds and we moved from Texas, where we lived in a mansion, to that freaking rain forest, where we lived in a thatched-roof hut, I was not the kind of child open to new experiences, culinary or otherwise." She ran a finger across the condensation on her water glass as she remembered. "But then . . . well, I guess I was forced into being a different kind of girl."

Billy nodded. "When I was a kid, my fantasy of the perfect life was to stay in one place—some town in America that looked like a Norman Rockwell painting—picket fence, bike, basketball hoop in the driveway, Cub Scouts, and Little League." He shook his head. "Man, I wanted that so much. But instead . . ."

Lydia knew the rest because Billy had already told her. When he was a boy, his parents had been stationed with the Foreign Service in a half dozen different countries around the globe. "So how did it change you?"

He shrugged and nibbled at his scone. "Who the hell knows? Maybe I decided to be a designer so that I could create my own fantasy worlds."

Speaking of fantasies—Lydia studied him. Hadn't she seen an entire wing of open staterooms when she'd toured the ship? Even if they'd been paid for, no one was in them yet, because everyone was eating dinner. Suddenly, her grumbling stomach was forgotten.

She put a meaningful hand on his thigh. "Oh, Will-i-am," she singsonged.

"Oh, Li-dee-ya," he sang back, teasing. "You might want to move your hand; the waiter is heading this way with the first course."

"I was thinking we could skip the meal. Let's find a stateroom."

"Oh, really." He smiled at her.

"Yes, really." She kissed him softly. "I have on the most killer lingerie. You really should see it."

She saw the flicker of lust in Billy's eyes. She'd seen the same look in Scott's eyes—as if their IQs had just slumped twenty points. Good to know that Billy was not impervious to her charms. Even if he was the coolest hetero male on the planet, he was still *male*.

The waiter placed the salad plates atop the gold chargers in front of them. Lydia gave Billy one meaningful gaze, then let her eyes flick toward the exit. She was sure he'd take the napkin off his lap and stand up. Then she'd rise. Then he'd take her hand and lead her to a stateroom. They'd lock the door. He'd kiss her wildly, passionately, then turn her around and slowly unzip her dress until—

"Mmmm, Lydia. Delicious."

Lydia snapped out of her fantasy, because Billy wasn't referring to her. He had just forked a bite of apple and something brown and pasty-looking into his mouth from the appetizer plate.

"You're *eating*?" Lydia couldn't believe it.

Billy pointed to his plate with the fork as he swallowed. "This has to be the foie gras."

Now she was getting pissed. "I am wearing an eight-hundred-dollar Chanel dress, under which is three hundred dollars' worth of lacy silk, under which is priceless silky me. You're telling me you'd rather munch that—that brown stuff?"

"No." He put his fork down and wiped his mouth. "Resisting you is right up there with world peace—damn hard to achieve."

"So, don't resist."

"We're not rushing into this, Miss Chandler."

"Who's rushing? I've been wanting to have sex since I was thirteen, but the only possible candidates were five-feet-tall, nearly naked spear carriers!"

He took her hand. "Look, I'm honored, flattered—all that—that you want it to be me, but . . ."

In a flash, Lydia understood. "Oh, damn. It's too much pressure, right? Performance anxiety. I read about it in *Men's Health.* Now *that's* a boring-ass magazine."

Billy broke off a piece of scone, put a dollop of foie gras on it, and offered it to her. "Eat."

She was about to protest, but changed her mind and took a bite. "You know, that's really good."

"So's waiting to do the deed, Lydia. Otherwise it's just lust."

Oh, *now* she got it. Lydia washed the food down with a large gulp of water. "That is just so sweet, Billy. You're not in love with me and you're such a gentleman that you don't want to use me for your wanton lust. But it's fine; I am heavily into wanton lust."

He burst out laughing. "I have a feeling you'd be the one using me. I'd like to get to know you before I *know* you. In the biblical sense."

Lydia folded her arms. "I am just really disappointed in you, William Martin."

He didn't seem the least perturbed by her comment, just

broke off another piece of scone. "I'll make it up to you, Lydia Chandler, in the long run." His dimples winked at her.

Lydia scowled. Of all the crapola. Billy didn't want to have sex with her until they had a real "relationship." Lust wasn't enough for him. At least not with her. She had managed to fall for the most romantic boy on the planet.

Damn. Talk about bad luck.

Kiley stood just inside the massive double doors that led into the *Queen Mary*'s ballroom and tried to take it all in: The orchestra slowly turning on the raised platform in the center of the massive room. The twenty-foot-tall Lucite martini glass that was already half full of tip money earned by the celebrity waiters. Breathtakingly beautiful women in couture gowns, dripping jewels that they owned or that had been loaned to them from places like Harry Winston and Tiffany.

Not only did she recognize Hollywood royalty, but because of the breathless preview coverage the party had received on TV, she knew there was actual royalty in attendance too. Kiley had watched Tori Spelling on E! interview an aristocratic-looking man with a narrow face and a receding hairline, named Count Brandino Brandolini d'Adda, who was from Naranzaria, Italy. The count told Tori that all the wine that would be consumed on the *Queen Mary* had been donated from his vineyards.

Kiley looked up. Women dressed as flappers were swinging on swings descending from the ceiling. She was pretty sure that the young woman on the swing directly overhead was Jessica Simpson.

"Make way, please, excuse us, please."

Four white-jacketed flunkies were clearing the way for a scarlet-sequin-gowned Mariah Carey. And over there in the stunning gold brocade gown with the sweetheart neckline—was that Hilary Swank dancing with Jimmy Fallon? The only people it seemed she hadn't yet spotted were Tom and Platinum.

Platinum, in fact, would be arriving even later than Kiley and had sent Kiley ahead in the Lotus while she stopped at Raymond's salon for a blowout by the master himself. Lori would be taking care of the children that evening. "Caviar on toast point, miss?" A white-jacketed waiter with a chiseled jaw-line held out a silver tray, on which there was a small bowl of tiny round black things, another bowl of minced onions and chopped egg, a tiny bowl of sour cream with a baby spoon, and a plate of small pieces of toast. She recognized the tiny round black things as caviar—fish eggs of some sort—but she'd certainly never eaten any. Frankly, it looked disgusting. But that wasn't why her jaw was hanging open. That was because the hands holding the silver tray belonged to Jim Carrey, who Kiley was pretty certain was the funniest human on the planet.

"Care for some caviar?" he asked.

"No," she replied, half-dazed. "But thanks."

"You're welcome. Have fun tonight. Killer dress, you look great." He moved off into the crowd.

A smile crept onto Kiley's lips. Had Jim Carrey just told her she looked killer? Wait until she told Nina. And her mom—her mom loved him. If only she'd gotten a picture of the two of them together. No, that would have been way too tacky. Oh wait, she should have tipped him; given him some money to throw into the giant martini glass. But she'd only brought, like, five crumpled one-dollar bills with her. Still, she should have—

"Caviar?"

This time it wasn't Jim Carrey. It was Tom, looking tall and tan and impossibly handsome in a black tuxedo. "I just saw Jim Carrey offer you some," he explained. "You looked . . . dazzled."

"I was. Am," she corrected herself. "So . . . hi."

"This is a surprise. I didn't know you'd be here."

Right. Because you didn't invite me. "I've got my own friends in high places," she joked.

Kiley thought she saw admiration in his eyes. "You look beautiful."

Wow. First a famous actor. Then Tom Chappelle.

"Thanks. I'd say 'This old thing?' But it's an actual Chanel and I actually own it," Kiley confided. "Platinum treated my friends and me to a shopping spree."

"Yo, what's up, man?" An extremely tall, extremely muscular bald black man called to Tom as he walked by with two plates of hors d'oeuvres in his massive right hand.

Tom waved a hand to return the greeting. "Shaq," Tom said.

"I met him at the premiere party for *The Ten*. So, how'd it go last night with Platinum? You guys get home all right?"

Something in Tom's way-casual attitude irked Kiley. "You'd already know the answer to that if you'd called me to find out."

Tom winced. "Ouch. You're right. It's just been crazy. Two more runway shows this afternoon, then photos, interviews . . ."

"Oh yeah, me too," Kiley deadpanned.

There was a long beat of silence; then Tom burst out laughing, and so did Kiley. "Okay, I deserved that," he admitted. "Hopefully I can make it up to you. Dance?"

They went down to the dance floor—it was no longer crowded, since so many people had gone to their salons to eat dinner. The orchestra was playing; the torch singer's eyes were at half-mast as she crooned into the microphone about finding love. Tom held his arms out; Kiley floated into them. They fit together perfectly. She leaned into him and he stroked her hair. He smelled clean and so . . . so *boy*. His arms tightened around her waist.

If ever there was a moment when Kiley wished that a song would never end, it was this moment. She was exactly where she wanted to be, in the perfect moment with the perfect boy.

When the singer finished the last ringing note, Tom kept his arms around her and gazed into her eyes.

"Song's over," she pointed out.

His arms stayed where they were. "Do we care?"

"No, we don't."

"Tom, there you are." Marym swept over to them looking perfect in a silver column dress held up by a diamond brooch on one shoulder, the other bare; silver satin sandals made her nearly as tall as Tom. Her hair was up in a simple bun at the nape of her swanlike neck; long pink diamond-and-rubellite earrings danced in her ears, nearly brushing her elegant collarbone. Other than that she wore no jewelry.

Suddenly, Kiley felt like a chubby little girl playing dress-up. The stony look on Marym's face when she realized who Tom was dancing with didn't help.

"Kiley." Marym's tone was icy. "That's your name, isn't it?"

"Yes."

"I brought her to your birthday party," Tom reminded Marym.

Marym's eyes stayed on Kiley's. "But we don't need to go back that far, do we?"

Tom looked puzzled. "What's this about?"

"Some people were picketing my house this morning," Marym seethed. "I watched it on TV. You were there. Don't bother denying it."

Kiley blushed. Tom looked shocked. Kiley was instantly sorry that she hadn't told him about it. After all, he was the one who had introduced her to Marym. Kiley could feel Marym's and Tom's eyes on her, waiting to see what she would say.

Gulp. But she'd done the right thing, she reminded herself. Marym was the one in the wrong here, not her. She could tough this out. She *would* tough this out.

"Yes, I was there," Kiley affirmed, standing her ground. "Marym won't let the public get access to the beach," she explained to Tom. "I was part of a peaceful demonstration across from her house in Malibu this morning." She took a deep breath and plunged on. "I'd do it again, in fact."

Marym put one fist on a jutting hip bone. "You were a guest in my home, Kiley. Did you even think about picking up the phone and calling to ask me about this?"

Kiley really did not like the way Tom was staring at her. "Um . . . no," she admitted.

"I just bought my house," Marym fumed. "I didn't know anything about the beach-zoning rules—I've barely moved in, my financial planner found the place and made all the arrangements, and I've been on the road half the time! I don't want to keep people off the beach!"

Kiley felt awful. "You don't?"

"No, I don't. Now that I know about it, of course I'll allow the public access."

"But—but on TV they said you wouldn't even do an interview!" Kiley sputtered.

"How could I do an interview?" Marym's eyes blazed. "I was at Ma Maison Sofitel for the night! You were willing to think the worst of me without knowing the truth."

God. Marym was right. "I—I don't—I'm not . . ." Kiley had no idea what to say. She should apologize. But her envy regarding Marym, and her possible—probable—relationship to Tom made that so difficult. Still, it was the right thing to do. "I'm sorry," she said quietly.

Marym didn't respond, she just folded her arms and glared.

Tom finally spoke up. "Hey, she apologized, Mar."

"Is that supposed to fix everything?" Marym snapped.

"She made a mistake," Tom said. "But it was an honest one. She was standing up for something she believes in." His eyes went to Kiley. "That's pretty great."

Kiley smiled at him gratefully. He really *did* understand.

Marym put an elegant hand on her clavicle. "Whose side are you on, exactly?"

Tom nudged Marym playfully. "Come on, get over yourself, diva. This is me you're talking to. Next time Kiley has a disagreement with you, she'll call; I'll personally give her your number. How's that?"

"Just because I'm beautiful and rich doesn't mean I don't have feelings," Marym sniffed.

Ugh. *What a clueless thing to say,* Kiley thought. Maybe when everyone treated you like you were the Queen of Sheba, you started to believe it. But, Kiley reminded herself, Marym was only eighteen, just a little older than she was. It probably was tough to be thrown into a glamorous, adult world overnight.

"I really am sorry," Kiley told Marym. "It's just . . . I love the ocean so much. That's what brought me to California, because I want to go to Scripps Institution of Oceanography and . . ." She realized she was rambling. Marym didn't *care* why she was in California. "Anyway, I need to look before I leap."

Marym nodded, but she still looked peeved. She slipped her arm through Tom's. "Come on, let's go to Sir Winston's Salon. They already started serving."

"We're seated with the host and hostess of the evening," Tom explained to Kiley apologetically.

Kiley tripped all over herself to sound casual. "Oh, that's fine. I mean, you didn't even know I'd be here or anything." She started backing away. "I'm already late to meet up with my friends, so . . ."

"Maybe we can meet later?" Tom asked.

"Oh, you know, whatever, I'll be pretty busy. Have fun, you two!" Kiley turned and sprinted off. Could she have made any bigger an ass of herself? Tom had defended her to Marym, but he was just being a good guy. Kiley had ruined *everything*!

She ducked into a quiet corridor and stood for a moment, trying to collect herself. What difference did it make if she impressed Tom or not? All you had to do was look at the way Marym touched him to know that they'd been together, in every sense of the word. Maybe Tom had flirted with Kiley a little on the dance floor, but as soon as Marym appeared, the magical bubble had burst. Kiley knew exactly why she'd been willing to assume the worst about Marym: because she was jealous as hell.

She ventured back into the ballroom and saw that the crowd had thinned further. She wondered momentarily about her friends. Wherever Esme was, she was busy with Easton and Weston. Lydia and Billy had probably made it halfway through the *Kama Sutra* by now. Tom . . .

Tom was with Marym.

Dinner was the last thing she was interested in. So she sat alone at a high cocktail table, chin resting in her hands, and watched the orchestra play for a dozen or so couples cha-cha-ing around the dance floor. Could this night get any worse? *Yes, actually, it could. Let's see . . . Platinum could come reeling across the dance floor naked, screaming that I'm her love slave.*

"Dance?"

A skinny guy with long reddish hair stood before her, flashing a jaunty grin.

"No, thanks," Kiley told him.

He slipped onto the high stool next to hers. "I'm Mark Goldfarb. I just started with Lieberman, Levitt, and Goldfarb—you know, the accountants. We do a lot of the stars. Yes, Jerry Goldfarb was my grandfather. I plead nepotism." He glanced around and shook his head. "Man, we didn't have anything like this in Boulder."

"I'm from Wisconsin," Kiley admitted.

He pointed at her. "See, I could just tell you weren't one of these jaded prima donnas. I just graduated from the U of Colorado. Business major, skiing minor. So how about you?"

"I'm a nanny to a famous alcoholic drug addict," Kiley replied.

"Courtney Love? Only kidding! Oh yeah, these people are wild. I'm amazed by the kind of stuff they do." He leaned a little closer. "So who do you really work for?"

At that moment, Jim Carrey was making one last round with his tray. He leaned toward Kiley. "Don't tell him jack, he writes for that gossip rag, *The Insider.*"

Kiley whirled on Mark. "Is that true?"

Mark held his palms up to her. "Hey, cut me some slack, I'm just a hardworking reporter."

"You're just a lying little toad," Kiley shot back, and hopped off the stool. Maybe she should just leave. It wasn't like she was having a good time. Or even a decent time. She made a quick decision: she'd go up top, take a look at her ocean under the stars, and drive back to Bel Air.

Maybe she'd stop at Blockbuster and rent Jim Carrey in *The Majestic* before she went home. Critics had hated that movie, but she'd loved it. Or maybe she'd just go home and finish the damn letter to her mother, someone who actually cared about her.

But she didn't leave. Instead, she went on deck and stared out into her ocean, lost in thought for a long time. The ocean air, salty and sharp, filled her lungs. She gazed at the huge Long Beach marina, then at the city of Long Beach's modest skyline, and then out to sea. Just looking at it made her feel better. What was it about the ocean that she loved so much? Her mother used to read her a picture book about selkies—creatures that were half woman, half seal. When these women felt the sea beckoning, they returned to the brine and swam away to an entire other world.

That's what I want, Kiley thought. *To swim away to another world.*

"Watching over your ocean, Mistress of the Deep?"

Kiley turned her head to see Tom behind her, alone, wind rustling his blond hair.

"You're supposed to be eating dinner," she told him.

"Overrated." He joined her by the rail, both of them gazing out to sea. "I figured I'd find you up here."

"Marym will miss you."

He frowned. "Since when are you so concerned with Marym?"

I'm not. She leaned her back against the rail. "Can I ask you something? About you and Marym?"

"Sure."

It was on the tip of Kiley's tongue: *Are you sleeping with her? Did you ever sleep with her—say, at your hotel suite, for example? Are you even attracted to me?*

She opened her mouth. And nothing came out. She couldn't ask him such personal questions. "Never mind." She shook her head. "It isn't important." She sighed. "I was a bitch to your friend."

"Kiley." He put a finger over her lips. "You were standing up for something you believe in. That's more than most people ever do."

Her eyes met his. How could one boy look so absolutely, stunningly perfect? Before she could talk herself out of it, she leaned forward, raised her chin, and kissed him. Softly. For just a moment, eyes closed. Then she opened her eyes and realized something scary.

He hadn't kissed her back.

Oh, crap, he really *did* think of her as a little sister. Now he'd be all embarrassed and feel sorry for her and try to explain that he didn't like her *that way* and—

The next thing Kiley knew, Tom was pulling her to him, kissing her the way she'd always dreamed of being kissed, until the world went upside down and her insides melted. At that moment she knew—the fumbling, uncomfortable, did-we-or-didn't-we moment she'd endured with her ex-boyfriend wasn't sex and couldn't have been sex. If one kiss from the right boy could make her feel like this, then sex with the right boy had to be the most momentous, amazing, fantastic experience in the world.

They parted, breathless, his arms still around her waist. "Wow," he murmured.

Was this really happening? Kiley felt as if she could levitate with happiness. "I was so afraid you thought of me as your little sister or something—"

"Are you kidding? I've wanted to kiss you ever since you gave me that lame story about being called Krazy with a *K*."

Her words tumbled over each other. "But you never— I never knew—"

"I didn't want to come off as some asshole model, all full of himself. And my life is so busy, I'm on location half the time, it's insane, so—"

"Tom." His name on her lips was as sweet as the kiss.

"Yeah?"

They were kissing again; she was lost in him, and she never, ever wanted the moment to end. It was like the movies; she was hearing bells.

"Your cell is ringing," Tom murmured against her ear.

It took Kiley a moment to reconnect with reality. Real bells. Coming from her purse, which she'd dropped at her feet sometime during the festivities.

She retrieved it and snapped the phone open. "Hello?"

"Ki-ley?"

"Sid?" She went on instant alert, as there'd been snuffling between the syllables of her name. Sid never called. And he never cried.

"It's . . . can you . . . ?" He started crying again.

"Sid, what is it?" Kiley demanded. Tom looked at her quizzically, but Kiley was completely focused on the call.

"It's Serenity," Sid wailed. "She's . . . really sick!"

Kiley tried to stay calm, though her mind was racing in a million directions. Why was Sid calling her instead of his mother? Where was the babysitter? "Where's Lori?"

"Bruce came home and told her she could leave," Sid sniffled. "So she did. But then after that Bruce left too."

Kiley gritted her teeth. Lori left the kids alone just because a fourteen-year-old told her it was okay? What an airhead. "Where's Mrs. Cleveland?" Surely the cook would be there.

"It's her day off, I think," Sid said. "No one is here!"

Damn. "Tell me what's wrong, Sid."

" 'Kay, well, Serenity has these big red bumps all over her skin. And her lips are getting all huge and she's crying and I'm really scared!"

Hives, Kiley thought. *An allergic reaction to something.*

From the background, Kiley heard Serenity. "I want my mommy!"

"I tried to call Mom," Sid told Kiley, "but she didn't answer her cell."

"Listen to me, Sid; I think Serenity is just having an allergic reaction to something. It's going to be okay. Put her on the phone and I'll explain."

"She's shaking her head. Can you come home?"

"I'm an hour away from you, sweetie," Kiley explained, pacing the deck with the phone. "Is Serenity breathing okay?"

She heard Sid asking Serenity but couldn't hear the little girl's answer. "She said if she wasn't breathing she couldn't answer your stupid question," Sid reported.

Good to know she hadn't lost that Serenity edge. "Did she eat anything unusual, Sid? Or touch anything unusual? I'm trying to figure out what she's allergic to."

Silence from the other end of the phone, then: "Promise you won't get mad?"

"I won't get mad."

"Well, see, Mom left some of her stash in the living room. Serenity was showing off, so she put some of the reefer in the bong and took a hit."

"She *what*?" Kiley screeched.

"You said you wouldn't get mad!" Sid whined.

Kiley forced herself to keep her voice even. "I'm not mad, Sid. Go on."

"Okay, so she took a really big hit and started coughing and stuff. Yeah. And then she started getting the rash thingie, like, a little while later."

Kiley sighed. That was just so Platinum, to leave her marijuana out where the kids could get to it. "Put Serenity on the phone, Sid."

"Kiley!" It was Serenity. She sounded like she was gasping for air. Panic attack, Kiley figured. Well, she had a lot of experience with those; she'd talked her mom through dozens of them. "I can't breathe!"

"It's because you're scared," Kiley reassured her. "Your heart is pounding and it feels like the whole world is closing in on—"

"No!" Serenity sucked air into the phone. "Like in my throat!"

Kiley had seen a really bad allergic reaction once in her life, when a yellow jacket stung Nina on a Girl Scouts camping trip. Nina's throat had closed up and they had to rush her to the hospital. A person could *die* that way.

Kiley forced her voice to sound steady. "Serenity, sweetie, I want you to lie down on the couch and take slow, deep breaths, okay?"

" 'Kay." Serenity's voice was tiny.

"Put Sid back on the phone."

"You have to come home right now!" Sid demanded.

"Listen to me. I think your sister is in something called

anaphylactic shock. I need to call nine-one-one." Kiley's hand was white-knuckled on her phone.

"Okay."

"I'll tell them to send an ambulance," Kiley instructed. "I'm calling now. Then I'm coming home."

There was no traffic on the freeways for a change, so Kiley and Tom—he'd insisted on driving, saying that Kiley was too upset—pulled through the gates of Platinum's estate exactly forty minutes after they'd sprinted off the *Queen Mary*. The first thing Kiley saw was the emergency vehicles—a City of Los Angeles ambulance with its lights flashing, plus a Bel Air Police cruiser. There was also a white panel van with the city seal on the front door. No sign of Platinum or Lori, or any of the staff.

Kiley parked and ran into the house, calling for the kids as her heart thudded in her chest. A short, muscular cop blocked her way as Tom joined her. He looked them over. "You two are—?"

"I'm the nanny, Kiley McCann. He's a friend. Where's Serenity? Is she okay?"

"Kid's fine," the cop reassured her. He had a strong New

York City accent. "An injection of epinephrine and she's a hundred percent. No harm, no foul."

"Thank God." Kiley heaved a sigh of relief. She felt Tom's strong hand land comfortingly on the back of her neck.

"Your friend needs to wait outside," the cop declared. "Until we get this situation under control."

"But you said Serenity is fine."

"When we arrived, miss, we found no adult or caregiver in the home. We need to limit the domicile strictly to relevant parties."

"It's no problem," Tom assured Kiley. "I'll be in the truck. Holler if you need me."

She gave him a grateful smile as he slipped out the door. Then she faced the cop again. "Serenity is in her room?"

"Her brother's room. They're playing that fantasy card game. What's it called—my kid plays it all the time—Yoogi something."

"Yu-Gi-Oh!" Kiley filled in. She knew it was Sid's passion in life. "Thanks." Just as she reached the staircase, a huge commotion broke out behind her. She whirled around. There was her boss, trying to get past the policeman who was blocking the way with his body.

"Move the hell out of my way!"

Platinum had arrived. She wore a white leather Versace minidress with the sides cut out, and white thigh-high stiletto boots. She pushed against the burly cop's chest—he wouldn't let her into her own house. "You need to wait here, ma'am," he insisted.

Platinum spit on him.

Oh, crap.

The cop raised a shoulder to wipe the spit from his jaw, then spoke into his walkie-talkie, informing whoever was at the other end that the mother had just entered the domicile.

"It's not a domicile. It's my freaking house, asshole!" Platinum screamed.

"Please come with me, ma'am." The cop locked her upper arm in a viselike grip and maneuvered her outside as Platinum bellowed about police brutality and lawsuits. At the same time, Kiley had to make way as another burly cop, a paramedic, and a young African American woman with close-cropped hair came downstairs. Right behind them were Sid and Serenity.

Serenity flew into Kiley's arms the moment she saw her. "You came."

"Of course I came." She held the girl tight, under the watchful and concerned eyes of the authorities. "This is my nanny," Serenity told them. "The one I told you about."

Platinum burst back inside, somehow having gotten free of the cop. "I'm going to sue you assholes for every penny you've got!" she bellowed. "I have civil rights, you know!" Her eyes landed on Kiley. "You're a witness, Kiley!"

The burly cop reentered, shaking his head. "Platinum, you're going to have to come with me. Don't make this difficult."

"Come 'ere, kids," Platinum told the children, reaching out for them. "I love my kids." But the other policeman stepped between the children and Kiley as the African American woman approached her. "I'm Tonika Johnson, City Department of Social Services. You're—?"

"I told you, my nanny," Serenity said, burrowing closer into Kiley's leg.

"Fine. Serenity, just stay with your nanny for right now," the social worker said.

Kiley wrapped them both in her arms. "It's going to be okay," she told them in a soothing voice, though she had gathered that nothing was going to be okay; that "okay" was a big fat lie and the truth was right in front of them.

"My babies," Platinum moaned loudly, holding her arms out toward the kids and wriggling her fingers. "I need my babies."

The first policeman grimly unfastened his handcuffs from his belt. "Platinum, you're under arrest for possession of a controlled substance and the reckless endangerment of two minors," he declared. "Please extend your arms."

Platinum shook her head violently. "Come on, man, you can't do this shit."

Kiley was stunned—they were *arresting* Platinum? In front of her *children*?

"Kids, why don't you go back upstairs with Ms. Johnson," Kiley prompted. "I'll come up in a little while."

"That's a good idea," the social worker agreed, coaxing the children back upstairs. "You can show me your toys."

Kiley was afraid they'd refuse to go, that they'd fly into their mother's outstretched arms. To her shock, they meekly obeyed the social worker without even a backward look. Meanwhile, the cop slapped the cuffs on Platinum, then read her her Miranda rights.

". . . if you cannot afford an attorney, one will be provided to you. Do you understand?"

"How could you take me away from my kids?" Platinum wailed, bereft.

"You did it to yourself, ma'am. Did you understand everything I said? Do you need a court-appointed attorney?"

"Are you shitting me, asshole? I have six of my own on retainer."

"Good," said the lead cop. "You're going to need them."

Platinum looked past the cop to Kiley as both policemen started to lead her away.

"Kiley, take care of my babies! Call Shapiro, my lawyer, the number's on the refrigerator. Tell him to meet me at the Bel Air police station and to bring his checkbook. They'll take me to night court and set bail, I'll be out by two, three at the latest, so tell the kids not to worry."

Kiley nodded. How insane was all this? The only way Platinum could know exactly what to do and how long it would take was if she had had exactly this experience before.

With Platinum taken away to the station house for processing and the two children safely upstairs, Kiley sat on the white living room couch with the social worker while Tom continued to wait outside in the truck, at the social worker's insistence. The two police had been replaced by a battery of detectives, who were searching the house from top to bottom. They'd declared the whole place, including Kiley's guesthouse, a crime scene.

"The city and state have responsibilities, strict rules regarding the welfare of children," Ms. Johnson was explaining matter-of-factly.

Kiley nodded, dazed. She felt as if she was in a scene from a movie or a TV show and was in way over her head. "I'll take care of them until Platinum gets back later tonight, I promise. I really care about them."

The social worker rubbed her forehead. "I don't think you quite understand. How old are you?"

"Seventeen," Kiley said. "But I'm a very responsible person."

"Oh, brother," Ms. Johnson muttered under her breath. She stood, gathering a few files from the coffee table in front of her—the same one that had recently supported Platinum's marijuana stash and bong. "It's like this, Kiley. We don't treat a case differently because of the celebrity or notoriety of the deficient parent. Our sole responsibility is to the children. As a social worker, that's what I do, day in and day out. So by the powers vested in me by the State of California and the City and County of Los Angeles, it is my responsibility to remove the minor children from this home and bring them into a safe and secure environment."

Now Kiley finally got it.

"Wait, wait, you can't do that!" She jumped up.

"All this is pending a permanent disposition by the court system, of course."

"But—but—" Kiley sputtered. "You don't have to take them away. I'm here."

"It's not my personal decision to make. Besides, this is a crime scene. I think we should go upstairs and talk with Serenity and Sidney—"

"Siddhartha," Kiley corrected, an edge to her voice. "His name is Siddhartha. And there's another kid too. Bruce. You know about him?"

"I do now. Where is he?"

"Serenity told me on the phone he went to his friend's house."

"Fine, we'll locate him. And I'll call so that they'll be ready for three, not two."

"Who are you talking about?" Kiley demanded. "A shelter? *Foster care?*"

The social worker patted Kiley's arm. "I know it seems harsh. But it's what's best for these kids."

"No, no, it isn't," Kiley insisted. If only she could make this woman understand! "You don't know them, but I do. I can take care of them, really, I swear I can."

"I'm sorry, Kiley. That is not an option."

Kiley felt sick to her stomach with guilt and anxiety. It was bad enough that Platinum had let down her kids. Now they would think Kiley was abandoning them too. Besides, this was partly her fault. If she hadn't called 911, none of this would be happening. No call, no arrest. It was very simple.

"When are you taking them?"

"My intent is to have them at our local shelter within two hours."

"Well, when does Platinum get them back?"

"Kiley, this isn't about Platinum anymore. If the judge grants bail, she'll come back here, she can even live here eventually, once the police have collected all the evidence . . . and I'm sure there's quite a bit to collect. I imagine there'll be court-mandated rehab. But to get her children back, she's going to have to prove to a judge that she's responsible enough—"

"How long?"

"Weeks, months. Maybe never."

Kiley's hand went involuntarily to her mouth. This was unspeakable.

"I understand it's upsetting. Since the kids know you, perhaps you can help me convince them this is in their interest."

"No," Kiley snapped. "It *isn't* in their best interest."

"The children are coming with me one way or another. Now, do you really want to make it even harder on them?"

Kiley let her head rest on Tom's shoulder as they gently rocked in the old-fashioned wooden swing in Platinum's yard. The police were busy searching her guesthouse for evidence; they'd told her she could wait on the swing. Then she'd have five minutes to gather her belongings and leave. The place was a crime scene and she couldn't stay there. Tom had suggested that she spend the night in the extra bedroom in his suite at the Hotel Bel-Air, an offer she'd gratefully accepted.

Funny. During the entire horror story of Platinum's arrest and the social worker taking the children away, she'd completely forgotten that he'd been waiting for her in his truck. Had it really been only a few hours ago that she'd kissed him, and he'd kissed her back, and everything had been absolutely perfect?

"I hate myself," Kiley told him. "This is my fault."

"It's not your fault that the kids got taken, Kiley," Tom reminded her.

"Yeah, it is. If I hadn't called nine-one-one—"

"Serenity could have died," Tom interrupted her. "You did exactly the right thing."

Kiley felt the tugging at the back of her throat that always came right before she cried. "But the look on her face . . . I'm just one more person who betrayed her."

Tom put a comforting arm around her. The night was warm, the air soft, scented with orange blossoms. "Maybe it's for the best," he said. "That family couldn't keep going like it was going. Maybe this will shake things up, in a good way."

"I should have stopped it," Kiley insisted. "I should have sat down with Platinum after that newspaper reporter came and warned her what was probably going to happen."

"You think she didn't know?" Tom challenged. "My dad always said, If you know a guy is determined to stick his arm in the wood chipper, all you can do is get the towels."

Kiley grimaced. "Not a pretty image."

"You know what I'm talking about. On some level, I think your boss wanted this to happen. When's the newspaper story coming out?"

Kiley shrugged. "I bet there'll be something in the *Times* tomorrow. . . ." Her voice trailed off, and she buried her face in her hands.

"What's wrong?"

"It's going to be in all the papers."

"Yeah," Tom agreed. "And?"

"The town you come from is even smaller than La Crosse, but you've still got a newspaper, right? And all those celebrity TV shows?"

"Yeah. We have a satellite dish. What about them?"

"Well, tomorrow one of Mom's regulars at the diner is going to come in just as Mom is pouring the coffee and say: 'Hey, Jeanne, isn't your daughter working for that rock star in California?' And my mother is going to say: 'Gee whiz, Louise, she sure is.' And then the customer will say: 'Well, that rock star's in jail now, and they took her kids away, I just saw it on TV.' And my mom is going to have the mother of all anxiety attacks until I get my butt back to La Crosse."

"Well, just explain to her—"

"No, I can't! You don't understand. My mom flips out if she reads that crime is up in Milwaukee. She tests the batteries in our smoke detectors every day. She wouldn't go on the tour at Scripps with me because all the people made her too nervous. My mother is not *rational*!"

"Your dad—"

"Trust me, he won't be helpful." Kiley rubbed her forehead. "I have to think."

"I suppose staying with me at the hotel wouldn't fly," Tom ventured.

Kiley snorted at that. "Let me put it to you this way. Are you ready for the Wisconsin National Guard?"

"Friends, then?"

Kiley mused a moment. She *did* have friends in Los Angeles—Esme and Lydia. She explained this to Tom. "They're nannies too. Esme works for the Goldhagens."

"Goldhagens, like Steven and Diane, the hosts of the party tonight? I met their son, Jonathan, at dinner. Good guy."

Kiley stopped the rocking of the swing, then started it again. "It doesn't matter. I can't impose on either of my friends. I don't think their bosses would take too kindly to their having a houseguest in their guesthouse." She threw her head back. "Let's face it. I am so screwed."

"Look, there has to be something—some path we didn't think of. . . ."

Kiley smiled at him sadly. He'd said "we," which was touching; as if they were in this together. But they weren't. His future wasn't in jeopardy; only hers. *Her* guesthouse was being searched from top to bottom and was being put off-limits by the police. *Her* boss was probably in a courtroom that very minute. *Her* kids—she really did feel responsible for them—had been forcibly removed from their home, maybe never to return.

She had no place to live, no job, no money, and no way to stay in Los Angeles. The fact was, every path she could envision led directly to the last place she wanted to go: her parents' house in La Crosse, Wisconsin.

Though Esme hadn't seen Jonathan after their brief encounter in the ship's corridor, she'd spotted him later in Sir Winston's Salon, dining with a large tableful of his friends. Mackenzie sat next to him, draping an arm around the back of his neck, leaning her head against his shoulder, murmuring to him in one ear. Everyone at the table was beautiful, young, and white, with the privileged air of those born to wealth. That, Esme thought, might be what she resented most of all.

Fortunately, Diane didn't make Esme stay at the party for long. She showed the twins off in their little flapper outfits, letting all the stars who'd sent adoption gifts *ooh* and *ahh* over the children, and that was that.

The girls had fallen asleep almost instantly. There was a Ukrainian night nurse named Olga on duty, so Esme was able to put the children to bed and return to her guesthouse; appropriately named, she thought, since she still felt as if she was living there as a guest.

Now it was two hours later. She was in bed, trying to sleep but staring at the shadows on the ceiling cast by moonlight filtered through tree branches. The bathroom faucet was dripping; the sound felt as if it was hitting Esme in the middle of the forehead over and over, like some medieval torture device. Sheer masochism prevented her from getting up to do anything about it—she liked the pain. No, she *deserved* the pain. She punched her pillow into a better shape and rolled onto her side.

Drip-drip-drip. Damn sink. When Jonathan was there with her, she never noticed a dripping sink, or shadows, or much of anything. All her senses were filled with him. She was such a foolish, foolish girl. *Drip-drip-drip.*

That was it. She decided she could at least make herself useful, threw back the covers, and went to get the tool kit under the kitchen sink. Then she took it to the bathroom—the room where she'd first met Jonathan, when she had been helping her father repair the toilet. The repair had been unsuccessful and the toilet had overflowed, soaking her sandals and feet. Jonathan had witnessed her humiliation.

Her father, who was good at almost everything, had taught Esme to be self-sufficient, a lesson she'd learned well. Her mother had taught her to be proud and strong, a lesson she now realized she hadn't taken to as well as her father's. If she had, she would have heeded her mother's warnings about getting involved with their boss's son.

Here's to you, Papa, she thought as she loosened the faucet and removed the index cap. How ridiculous it was for the Goldhagens to have kept the original fixtures in this old house, rather than replace them with new, modern ones. Diane had used the word "quaint" and was proud that Cary Grant had once lived there. Big deal. There was no reason to have plumbing fixtures as old as Grant would be if he hadn't died ages ago. Esme checked the cartridge stem and the retaining ring and found the problem—the pressure on the washers had loosened. She tried tightening the packing nut, but the faucet still dripped. It meant that the packing itself needed to be replaced. Unless . . .

She went back into the kitchen and rummaged under the sink; sure enough, her extremely efficient caretaker father had left a second box of useful items—masking tape, superglue, twine. She took the twine to the bathroom and carefully wrapped it around the compression stem.

This is how you fix a faucet for free, niña, he'd tell her; *it is shameful to waste money.*

She replaced all the parts once more, then turned the water on and off. No drip. "We can't go on meeting like this," said the voice from behind her.

Jonathan. Of course, Jonathan. Damn him.

She knew she looked a mess. She was wearing polka-dot short pajama bottoms and a MEXICO T-shirt that had been the party favor at a friend's *quinceañero* celebration back in Fresno. Her makeup had long been scrubbed off; she could feel the tingling of a coming cold sore on her lower lip. He still wore his perfect tux, the tux shirt unbuttoned at the neck, the tie charmingly askew.

Oh, how she'd fantasized about staring him down and

telling him off. But in those fantasies she'd always looked fantastic and felt in control. She hadn't imagined him in a tuxedo that cost more than she made in a month and her . . . like this.

"Get out," she told him, trying the faucet again even though she didn't really have to.

"If that's really what you wanted, you would have locked your front door."

She forced herself not to look at him and instead deliberately replaced all the tools in the toolbox. "Why are you here? Shouldn't you be at your parents' party, dancing with Mackenzie?"

"I'm not 'with' Mackenzie. I haven't been with her for a long time."

"Don't hand me that shit, Jonathan. 'I had so much fun yesterday, Jon-Jon.' " She did a whining imitation of Mackenzie. "Move."

He stepped aside and she carried the box and twine back to the kitchen.

"Come on, Esme. We played a charity tennis match together," Jonathan explained as he trotted along behind her.

"What was the score? Love-love?" Esme shoved the supplies back under the sink and banged the door shut for emphasis.

"Why are you so willing to think the very worst of me?"

"*Mis padres no criaron una tonta*. My parents didn't raise a fool." She forced herself to pretend she still had on the armor of her designer dress, her beautiful hairstyle, and her high heels as she swept past him once again, this time into the living room, where she pushed open the front door.

He didn't budge. "I'm not leaving until you hear me out."

"What's to hear? You played me."

"God, Esme. I didn't play you!"

"What do you call crawling into my bed every night and then leaving before the sun comes up, eh? So no one would know?"

"I call it what you wanted."

Of all the nerve. "What I—"

Jonathan cut her off with a wave of his hand. "You said Diane still has you on probation, that you were afraid you'd lose your job if she knew we're involved. Isn't that what you told me?"

"I . . . I . . ."

Her heart was pounding so hard she could barely think. Yes. She recalled how she had said something along those lines, but the explanation was too damn easy.

"How convenient for you that you never questioned it all this time," she shot back. "You didn't have to face your stepmother, or introduce the *chica* from the Echo to your friends. You could blame it all on me and take the easy way out, because that's the only way you know."

She saw color rush to his cheeks and knew she'd hit her mark. "C'mon, Esme," he said. "I asked you and the girls to go for ice cream yesterday. Why would I do that if I didn't want things to change?"

"Gee. Aren't you the macho one? Big brother taking his little sisters for a snack and the nanny tags along," Esme jeered.

Jonathan's eyes flashed. His jaw set hard. "Fine. Be that way. Like I said, you never locked your door. Not even tonight. You wanted me here. You loved every minute of it."

"Screw you."

"You did. Which makes you just as responsible as I am."

Ouch. That hurt. Esme didn't want to admit how much it hurt, especially because it was true. She turned away.

When she finally turned back to him, she was careful to maintain her dignity and spoke in a quiet, controlled voice. "It is my fault too," she allowed. "That you used me makes me sick. That I *let* you use me makes me even sicker. Satisfied?"

"No. Not at all." He edged toward her. "Esme—"

She backed away. "Don't even think about it."

"Shit." He swung around, made a fist, and drew it back as if to power it through her living room wall, then stopped himself. She was shocked to see tears in his eyes. He let his arm fall to his side. "I hate this. How did it all get so damn complicated?" He ran a hand through his hair. "Okay. There's some truth to what you said."

"I hope you're not waiting for me to disagree with you."

He almost smiled. "You're *such* a pain in the ass. I'm sorry. I screwed up, okay?"

Was it? Could it ever be okay? Esme thought about Junior, hooked up to an IV in the hospital. She thought about how being with Jonathan meant risking not just her job, but also her parents'. The Goldhagens weren't likely to keep her parents on if they fired her—it would all be just too awkward. And there were plenty of off-the-books replacement caretakers and housekeepers who Steven and Diane could hire. All they had to do was go to any bus stop in the Echo or any street corner in Van Nuys.

And what about what Jorge had said; that a relationship with Jonathan was doomed to failure, because the two of them could never be equals? Was that true? If so, was it worth risking everything for what would, in the long run, be a crash-and-burn?

"Esme?" He moved to her, a question in his eyes.

"I don't know," she whispered.

"But I *do,*" he insisted. "I know that I don't want to lose you."

From outside the front door came high-pitched canine yapping.

"Cleo?" Esme questioned.

"I took her for a walk. It was supposed to be my excuse in case you asked. She's tied to the pole of the basketball hoop. Esme, please—"

He was interrupted by loud barking, followed by a low growl.

He exhaled loudly with frustration. "She must have spotted a rabbit or something. You mind if I bring her in?"

"Okay." Esme sighed, sat on the couch, and waited for Jonathan to get the peach-toned, pampered pooch. Her head was pounding. She knew what she ought to do—end things, even if he was right that their secretive relationship had been just as much her fault as it was his. It was just that—damn—it had been so much easier when she could blame him.

Jonathan led Cleo inside. The dog, dragging its leash, leaped onto Esme's lap and licked her face.

"Down, Cleo," Jonathan commanded as he slid in next to Esme. The dog bounded down to the floor, panting and scurrying around, her tail zigzagging with happiness.

"So, am I banished?" He reached out a hand and tenderly stroked Esme's hair.

Her eyes closed. The same old feeling came over her: wanting him so much that she could barely breathe, like walking a tightrope without a net; exciting, dangerous. How could she give him up? He'd apologized, hadn't he?

But words were cheap. He hadn't said one word about how things would actually change. *Un árbol que crece torcido jamás su tronco endereza.* A tree that grows crooked will never straighten its trunk.

"I'd be a fool to start up with you again," she declared.

"It would be different." He ran one finger lightly over the back of her neck.

"Different how? Not just sex? *No* sex?"

"If that's what you want."

"Liar."

"Okay," he admitted. "I'm incapable of keeping my hands off you, I admit it."

She swiveled to face him. "Listen to me. It would have to be more than that, Jonathan. I won't settle for—"

"Jonathan?"

Cleo barked twice and bolted to the front door as Jonathan guiltily swung his arm out from around Esme. There was Diane, hands on hips, still in her party dress—a Dolce & Gabbana gold lamé sheath—staring daggers at Esme. She'd never felt so inspected—no, *dissected,* pinned down by Diane's stare.

"I took Cleo for a walk," Jonathan explained lamely.

"I see." Diane's eyes never moved. "Esme, I thought I made the rules very clear. No male guests in your guesthouse. No male guests means no male guests. What part of 'no' don't you understand?"

Esme felt sick to her stomach. Her mother had warned her. Jorge had warned her. She'd warned herself. Obviously, her parents *had* raised a fool. She made a quick decision to depart with dignity, not to insult herself or her boss with begging, some charade about how she'd forgotten the instructions, or some lame-ass excuse about how Jonathan had walked in on her uninvited.

She stood up. "The rules were clear, Diane. I'll leave immediately, or as soon as you find my replacement, whichever you want. I hope you won't penalize my parents for my mistake; that's all I'm asking."

"Whoa, hold on here, both of you," Jonathan interjected, jumping to his feet and forming a "time-out" T with his hands. "We need to talk about this, Diane."

"There's nothing to talk about." Diane bent over and picked up her dog's leash. "Come on, Cleo."

Jonathan moved to block her path out the door. "Yes. There is."

Diane eyed him coldly. "If I can't trust Esme on this one, how can I expect to trust her with my children? Now, please get out of my way."

Jonathan didn't budge. "*You,* of all people, are talking about *trust*? You were playing hide the kosher sausage with my father way before he even thought about the word 'divorce.' "

Diane flushed guiltily. *Oh my God,* Esme thought, *that must be true!* And Jonathan was standing up to Diane in defense of his relationship with Esme; even though he didn't know if she was going to agree to *have* a relationship. A boy who just wanted sex would never do that, she reasoned. It was . . . amazing.

Diane tugged on Cleo's leash and looked away from Jonathan. "I'm not discussing this with you—"

"Fine. Don't discuss it. Just hear me out. Esme and I have been seeing each other since the premiere party for *The Ten.* She didn't want to break your rules, so she told me to leave her alone. I came here *begging* her to take me back. If you're going to blame someone here, blame me."

His eyes went to Esme. "I care about her. A lot. And I think . . . I *hope* . . . that she cares about me, too."

She does, Esme thought, returning his gaze. *So much.*

Cleo was ignoring the tugs on her leash, so Diane swooped her up. "Why didn't you just tell me?"

"Because of exactly what's happening right this minute."

Diane stroked Cleo's fur during a silence that, to Esme, felt as if it went on forever. Finally, she spoke. "It's been a long night. I need to give this some thought. We'll discuss it tomorrow, Esme." She nodded at Jonathan, indicating that he should move out of her way.

He held up a finger. "One last thing. Easton and Weston adore Esme. Firing her would be the worst possible thing you could do to your own daughters."

"Thank you, Jonathan. But I don't need you to tell me how to raise my children."

He didn't budge. "My *sisters.*"

There was a beat before she said goodnight and carried her little dog away with her.

Jonathan closed the door and turned to Esme. "You're safe."

"How do you know?"

"I'll go to a higher authority."

"I don't know that prayer will help," Esme said.

"Trust me, Esme." He pointed upward. "He's the one with the power around this place. That would be my father."

She sank into the couch, digesting everything that had just

happened. Jonathan sat next to her again. "Tomorrow when you get off work, let's do something."

She eyed him warily. "What?"

"Something *public*." He grinned. "Let's be crazy. Let's . . . let's skinny-dip on Venice Beach. Run naked down the Sunset Strip. Hell, I'm a little famous—it'll end up on *Entertainment Tonight*. Then the whole world will know we're together."

"Is that what you want?" she asked cautiously.

"Is it what *you* want?"

"I asked you first."

He grinned. "Come with me." He marched out her front door and stood under the basketball hoop, moonlight streaming down on him through the eucalyptus trees. He threw his hands wide and howled up at the moon: "Attention, Bel Air residents! I really, really, *really* like Esme Castaneda!"

"Shut up, you idiot!" Esme cried, giggling.

He pointed at her. "Say you really, really, really, *really* like me, or I keep going." When Esme hesitated, he cupped his hands around his mouth. "Attention, Bel Air res—"

"Okay, okay! I really, really, really, *really* like Jonathan Goldhagen."

In two giant steps he was with her, his arms around her waist. "Tomorrow we go public, yes?"

"Yes," she whispered into his chest.

He cupped her chin and raised her face to his. "You do know why I'm doing this, don't you?"

"Because you really, really, really, *really* like me?" Esme teased.

"Bullshit. Because I need you to finish my damn tattoo."

Esme punched his arm playfully. Then she kissed him, and

the sweetness of it melted her heart the way the first Popsicle of the summer melted on her tongue. She was done with hiding, with being afraid. She and Jonathan were together. She would have to tell Jorge, and her friends. She would have to tell her parents. And Junior. None of it would be easy, but at least, at last, it would be the truth.

Goodbye, dreams. Goodbye, Scripps. Goodbye, Tom.

Being in Tom's suite at the Hotel Bel-Air was surreal. During the filming of *Platinum Nanny,* she'd been right on the other side of his bedroom wall, hoping and praying that she'd win and become Platinum's nanny so that she could stay in California. She had never in a million years dreamed that she'd end up with Tom, in his suite. Well, that wasn't true, exactly. She'd met him, and heard his lust symphony with some other lucky girl whose initials were probably *MM,* and she had *definitely* dreamed about it. But it wasn't one of those dreams that she ever expected would actually come *true.*

While Tom made coffee in the kitchen, she wandered around, feeling nervous and awkward. Two bedrooms, Persian rugs on the floor, twentieth-century art on the walls, big-screen TV in the living room, full kitchen in Swedish modern, fresh fruit basket on the table. A side table in the living room supported a flat-screen computer monitor, keyboard, and small printer. It looked exactly the same as the suite next door.

She stared out the window of Tom's room, lost in thought. Finishing up at Platinum's had been easy. Under the watchful eye of a Bel Air detective, it had taken Kiley five minutes to change into jeans and her dad's bowling shirt, then pack all her belongings into her tattered suitcases. She made sure to take the house keys and Platinum's American Express card; she'd mail them to Platinum. Certainly she'd still be able to get her own mail, wouldn't she?

She tried to stop herself from crying as she closed the door to the guesthouse for the last time and the detective resealed it with yellow crime-scene tape. Then, it was a brief, silent drive from Platinum's mansion to the Hotel Bel-Air.

Tom found her staring out his bedroom window. "Want coffee?" he offered.

She shook her head. "It was really nice of you. To let me stay here tonight."

"It's not like it was a tough decision, Kiley." He turned her around and gently brushed the hair off her face. "You okay?"

"No," she admitted. He wrapped his arms around her. Kiley wished she could stay there forever.

"The offer still holds, you know," he said. "You can move in here. I'll take on the Wisconsin National Guard for you. Heck, I won all kinds of merit badges in Boy Scouts."

God, he was so sweet. And she finally knew that he really liked her, just when she had to leave! It was so horribly unfair. But she had to face facts; there was simply no way for her to stay.

Sensing that she needed some time alone, Tom offered to go

get a drink at the hotel bar. Kiley was grateful. She didn't want to break down in front of him.

He kissed her softly before he left. Then she sat down at the computer and logged on to Hotwire. There was a cheap flight the next morning from LAX to La Crosse, connecting in Minneapolis. She'd have to be at the airport at nine for the eleven o'clock departure. She booked and paid for it using Platinum's credit card, then printed out the boarding pass.

The only thing left to do was call Esme and Lydia, to tell them what was going on. Seeing as how it was two in the morning, she decided to wait until dawn. They weren't exactly conversations she was looking forward to having. She felt that ache in the back of her throat again. God, she was going to miss them so much.

She was just setting the alarm in the second bedroom for seven o'clock in the morning when she heard two quick raps at the front door. *Tom,* she thought immediately, and went to open it. He must have forgotten his key card.

She swung the door open. There stood Esme and Lydia. Esme was in jeans and a T-shirt; Lydia wore cutoffs and a Houston Oilers jersey cropped above her belly button.

"What in good God's name do you think you're doing?" Lydia demanded.

Kiley's jaw fell open. She was speechless.

"Why the hell didn't you call us?" Esme asked.

Kiley couldn't put the puzzle pieces together. "I— How did you—?"

"Tom," Esme reported. "He just phoned Jonathan Goldhagen from the hotel bar—they met at the FAB party tonight—

and Jonathan told me. I called Lydia, Jonathan loaned me his car, and I went to pick Lydia up. And . . . here we are."

Kiley still didn't get it. "Jonathan woke you? For this?"

"Actually, no. He was with me when his cell rang," Esme admitted, coloring. "We're . . . together."

"Yessiree, it's been a fun night of surprises all around," Lydia sang out. "Evidently Miss Esme here has been line dancing between the sheets with Jonathan since the *The Ten* party; somehow she neglected to tell us."

"This isn't about me, okay?" Esme reminded her.

"And thank you, Kiley, for inviting us in," Lydia added. "That is just *so* polite."

Still bewildered, Kiley ushered her friends into Tom's suite. Instead of the couch, Lydia sprawled on the Persian rug, while Esme settled into one of the plush chairs.

"Nice digs," Lydia commented.

Kiley perched on the armrest of Esme's chair. "It's unbelievable. That you guys came over here, I mean."

Esme nodded. "Yes, it was."

"How much did Tom tell you?"

"Everything, I think," Esme replied. "Platinum's under arrest. Social Services took the kids. The mansion is a crime scene."

Lydia rolled over, reveling in the lush rug. "Mmm, this feels sooo good. Tom said you're leaving town. That can't be true."

Kiley fished the boarding pass she'd printed out from her back pocket and waved it at them. "The police told me I can't stay at Platinum's. It's officially a crime scene. I'm due at LAX at nine."

"What, just like that, *adiós*?" Esme looked shocked.

Lydia sat up. "I never took you for a big ol' quitter."

"Don't do this to me," Kiley pleaded. "You're not making it easier."

Idly, Lydia reached over to the coffee table and picked up an old copy of *People* that Tom had left there. It was from when *Platinum Nanny* was first announced; the rock star was on the cover. "They airbrushed the hell out of her in this cover shot." She tossed the magazine aside. "Platinum's one sick puppy. She's got problems, you've got problems, all God's children got problems. You know what you do with a problem, Kiley? I'll give you a hint: cut and run is not the answer, you wimp."

Lydia's words felt like a gut punch. "My job is over, Lydia!" Kiley cried. "How the hell am I supposed to stay here?"

"Duh, girl, get another job."

"Not an option. It was hard enough convincing my mom to let me take this one."

"You can't just give up without a fight," Esme said softly.

"What are you, a capybara?" Lydia challenged.

"A *what?*"

"Cap-y-ba-ra," Lydia intoned slowly, as if Kiley was six years old. "It's this animal in Amazonia that looks like a cross between a guinea pig and a mini-hippo. Ugly-ass thing. It's the biggest rodent in the world, but it's scared of its own shadow. Which is why as big and ugly as it is, it gets caught."

Kiley shook her head. "And?"

"And it's not a fighter, Kiley. At the first sign of trouble, the capybara rolls over and plays dead. I've killed dozens of 'em. Good eating. Especially fried."

Kiley hung her head. Lydia was used to taking care of herself in difficult, even deadly, circumstances. So was Esme—Kiley had seen where she'd grown up. But what was the biggest hardship that she, Kiley McCann from La Crosse, Wisconsin, had ever had to overcome? Her mother and her father? Gawd. Compared to Lydia and Esme, she really *was* a capybara.

Kiley took a deep breath. "Look, you guys are my friends and . . ." She gulped down the lump in her throat. "I really care about you. I'm not cutting out because I want to, you have to know that."

For the next five minutes, she laid out all her concerns, one by one, in excruciating detail. She'd never be able to convince her mother to let her stay in Los Angeles. Where would she get money? Where would she go to school? Where would she live? The questions piled up like cars in a train wreck, except the train wreck was her life.

When she finished, Lydia scrambled to her feet. "Kiley McCann, you are so full of horse dooky." She began ticking points off on her fingers. "Fact: you were supposed to be the corn-fed yokel joke of *Platinum Nanny.* The day we met you at the country club, there was a challenge that was designed for you to fail. Fact: you kicked ass anyway."

"That was different," Kiley muttered.

"No, it wasn't," Lydia insisted. She took Kiley by the shoulders. "Amas never run from battle. Not men, not women. They're warriors. Kiley, *be a warrior.*"

Be a warrior. Right, Kiley thought.

"All right, first things first," Lydia went on, tapping a forefinger against her lips. "A place to live. Not here, obviously. Your mom would kill you if she found out, although it might be worth it. Why don't you stay with me?"

Kiley gave her a jaundiced look. "Oh yeah. That's what I always wanted to do. Get you fired."

"I'll hide you," Lydia declared brightly. "We'd have to be real careful, though. The not-so-merry matron of Moscow—otherwise known as Anya—knows I've been kinda veering from her schedule. And she had this big ol' list of all of Aunt Kat's clothes that I borrowed. And she caught me feeding Martina a milk shake, and—"

Kiley raised a hand to stop her. "It's not gonna happen, I'm not staying with you."

"Esme?" Lydia prompted. "You want to step on in here?"

"I'd love to, but . . ." Esme scuffed her sneakers into the wooden floor self-consciously. "Diane caught me with Jonathan an hour ago."

"Oops," Lydia muttered.

"She might fire me; I don't know yet."

"It doesn't matter, I'm not staying with you, either," Kiley insisted. She looked at her watch. Two-thirty. She was bone-tired and ready for her friends to leave. All this was doing was prolonging the inevitable. "Listen, you guys, thanks for trying. I mean it."

Instead of rising, Esme took out her cell phone. "I have an idea."

"No," Kiley joked lamely. "I am not working for Evelyn Bowers, I don't care how much she's paying."

"After Junior's *cholos* beat up Jonathan, you were there for me, Kiley," Esme reminded her as Lydia nodded. "Now do me a favor. Let me be there for you."

32

Dear Mom,

Since I never did get around to mailing the letter I wrote to you, I can include this postscript. I'm so glad we talked early this morning. It was just as shocking to me as it was to you, but when you live out here you learn how much the tabloids and the TV shows exaggerate everything. It turns out that so much of what happened was based on misunderstanding, and the media jumped to conclusions. Platinum was just practicing for a role in an upcoming movie where she is going to play this down-and-out hooker with a heart of gold. So she had all the stuff in her house to get ready for the role. Mom, you have to disregard any slanderous things you hear on the news or read about in the paper. It's just malicious Hollywood gossip.

Platinum is fine, the kids are fine, and I'm more than fine, so don't worry.

Oh, this is so cool, Platinum let me redecorate my guesthouse. I had the walls painted pale green, and brought in some paintings I got at a street fair in Los Feliz. I'm looking at those paintings right now and they are SO beautiful. Plus, even though Platinum has a gate, she was thoughtful enough to have double locks put on the front door, so you don't have to worry.

Kiley chewed nervously on the end of her pen. Maybe the it-was-all-research-for-a-film thing and the I-redecorated-the-guesthouse thing was overkill. Her mother was anxious, not stupid. On the other hand, maybe since the letter was so over the top, her mom would think, *Well, anything that over the top* has *to be true.*

True. Ha.

Kiley looked around the small room in the Echo Park bungalow that was, at least for the moment, her new home. It was stiflingly hot, with barely a breeze. There was a shelf filled with books on philosophy, poetry, and various classic novels in Spanish. Other than that, the room was fairly bare, with two cloth rugs, a battered desk, a dresser, and a neatly made single bed under a large crucifix on the wall.

Raucous Mexican music from someone's lowrider on the street poured in with the heat through the barred window. The air was pungent with spices. Someone was cooking tacos.

If my mom knew the truth, Kiley thought, *she wouldn't just have a panic attack, she'd have a heart attack.*

Fear prickled the back of her neck. She'd told so many lies in this letter. If lying sent you to hell, which is what her grandmother believed, then Kiley would be doing eternity in the Big Inferno.

There was a knock on the door.

"Come in," Kiley called, flipping the letter over so that whoever it was couldn't read it.

The door opened. Jorge Valdez, Esme's best friend, walked in. "Hi. I just wanted to see how you're doing."

"Fine," she answered automatically, even though it was far from true.

Jorge sat backward on the scarred chair at the small wooden desk. He looked around. "Sorry, it's kinda stark in here. My bro' wasn't big on decorating. His dorm room at Cal probably looks like a prison cell." He nudged his chin toward the cross on the wall. "My *abuela*—grandmother—put that up. Carlos would take it down, she'd put it back up."

"Oh, it's fine," Kiley insisted. "Really."

Jorge nodded and rubbed his jaw. He wore an open black shirt over a white undershirt, and black jeans. He was thin, medium height, not at all wimpy. Actually, Kiley thought he was very handsome. Not in a Tom way, maybe, but in a more interesting way. His dark, luminous eyes seemed to take everything in, in a way that most people's did not.

Of all the people Kiley had considered that Esme might have called the night before, she hadn't imagined it would be her friend Jorge. But Esme knew that Carlos was away at college and that there was an empty bedroom at Jorge's house. Jorge hadn't hesitated. If Esme was doing the asking, Kiley could stay for as long as she needed.

Tom had driven her to Jorge's at ten because he had an afternoon photo shoot up in Malibu. Even through her sheer terror, Kiley had noticed that the two guys seemed to be sizing each other up. It was ridiculous. One guy was Esme's friend and the other guy wasn't even Kiley's official boyfriend. Maybe that was just how guys were.

Jorge's mom had shown Kiley to her new room. She was a short, round woman, with high cheekbones and a musical laugh. A schoolteacher for L.A. Unified, she had the summer off. She tried her best to make Kiley feel comfortable, plying her and Tom with delicious homemade cookies even though it was before noon. Tom left a half hour later, promising to pick Kiley up that night and hook her up with Esme and Lydia. It wasn't like she was alone, even though she felt like she was.

"So . . . you need a job, right?" Jorge asked.

Kiley nodded. "The only experience I have is babysitting and waitressing, though."

Jorge folded his arms and leaned them on the back of the chair. "There's this coffeehouse in the neighborhood called La Verdad—it means the Truth—I do some rapping there, hang out, play chess, you know. It's a good place; they don't allow any gangbangers. They need a waitress."

Kiley's heart pounded. She hesitated. A Latino club in Echo Park? Her Spanish was nonexistent. She'd stick out like . . . like exactly who she was.

"You're afraid you'd be the only white girl there," Jorge guessed.

She nodded, embarrassed.

"You won't be," Jorge assured her. "One of the other waitresses is from Kansas. Wants to be a screenwriter. Cheapest apartment she could find was here in the Echo. Whitest girl I've ever seen. Anyhow, the place is cool. If you want to check it out, I can take you over tomorrow night."

"That would be great," she said softly, overwhelmed. "This is so nice of you, I just—I don't even know what to say."

"*De nada*—it's nothing," Jorge insisted. He stood. "You hungry?"

She had to admit that she was. She hadn't eaten more than a single cookie. Too nervous.

"I need to introduce you to Bettina's down the block. Little hole in the wall. The woman has a gift with *huevos rancheros*. Come on."

"Now?"

Jorge shrugged. "Why not?"

Kiley bit her lip. "I just have to finish writing a letter first. Can we mail it when we go out?"

"Works for me. I'll be on the front stoop when you're ready." He flashed a dazzling smile and looked at her with those penetrating eyes. "It's gonna be okay. You'll see."

When he was gone, Kiley went back to the letter, determined to finish it and get it out of her hands before she lost her nerve.

Remember, Mom, how you told me not to let fear hold me back? That's probably the best advice you ever gave me. I used to be such a wimp. But now . . . I've decided to try and be a warrior.

All my love,
Kiley

P.S. Give Dad a hug from me.
P.P.S. Don't worry!

About the Author

Raised in Bel Air, Melody Mayer is the oldest daughter of a fourth-generation Hollywood family and has outlasted countless nannies.